DAVID MARTIN'S

The Beginning of Sorrows

"*The Beginning of Sorrows* is an impressive book, simply though powerfully written, eerily moving, aching with sorrow for life's too frequent wrong turns."
— *Newsday*

"David Martin's crackerbarrel prose—at once bizarre and familiar...unearths the mystery and spice of small-town America and conveys them beautifully."
— *Vogue*

"*The Beginning of Sorrows* is a mythical novel of life, death and rebirth on the Faulknerian scale."
— *Philadelphia Inquirer*

"Martin's people are trapped between motion and stasis, frozen at the point of flight."
— *San Francisco Chronicle*

"Themes of isolation and flight, love and betrayal, youthful promise and aging resignation occupy this taut, haunting, lyrical novel by a fine writer."
— *Booklist*

"A buoyant, mysterious book, with magnificent landscapes and dark portraits...a tour de force."
— *Publishers Weekly*

The Beginning
of Sorrows

ALSO BY DAVID MARTIN

Tethered
The Crying Heart Tattoo
Final Harbor
Lie to Me

The Beginning of Sorrows

. . . . .

DAVID MARTIN

Vintage Contemporaries

VINTAGE BOOKS

A DIVISION OF RANDOM HOUSE, INC.

NEW YORK

FIRST VINTAGE CONTEMPORARIES EDITION,
SEPTEMBER 1989

Published in the United States by Vintage Books,
a division of Random House, Inc., New York.
Originally published, in hardcover,
by Weidenfeld & Nicolson, New York, in 1987.

Library of Congress Cataloging-in-Publication Data
Martin, David Lozell, 1946–
The beginning of sorrows/David Martin. —
1st Vintage contemporaries ed.
p.   cm. — (Vintage contemporaries)
ISBN 0-679-72459-1: $7.95
I. Title.
[PS3563.A72329B4   1989]
813'.54—dc20   89-40156
CIP

Manufactured in the United States of America
10 9 8 7 6 5 4 3 2 1

To Marjorie Morris Martin and Curtis Charles Martin.
And to Beehart, long gone home again.

. . . . .

*The full soul loathes a honeycomb, but
to the hungry soul every bitter thing is sweet.*

—PROVERBS

. . . . .

Mr. Johnny Reace

1

IT IS June and winter is memory. I sit here on the large screened-in porch to the side of Beaker Mansion watching Junie bugs fly against the screens, get knocked to the ground, then resume their crashing flights. With me is a small and silent boy with the face of an old man. I am only forty-three.

Flanking my property are remodeled and restored houses full of bright people, the ones who speculate about the extent of my wealth and of my eccentricities and about the subscriptions hauled to my door each day. But these bright, new residents of my town weren't around fifteen years ago.

When I was twenty-eight. Johnny Reace and a bad winter came to Beaker's Bride when I was twenty-eight, and that's when the iron entered my soul. I was living with my son, Jess, and his grandfather, Bonner; I had been stuck in what was a dead town back then—stuck as if in a dream—when Johnny Reace showed up in a hailstorm and, following him, that bad winter. And, now, sometimes now I still awaken with a hope too short for being so great: *It's a dream.*

But it was a winter—a winter so bad that I carry it like something still within me. Let me tell you how it began: with September and ice and a splendid urgency at our front door.

2

BONNER HADN'T EVEN OPENED the door all the way before Alan Winslow shouted it: "He came up from the river!"

Bonner remained placid. He had been sitting in his large chair by the window overlooking the back lot, watching the hail. Ice fell too quickly for his eye to follow, so he had to watch the ground and the marble monuments because white chunks could be seen only on the rebound, leaping from grass and shooting up high off polished stone. "Who?" he asked Winslow.

"Right in the middle of that hail, he came up from the river and put a ladder to the side of Beaker Mansion! Going to rob it in broad daylight!"

Bonner looked past his neighbor, this small elderly man who held in his arms a struggling dog. It was more toward dusk than broad daylight, but now that the hailstorm had passed, there would be a sunset. People around town had, like Bonner, been at their windows watching the ground agitate with ice, pop ice like corn, push up more ice until enough white had been issued to lay a blanket inches deep. Already the white ice, lying quietly now in Bonner's front yard, had begun to redden with the sun. "What were you doing out in that weather?" Bonner asked.

"Taking the mutt for a walk."

Taking a dog for a walk in a hailstorm that dropped the temperature from sixty-three to fifty so fast you could feel it going down? Walking a dog in hail that battered gutters with an awful racket, ruined roofs, razored up crops standing in the field? "Taking him for a walk in that hail?"

"We got caught in it!" Winslow shouted, impatient with Bonner.

In the kitchen, Jess still hadn't digested Winslow's opening statement: *He came up from the river!* The boy, rocking from foot to foot, began a low singsong moan.

"I figured he was trying to use the hailstorm as a cover, but then I caught him," Winslow was telling Bonner. "The thing is, he went up on the roof anyways—even after I confronted him. You better go over there and see what's what."

In Beaker's Bride, Bonner was as close as people got to the law.

"I'm going, too," Jess whispered to Beehart, who shook his head and trembled. No way *he* was going to confront some man who came up from the river. "Coward," Jess whispered, feeling himself become braver in face of Beehart's fear.

·   ·   ·   ·   ·

FROM THE MANSION'S ROOF, Johnny Reace could see all of Beaker's Bride, a town resting in a sweet niche where bluffs and hard hills broke open here to cradle what had been a meadow once spreading green and yellow from rocky heights to water's edge.

High bluffs stood behind Beaker's Bride, to the east; the town's southern flank was guarded by a heavy forest brambly with underbrush and treacherous with rock outcroppings. As if to fence out whatever had once been bad in there, an old stone wall in great disrepair ran the length of this southern flank.

Train tracks bordered the other side of Beaker's Bride, tracks on which trains still traveled but no longer stopped.

This northern flank also had been the site of commerce, all closed down now: abandoned depot with splintered platform, acres of empty switching yards, long-bare loading docks.

Railroad north, forest south, bluffs east—which leaves the west, the river, the Illinois. It flowed in front of the town, along the lower part of that former meadow, and water was what Johnny needed to see.

His view from the roof offered a generous length of river, which he drank in a long draught, taking time to watch the Illinois run, watch its current hurry south, watch an occasional barge work that course.

Then he looked more closely around him. A hundred houses were arranged in an irregular horseshoe shape with the stone mansion at the top, back near the bluffs, higher than anything else in town. Just below the mansion, a cemetery filled the open area of the horseshoe. Johnny could tell by the houses' condition, boarded windows and trashy yards, that no more than a dozen were occupied. Down by river road, a small business section stood empty, and in the residential areas Johnny could identify at least six abandoned churches and schools.

Someone called up to him. He didn't look to see who it was until he reached the ground, turning from the ladder to greet a boy, a collie, and a fifty-six-year-old man who looked astonishingly like Abraham Lincoln without the beard. The boy and dog were both eight. Johnny tipped what would've been a hat had he been wearing one and offered his hand and pretty teeth smiling. "Johnny Reace."

"Bonner Relee."

Johnny didn't catch the name but kept shaking hands vigorously, impressed by the famous face and trying his best not to laugh at the boy: his pants were too tight and cuffs too high, his gut hung over the belt, which had a six-inch length flopping free, and thick-lensed glasses magnified already large brown eyes. Jess hid behind Bonner the way you might expect a two-year-old to do.

"Something funny, Mr. Reace?"

Ah, a serious man. "No, sir. But I missed your name."

"Bonner Relee."

"Rally?"

"Relee. *R, e, l,* double *e.*"

"Nice to meet you." Johnny still had trouble understanding Bonner's speech, marked as it was by a kind of high-pitched gulping country accent, and Johnny continued to be distracted by the jarring Lincoln resemblance, heavy face, big ears, thick black hair, and especially those dark searching eyes. "This your boy, Mr. Ree . . ."

"Relee." Although he did not trust the stranger's instant friendliness, Bonner appreciated the assumption that Jess was his son. "My boy's boy. Jess. Shake hands with the man."

But Jess stayed on the far side of Bonner and waited to see if his grandfather recognized this man.

"What's her name?" Johnny asked, kneeling to look at the collie.

Jess wouldn't answer.

"Lady," Bonner said, adding a warning: "She ain't all collie. Got some kind of severe blood mixed in and she's been known to bite."

Again that grin and then: "I've known some ladies in my time who were notorious biters." Deciding abruptly that this was funny and no longer able to hold his laughter, Johnny let it out like sudden music.

He was short and stocky and sweet the way they talk of a prizefighter being sweet, sure of movement and a pleasure to watch—especially when he tossed back his good head and laughed so well that you hoped he would do it again soon.

Johnny's music agitated Lady, making her sweep the

bushy tail back and forth rapidly for a dog of her age, and then she dipped her head to Johnny and bumped him and leaned into him. After she performed all of this, he consented to touch her.

"Never knew her to take to a stranger that way."

"My effect on ladies, Mr. Relee."

Although unimpressed with Johnny's glibness, Bonner knew that something consequential was required to charm a normally solemn dog like Lady. "What were you doing up on my roof, Mr. Reace?"

"You live here do you?"

"We live in that frame house yonder." Bonner pointed.

"With all the statues out back?"

"Gravestones." Bonner took a pipe from his jacket. "But I own this here place, Beaker Mansion." He'd been working on it ever since Jess was born, but the stone mansion had sat empty a long time and it was too much house for one man to restore. "I hope you weren't cracking my slate."

Johnny looked toward the roof. "I was careful."

"Man walking on slate can crack it."

"But I guess that hailstorm didn't hurt it none, huh?"

"Nope."

"Never saw hail like that in my life."

"I want to know what you're doing here, Mr. Reace." Bonner spoke the way big, quiet men do, accustomed to being answered straight.

"Trespassing, clear and simple. Any way I can make it right with you?" Johnny Reace was fearless and possessed a short man's ready combativeness, though it was leavened in him by his great, grand sense of humor: he wasn't afraid of Bonner's size but of the man's disapproval. "I just had to get a good long look at the Illinois."

Bonner turned toward the river that swept, straight, past Beaker's Bride but made an artful bend downriver from town. "Best view in the state. Right here."

"I believe it."

He elaborated upon the pipe lighting to give Johnny an opportunity to explain himself.

"I was just passing through and—"

Bonner shook his head. That's what Alan Winslow had reported, of course—that the stranger claimed to be just passing through—but you had to travel old gravel river roads to get to Beaker's Bride and Bonner wasn't going to stand there and listen to the man lie to him.

Seeing this, Johnny eased a bit of Irish into his voice, amplifying its charm. "Have you got time for a story, Mr. Relee?"

Bonner tamped the coals of his pipe bowl with an index finger blackened and blunted; he put a great hand to the side of Jess's face and held the boy close as if to tell him now here comes a man's story so you listen carefully.

Johnny wove an elaborate tale of how he'd spent the summer in Chicago with a widow woman who owned a gleaming white sailboat on which she and he slipped through the colored waters of Lake Michigan, sails full and breeze sweet. Jess, who'd never seen a sailboat in his life, saw this one even without closing his eyes.

"I don't blame you for being a river man, Mr. Relee, living as you do on this fine stretch of the Illinois, but for greens and blues you need an ocean or a lake like Michigan. No painted waters in a river, Mr. Relee—not painted like that Michigan water, as if you could dip in a brush and use it on canvas."

Jess intended to report all of this to Beehart.

At the end of the sailing season, Johnny said, the widow wanted to keep him for winter the way she kept that white sailboat for summer's fun, and although he was sorely tempted, the living with her being free and easy, he did not wish to face winter in Chicago—winter's own territory—so he got into his little blue car and drove south with intentions of reaching someplace where winter doesn't. "Have you ever been to the Florida Keys, Mr. Relee?"

"Never."

"They step right out into the ocean and when you get to the end of the road, the only way to leave is to turn around and go back the way you came."

"Sort of like Beaker's Bride."

Johnny smiled. "The women down there are sweet-tempered and brown all over."

"Now *that* ain't like Beaker's Bride at all." Bonner's own smile cracked his face.

Encouraged, Johnny went on to explain how he left Chicago and drove down the middle of the state and then when he couldn't stand another hour being away from sight of water, he turned right and struck west for the Mississippi. " 'Course, I ran into the Illinois first. Then got caught short by that hailstorm, went off on back roads, found myself lost—slid into a ditch in front of your town here."

Johnny knelt to put his eyes on a level with Jess's and he spoke directly to the boy. "Thought this was a ghost town. Went walking around in those woods like a damned fool, and you know what? I found a cave to sit out that hail. It was dark in there and I had a feeling something big was in there with me. I heard growling."

Jess was a statue.

"Not throat growling but stomach growling—which made me all the more nervous. Something big and smelling bad jumped on me and we had a terrible fight, truly terrible. But I thought I got away free and clear. Ran back to my car and sat there taking stock. Counting fingers. Kept coming up with nine."

Johnny quickly put his hands, fingers spread, in front of Jess's face. The ring finger on the left hand was all but missing, just a rough half-inch stub remaining—some old wound that had healed badly. "I figure a bear's in that cave with my finger in its belly."

Seeing the boy's face, and having been caught by the finger trick himself, Bonner removed the dead pipe from his mouth and laid back Lincoln's head to laugh—a laugh lower in pitch than his speaking voice, arising from deep in his long torso and taking time to come out but then tumbling free in a train-car series of boiling, gurgling, breath-strangling chokes-gulps-sobs.

Jess couldn't remember his grandfather ever laughing quite like that before.

And Johnny was astonished, too, this world-class laughter arriving so unexpectedly from a man who seemed otherwise afflicted by bone-deep sadness.

So Johnny laughed, too.

Then Jess laughed, shyly at first but soon boldly. Bonner's hands rested like yokes on the boy's shoulders as the three of them continued to laugh, joyous in the spirit and investing in Lady an unbridled delight that made her smile the way a collie will, twisting up the back of her mouth, and caused her to paddle front paws on the ground in an old dog's dance, soon barking.

The two men and the collie eventually quieted themselves, but Jess's laughter had gone beyond what he could control—growing into something bordering on hysteria, crying, making animal noises that alarmed Bonner and led him to press down on the boy's shoulders. Jess twisted loose and threw himself onto Lady, knocking both of them over and losing his glasses and still he laughed and cried and made noises.

Johnny reached for him.

"Leave him be," Bonner ordered. This was family, and Bonner had seen these fits before.

Johnny couldn't stand to watch the child act so desperately. He grasped Jess by the upper arms and pulled him nose-to-nose close.

"I said leave him be."

But there was iron in Johnny, too. He ignored Bonner and studied the boy's terrified face, unchildlike in its heaviness of flesh, its redness, its large and troubled features.

"I can see something in your eyes, boy. *Something* in there and you know what it is, too, don't you? Something . . . magic! Yeah, I see it in your eyes. You can do something magic, can't you? What is it? What's the magic you can do?"

Jess stopped struggling and became quiet. How did this man know? Did he really know?

"Something magic in those big brown eyes of yours. Tell me. Go on, tell me."

Jess spoke hoarsely: "I can fly."

The statement made Bonner grimace, but Johnny smiled like shades popping to light a room.

"I *can* fly," Jess insisted.

Johnny laughed at this gospel. "Me, too, buckaroo—me, too!"

That Bad Winter

3

BONNER invited him to supper.

Walking back to the house, what light the two men and boy had came from a sun already set and, with that light, Beaker's Bride became a diorama in red—a three-sided box, railroad embankment to the north and forest to the south and the bluffs in the back: a box filled with light of such redness that white houses were tinged, their three faces were bronzed, and the remaining ice looked as if it had begun to rust.

Johnny was going to comment on all this, but Bonner's silence had a way of discouraging light observations. "Are you sure the missus won't mind?" Johnny asked. "Springing someone on her for dinner like this."

Bonner didn't reply until they reached the house. "There's no missus. Just Alva." Then as he opened the front door, he added something Johnny didn't know how to take. "She needs the company."

Alva got caught in the hallway.

"This here's Mr. Johnny Reace," Bonner told her. "He's come to supper." As an aside to Johnny, he said, "Alva. The boy's mother."

Johnny thought at first she was a teenager—thin, not tall but long-legged, dressed in a blue workshirt and jeans, flyaway black hair cut short. But when he looked closely at her face, he could see she was fully a woman, more intriguing than pretty and with the largest eyes that Johnny couldn't figure out. Were they opened so wide from fear or from surprise and delight?

Extending his hand, he advanced on Alva as she tried to hold her ground. But she could not. He came toward her so quickly and he was such an unexpected presence in that house. Something dry-feathered beat in her chest and then fluttered up her throat; Alva couldn't speak. Johnny, still smiling, kept coming.

Then she stiffened. And when Alva stopped retreating, Johnny nearly bumped into her and stood so close that she could smell him all whiskey and spice, his breath on her like something she hadn't inhaled in a long time.

"I apologize for barging in on you like this," Johnny said, still holding her hand.

"Pork chops, Mr. Reace." Alva had regained an old composure.

Johnny laughed that music of his, and Bonner stood there as Jess went tearing for the kitchen.

"He loves pork chops," Alva explained.

Johnny leaned back his head and closed his eyes. " *'Don't need no coat and don't want no bed.'* " Singing these blues mockingly, softly and off-key. " *'Don't need no pork chops, just give me gin instead.'* "

Alva and Bonner looked at each other. Johnny laughed.

"Actually, I never touch gin," Johnny said, loudly enough for Alva to hear—she had gone off to the kitchen. "Wouldn't mind something brown, though. Anything you happen to have, a little bourbon or Scotch or even—"

Bonner spoke abruptly, in a quiet voice that made Johnny feel as if he'd been shouting. "You're welcome to our hospitality."

"I certainly appreciate it, taking in a stranger like—"

"But don't bring anything bad into this house, Mr. Reace. We've had enough bad to last us."

"I have no intention—"

"It'll be time to wash up for supper then."

Johnny nodded. Even he could learn something about theatrics from this big and ugly man who knew how to step on your lines and make you feel foolish.

· · · · ·

THROUGHOUT dinner, Bonner sat there like a beacon issuing not light but darkness—his eyes absorbing energy so that when Johnny said something funny, the good mood didn't last long.

He was six feet four inches tall when he stood straight, but Bonner's gangling powerful body slumped as if he roped an anvil to his shoulders each morning. Even for his height he was unusually long-limbed, with massive hands and feet that appeared too large for their thin wrists and ankles. Bonner's fingers seemed deformed in their length. He was nearsighted but refused to wear glasses, making his stare all the more intense, as if looking through you in his effort to focus. Like Lincoln, Bonner owned a great generosity of mouth.

And like Lincoln, Bonner was involved in a long and inevitable war that somehow was of his own making and that sometimes seemed to be extracting too high a price: to keep Beaker's Bride alive so it wouldn't end up like Millerway, six miles south, where Alva grew up. Ten years ago, when Alva's mother died, leaving the town empty, Millerway was abandoned to scavengers and vandals. Bonner didn't want that to happen to his town.

Beaker's Bride had been in a long decline ever since the rail yards shut down. When the schools closed and families with children moved away, the last store and gas station went out of business and the final church shut its doors. The only commerce done in Beaker's Bride now was the cemetery's.

Bonner's wife left him when their son, Matthew, was a

boy. Now all that Bonner wanted to do before he died was put Alva and Jess in Beaker Mansion.

After the meal, with Johnny in the living room waiting for a drink, Bonner came to the kitchen, where Alva and Jess were cleaning up. "Leave that and come sit with us," Bonner told Alva. "You too, pup." Then he poured whiskey for himself and Johnny, gin and juice for Alva, and for Jess Bonner made a special mixture of ginger beer and cherry juice. He carried all four glasses in his big hands, needing no tray.

When they each had a drink, Johnny raised his. "Better days ahead," he said with a hopelessness that suddenly showed you a different side of him.

After he could feel the whiskey in his belly, Bonner spoke to Johnny. "Alva was down in them Keys where you said you went."

Alva spoke quickly and with a defiance she hadn't yet shown Johnny. "When Jess was four, I ran away and stayed gone for two years. It's a sore Bonner won't let heal."

Bonner hunkered down, saying nothing.

But Johnny proceeded brightly, asking Alva if she remembered how the sun set in Key West. "Like fiery butter, showing green flashes, and the light there at the end of the day makes you glad for eyes. Do you remember it, Alva?"

She nodded, looking at him with equal parts of curiosity and mistrust.

Bonner asked him, "What's your trade, Mr. Reace?"

"Johnny. Call me Johnny. I do a little of this and a little of that. What's your trade, Alva?"

She shrugged. "I went to college."

"She didn't go but half a year," Bonner said, getting out of his recliner to collect the glasses. "Another drink."

With Bonner in the kitchen, Jess offered some information from the floor. "He said a bear bit off his finger."

Johnny held up his left hand. "Actually, now that I remember, this finger was bit off by a barracuda in Key West."

Sitting at the opposite end of the couch from him, Alva wanted to make sure Johnny saw her face—how totally unimpressed she remained.

Bonner returned with the drinks just as Johnny was asking Alva about her husband. "My boy's dead," Bonner said. "Drowned in the river. Jess is his son and she's Jess's mother but there ain't no husband involved."

Johnny wasn't accustomed to someone else controlling the conversation.

"Jess is the only child in town," she said flatly.

Johnny pointed at the boy. "The heart of Beaker's Bride."

"He's that," Bonner agreed.

"A dreamboat," Alva added.

To escape this attention, Jess grabbed Lady by the sides of her head and looked as hard as he could into her calm eyes.

"Of course," Alva continued, "I wish he'd learn to stay out of my chocolate chips. Oh, I saw what you did to that last package, mister. I was going to make Toll House cookies for after supper but then I found the package half gone. For once, I'd like to look in that cupboard and find an unopened—"

She was interrupted by a knock at the door. Bonner left the room with Lady watching intently to see who had come visiting at night like this.

"As if that hailstorm wasn't news enough," Alva said, talking to the room. "A stranger in town, too. My, my. A big noise in Beaker's Bride."

Bonner brought in Mr. Gibsner and Charlie Warden, two old men who shared a house on the southern edge of town a few yards this side of the stone wall that kept out that deep and brambly river forest.

Mr. Gibsner was short and round and dressed like the

farmer he used to be except now his bib overalls were store-new and he hadn't carried pig shit on his shoes or grease under his fingernails in more years than Alva had lived.

Charlie Warden was the opposite: tall, thin, quick to smile, and ready to agree with anyone except Mr. Gibsner; Charlie, a retired gandy dancer, played a wifely role to the other man's gruff aloofness.

Once in the living room, both men stared boldly at Johnny as if he were a curious display at some roadside attraction they had paid to see. Bonner made the introductions.

When Mr. Gibsner and Charlie Warden each had a bottle of beer in hand, they sat in chairs at opposite sides of the room and said nothing.

"Some hailstorm today, huh?" Johnny offered.

"Worst I ever seen," Charlie Warden agreed.

"Crop damage," Mr. Gibsner said.

Then another knock at the door—Alan Winslow coming in for a close look at Johnny. "Don't have time," Winslow said when Bonner offered him a drink.

"I see you out in that hail?" Mr. Gibsner asked.

"Be a damn fool to go out in that hail," Winslow replied and then left.

"Strange bird," Mr. Gibsner said.

Then nothing but the clock.

"Helen and them others that keep chickens," and this was Charlie talking, "they lost two dozen in that hail. So I heard."

Mr. Gibsner was shaking his head. "Lost more than that, I heard. Damn fools for not getting them in the coop."

After another round of drinks, Mr. Gibsner asked Johnny where he was from and Johnny said he came down from Chicago, but Mr. Gibsner seemed uninterested in the answer. "I remember a hailstorm back in 'forty-one lots worse than this here one today," he observed. "Lost me forty acres of new corn, stripped it bare till there wasn't nothing but straight stalks sticking in that field. Had an old Tennessee walker go crazy on me so's you couldn't ride her anymore at all after that hail. 'Course, she's high-strung to start."

"I remember that hail, back in 'forty-one," Charlie Warden said. "It lasted longer than this one today but I'm telling you the stones wasn't as big and they didn't hit as hard."

"Hit hard enough to crazy-up my Tennessee walker and strip forty acres of new corn. Can't hit much harder than that."

Alva became impatient. "Time for bed," she said to Jess. "You got school in the morning."

Mr. Gibsner and Charlie Warden stood in unison, Charlie smiling and nodding and thanking Bonner for the beer, Johnny for the pleasure of meeting him, Alva for her hospitality. Mr. Gibsner waited sober-faced for the niceties to be completed.

When they had gone, Alva stood. Just looking at Johnny Reace gave her a feeling she didn't entirely like. She walked over and nudged Jess with her toe.

"Come on, dreamboat."

The boy squirmed away.

"Leave him be," Bonner said. Then to Johnny: "Want to call it a night?"

"Not me. I was born two drinks down and a story short. Bring in that bottle and talk on, commander, talk on."

"I'll be in bed, then," Alva said, shaking her head and leaving Jess to sleep on the floor. Men and their stories. She escaped upstairs, turning once to look at Johnny, who was still watching her.

"What I want to know," Johnny said, returning his attention to Bonner, "is how this town got its name." It was, in fact, the town's odd name on an old map and not a desire to see water that had made Johnny take a right and strike west.

"Opinions differ," Bonner said slowly. "You have to start with Big Ed Beaker out of Chicago. He owned the railroad, least he ran it. Used to ride his private car through these parts, watching out the window to see what he could see. Farmers used this spot as a natural holding pen for their stock. They'd drive their hogs and cattle along the river and put them back along the bluffs here to wait for the barges that would take the stock on down to St. Louis. So Big Ed Beaker, he figured this would be a good place to put switching yards and loading docks—transfer everything from the trains to river traffic and the other way 'round. He takes one look at what used to be a meadow here, and he sees right away what a sweet spot it is.

"The town was first known as Beaker's Pride. But then Big Ed built his mansion, and on his visits he brought young women, a different one each trip: chorus girls and working girls and secretaries from the railroad's office in Chicago. Whenever someone asked about the young woman on Mr. Beaker's arm, his cronies would say she was Big Ed's bride and the two of them were on their honeymoon—no matter that every year there might be four or five of these honeymoon trips and each with a different bride. Got to be a joke. Folks took to calling the town not Beaker's Pride but Beaker's Bride."

Bonner set aside his drink so he could talk with both hands. "Old Edward Beaker arranged for the town cemetery to be put between his mansion and the river so that other houses could never be built there and interrupt his view of the Illinois." Bonner talked about the cemetery and the stones and monuments that Ed Beaker brought down from Chicago—statuary that Bonner now owned and sold and set for the cemetery's new residents. He talked about why he dug graves by shovel and never called in a backhoe even when the ground was hard. He told stories about farmers fattening their pigs on trash fish seined from the Illinois and its tributaries. The man spoke epics.

When Johnny interrupted to ask if Jess was okay sleeping on the floor, Bonner replied, "He's fine." Bonner required Jess nearby now for the same reason he would on occasion sit at his grandson's bedside and talk as the boy slept, the mind filing in a finer place what it hears overheard like dreams—so let him lie there on the floor with his dog and hear how it is that men tell their stories.

· · · · ·

TOWARD dawn, Bonner carried the heavy child upstairs, making enough noise to awaken Alva. She listened as Bonner came out of Jess's room and hesitated in the hallway before pushing open her door and standing there for the longest time.

"Alva?" Bonner stayed by the doorway.

It had been more than a year now.

"Come here, baby," she whispered, folding back the covers.

"No."

Alva pulled up her nightgown and recalled how odd he looked naked in bed with her—Bonner's long toes and dangerously long fingers and those long arms and legs. His great lengths had to be dealt with in bed.

This time, however, Bonner did not take off his clothes or get into bed with Alva. "I put him up for the night. He's going to stick around awhile and help me with Beaker Mansion."

She had assumed Johnny would be there for breakfast and then leave; the prospect of his living with them, even for a few days, made her belly go funny.

Bonner stood a moment longer, as if measuring something more to say, but then left saying nothing. Alva started to pull down her nightgown but looked into the hallway and thought better of it, leaving the flannel gathered high around her waist with the covers still off.

4

"AGNES, dear sweet old Agnes, guess what? We're having a party and *you're* invited! I know it's rather late notice, dear, the party being tonight and all, but we're a rather impulsive lot. You don't have another engagement, do you? Well, you simply *must* fly out of bed this instant and I'll help you pick out a party dress."

One of Alva's jobs, along with the other women in Beaker's Bride, was to care for Agnes who lived alone, bedridden and occasionally lucid. But unlike the other women in town who actually bathed Agnes and changed her bedclothes, Alva used her time in Agnes's house to play around—talk silliness to the woman, tease her, ridicule her, listen to her mumble and murmur. Alva wasn't about to touch the woman's body. *Old?*

· · · · ·

AGNES WAS OLDER than water. Caught in a body for which mobility was a past dream rusted through, a body with only enough juice left to keep her in music and memories, Agnes traveled in bed. She tuned in the old stations, recalling God-wonderful details transmitted from Jacksonville and 1937, from a two-flat on Center Street and the World War. She remembered her long life in dialogue and snapshots and scenes: her sister calling "Agnes, Agnes" of a morning, the whiteness of pearled gloves on summer Sunday afternoons, her man coming down the stairs, holding babies sweet from their bath.

. . . . .

"IF YOU GET DRESSED UP real fancy, some old beau
of yours might ask you to dance."

Alva, airy light, danced around the room that smelled of
Agnes's age. Although Alva had slim hips and the tight
small butt of a teenage boy and although her breasts hadn't
advanced beyond the stage they reached when she was
sixteen, when Alva danced she felt voluptuous.

"Agnes, do you think I dance divinely?"

The ancient one did not, of course, answer—Agnes was
away somewhere else.

"I made a special trip over here to invite you, dear. I'm
supposed to be getting the house ready for tonight. And I
knew Jess wasn't about to come up here and invite you
himself. Did I tell you? Johnny somehow convinced Jess to
go around town and invite everyone *personally* to tonight's
party. That's what the little creature is doing right now. I
don't know how Johnny talked him into it.

"Johnny is the strangest man. He'll come downstairs
of a morning and pull a quarter from Jess's ear, and Jess
just stands there with his bulging eyes bulging all the
more. Or Johnny'll grab one of the eggs I'm about ready
to fry for breakfast and make it disappear right in his
hands. Jess claps. When we walk in the house after I
bring Jess home from school, Johnny shouts out, 'My
beamish boy!' Then they both go running around the
house with their arms out like they're airplanes. It's been
crazy times this past week.

"Johnny and Bonner are getting along famously, too.
Staying up late drinking and telling stories, and then I
come downstairs in the morning and find one of them
sleeping it off on the couch or a lamp broken.

"The only one around the house who isn't getting any of
Mr. Johnny Reace's attention is yours truly. Oh, I don't

know—maybe I intimidate him. Men have told me that before, how they find me intimidating. Can you imagine?"

Alva took a sewing needle from under the lamp on the bedside table and jabbed Agnes lightly in the upper arm, just enough of a prick to cause the old woman to lose for a moment that faraway stare of hers—to lose her place among the memories and music.

"Do you tell Bonner I give you these shots? Oh, I know you talk to *him.* To the other women, too. I don't see the point of keeping your secrets from me. Maybe another jab'll bring you around. No? Well, I was going to be a nurse, you know. Agnes? Your eyes are open, dear, but I can never be sure if you're awake or asleep—or dead."

. . . . . .

AWAKE OR ASLEEP mattered only a breath to someone living on memories' juice, and Agnes thought as a whale thinks or as some people would have you believe whales think, their great brains unbusied by articulating fingers and unopposed by thumbs—allowed therefore to loop thoughts back on themselves, loops and double loops, until over the millennia the thoughts of whales have become cosmic, grander than oceans, thoughts as untranslatable to us as ours are to worker bees busy building, these thought-whales sounding to the depths with their great godheads of thought traveling farther out than rockets and further in than philosophy, recalling how it had been to live on land and back before that to the sea the first time around, back to a cell dividing in the febrile saline sea and remembering all that had happened between then and now, now residing as a grand bulk buoyed by the sea: *able to remember evolution.* So what was reality except something pesky, like hunger or pain, something pesky that had to be endured like those little boats carrying little men throwing harpoons like little needles, deadly little needles. When Agnes's thoughts traveled like the thoughts of whales, she did not wish to be bothered by the airy light if painful reality that Alva pricked her with.

. . . . .

WHEN Alva saw the time, she quickly put the sewing needle back beneath the lamp and hurried out of the house because Jess should be finished inviting everyone by now and the men in her household would be wondering where she was.

On the way home, she passed Alan Winslow's place and stopped to look up at his lighted bedroom window. *He was dancing.* There was no mistaking the movements, crossing back and forth in front of that window and turning and holding his arms out to hold no one. Winslow danced alone.

Alva wondered how many people in the world were dancing at this precise moment. If you could race all over the world, into every bedroom, to all the nightclubs of all the cities, into high school gyms, on cruise ships steaming the oceans—how many? She turned a few airy light steps herself, down the darkening streets, glad to be counted in their number.

Alva had made up her mind: tonight she would seduce Johnny Reace, either by charming him at the party or by simply presenting herself after the party, in the middle of the night, down in the basement room where he slept.

5

JESS RELEE grew up in Beaker's Bride as the only kid in town, Bonner's boy's boy, and did not know until he went to school that he was an oddball, did not know he was uncoordinated until he went to school and baseballs kept hitting him hard in the belly because he couldn't get his hands in front of him fast enough. He grew up in Beaker's Bride, where people called him affectionate names, son and little man and dreamboat and Junie bug. Junie bug is what his mother called him during the summer days when those strange beetles came out, because Jess reminded her of a Junie bug the way he went whirring around the house as if to fly, blundering into furniture as Junie bugs crash against screens, get knocked to the ground, then buzz again to resume their reckless flight. Junie bug and dreamboat and son.

Jess did not know he was fat until he went to school, where kids called him tub-o'-lard and two-ton. They called him specs and four-eyes because of his thick glasses, which he had accepted as a natural part of himself until he went to school and kids confronted him by making circles of their fingers and thumbs and then holding those circles to their own eyes. He grew up in Beaker's Bride where no one laughed at him and Jess did not know until he went to school that he looked funny, feet turning out when he walked like a fat man trudging mud.

He had an adult's features: large round face, bulbous nose, fleshy lips, a mouth that hung open, a big belly over short legs, and his mother's dreamy eyes. Jess had never heard of Winston Churchill until he went to school and a teacher greeted him one day by saying, "Here comes little Mr. Winston Churchill."

Kindergarten was bad, but school got worse with each grade.

Jess grew up in Beaker's Bride hearing about his father, Matthew, who'd been the town's pride, a good kid and a bighearted man who couldn't do enough for you, so full of life and such a shame. Jess referred to his father as Matthew because that's the name everyone else used and saying "dad" sounded wrong. Matthew's golden reputation made Jess a mixture of pride and confusion. "The good die young," people said of Matthew, and Jess wondered what he possibly could do about that.

He knew how Matthew had died: drowned in the Illinois before Jess was born, while Jess's mother was still pregnant. Matthew's aluminum boat was discovered washed ashore miles downriver, but the body never surfaced. Jess didn't know what he could do about that, either, until Beehart suggested a course of action.

This happened back when Jess just started second grade, more miserable than first but not as bad as third was proving to be. It was late afternoon and Jess and Beehart were playing down by the river when Bonner called them home for supper.

Beehart wouldn't leave.

"Come on," Jess said. "You know how mad grampa gets when we're late to eat. And I'm hungry!"

Beehart just sat there.

"*Come on.* Don't be a horse's patoot." Jess wasn't sure what a horse's patoot was, but Mr. Gibsner said it so it had to be something pretty bad. "I'm telling grampa this is your fault, all your fault we're late."

But the good-hearted Beehart did not budge from the cottonwood log where he sat.

"What're you doing?"

Beehart said he was waiting for Matthew.

So Jess sat next to him and said, "Me, too."

Bonner had to come looking for him and Jess blamed everything on Beehart.

After that, the boys often waited by the river's brown width wondering if Matthew might really come ashore—or was this just one of Beehart's games?

.　.　.　.　.

FOR the past week, Johnny had been a joy in Jess's life. Beehart, however, could be vexing and Beehart almost made it impossible for Jess to keep his promise to Johnny about inviting everyone in town to the party tonight. Jess tried to tell Beehart there was nothing to be afraid of, but old Beehart wouldn't move from the base of the walnut tree where they discussed the day's plan.

"Sometimes you really frost my balls." The eight-year-old had no idea what this meant but he'd heard Mr. Gibsner say it and Jess liked the sound it made: frost my balls.

"I said I'd do all the talking. Crybaby. I am *not* afraid—you're the one. I could've been half done by now. We'll walk over by the mansion and then cut up to where Jenny and Sally live. You can wait outside. Mom told me what to say. Come on—I'll play the soldier's song when we get home, *promise*. Please? Okay, then, I'll go by myself but you're not sleeping in my bed tonight. You can sleep on the floor. I just hope that black widow spider I saw the other— Hey! Wait for me!"

But like always Beehart ran on ahead.

When Jess caught up, he asked Beehart if he believed Johnny's finger really had been chewed off by a bear in that cave, and Beehart said he did. Well then what about how Johnny told mom that some fish bit it off—and Beehart said he believed that, too. "You can't believe both. If one's true, the other ain't." But when it came to belief, Beehart had no trouble embracing contradictions.

Beehart was the boy's constant companion but also ever the provocateur. Like the time they forgot about the trash and Beehart said let's get up early and burn it in the morning so we don't have to go out in the dark—which Beehart was afraid of. When at midnight Bonner discovered trash sacks hidden on the back porch, he roused Jess from a sleep and told him gently but without room for compromise that it had to be done right then no matter the hour. You do your duty. All Beehart's fault.

Still, what would Jess have done without him? They were the river rats—that's what Bonner called them.

Something bad might be in that forest, so they didn't play there, and Jess was forbidden to go anywhere near the railroad tracks. The bluffs were too steep to climb. That left the river, where Jess and Beehart spent all their free time watching the barges and skipping stones and waiting for Matthew. Jess could smell the river even when he was in his room, smell the river dirt that the Illinois carried cutting diagonally across that well-soiled state. And the river bore other treasures the boys watched for, collected—it belonged to them and to their time, that stretch of Illinois.

Jess wanted to be down by the river today and wished now that he had told Johnny no, but Jess had trouble denying Johnny anything because he was a magical and scary man who had come up from the river to change life as it had been and who said things Jess loved hearing but didn't understand. It got so that Jess wondered what was the point of waiting any longer for Matthew.

At the door of the first house on their route, Jess turned to Beehart and spoke sternly: "Remember I do all the talking. And *you* stay outside."

He knocked. No answer. Knocked again. Getting ready

to leave when the door opened. Now he had to remember what Alva told him to say. "Uh . . ."

"Lord love us! Jenny, come look who's here. Come in, child, come in. Look how big you're getting. How old are you now?"

"I'm, uh . . ."

"I swear. Oh, Jenny'll have to see you. Jenny! Seems like yesterday your grandpa was carrying you around town on his shoulders like he discovered babies all on his own. You're going to be a big one like your daddy, yes. Jenny, come here! Matthew was the best. Got your mother's eyes, though. What would you like to eat, Jess, honey? You've always been the shy one, haven't you—not like your father. Jenny, remember how Matthew used to come over when he was a boy and talk our leg off?"

Jess blurted out the invitation, saying everything Alva had instructed him to say: "Mom and grampa are having a party tonight and they want you to come over about eight. You don't have to bring anything."

"Now, honey, when your momma says don't bring anything, she doesn't really mean it. Just her way of being polite. I guess she never did mix in with us too good— coming from Millerway, I guess. Why, Matthew couldn't stand it if we came visiting without bringing his favorite dish. Sally? Was it Matthew or Bonner who likes that mince pie of yours? Well you're going to have to bake up a couple this afternoon 'cause he'd never forgive us if we came over without one of his mince pies."

Not only were they going to bring food to the party, but the people Jess was inviting made sure he didn't depart without eating. On the next stop, they pushed cookies.

"Go ahead and finish them up, child, 'cause it won't take us no time to bake some more. Eight o'clock, did you say? My, a party. Marge and me are going to have to get some-one to drive us down to the store so we can buy the makings for ham salad. Unless we can get something defrosted in time."

And if not food, then they wanted to fill the boy with their memories.

"Ev and me always talk don't we Ev about how Matthew used to walk over here and ask us if he could play with that little sausage dog we had and this was back when he was about your age. You don't remember Otto of course. He died 'fore you even was born. When *did* Otto die, Ev?"

And after each visit, Jess told Beehart what he'd eaten: cookies, sandwiches, cake, pie, pudding left over from the night before so that it had that interesting thickness on top. He drank milk and pop, his stomach tightening until Jess thought he couldn't possibly add one more bite or gulp. Still, you had to eat what was offered, and Jess owned an appetite that would cause you to sit down and think about it.

"Oh come on now and stop trying to be so polite, nibbling around like that. Goodness, Jess, I changed your diapers. I'm no stranger you have to be polite to. If your mother said you shouldn't eat with us that's just 'cause she doesn't understand our ways. Dorrie and me we baked those oatmeal cookies yesterday and I never met a boy yet couldn't eat more than three oatmeal cookies so go ahead, help yourself. You like them without raisins, too? We make them both ways 'cause Dorrie can't tolerate raisins anymore. And bring him a big glass of cold milk, too, Dorrie. You can't eat oatmeal cookies without milk, can you child?"

This was taking all day, and Jess couldn't move very quickly between houses because his tightened belly made him walk in a kind of swayback waddle. He remained polite, however, and ate what was offered. Yes ma'am. Thank you. Yes sir. "Ain't he got manners?" "Well, sure, Bonner brought him up right—just like Matthew." The old people beamed upon the boy.

They were elderly sisters living together, widowed sisters with maiden sisters, long-married old couples whose children were moved away and who had themselves become elderly, a few bachelor men living with their sisters, widows three to a house, retirees, invalids, men and women who had paid for all their possessions but who lived now on meager pensions and on savings almost gone, wondering which would come first, death or penury, and who sometimes were unsure which conclusion they preferred.

But they were undesperate, solid and stolid and midwestern. They lived along a river and had insight into life's length: You marry a man and live with him thirty years, a lifetime, then he dies and you're alone seven years, a lifetime it seemed, and then another man as fine as the first and God gives you twenty-one years with him and now it's been what nine years since he passed on. All of that in just one life.

Here comes even more, this strange and wonderful child who must be loved by God—just look at him—and he's standing there in the doorway reciting an invitation to a *party*, of all things. At my age. So you fix him a sandwich asking constant questions about the kind of bread he wants and does he prefer butter or mayonnaise though he certainly can have both, just say, Jess, just you say. *A party*. Why, you can remember when we used to have those parties . . .

After some debate with Beehart, Jess decided not to invite Agnes. He knew she couldn't come to the door, which meant he would have to go into her house and climb the stairs to her bedroom and knock on her door there—and that was too scary because everyone talked about how old Agnes was and Jess didn't want to be the one to find her dead.

Skipping Agnes left only the Winslow house and then Jess could go home. It was getting on toward dark.

Alan Winslow didn't invite the boy in or offer to feed him; he just grilled Jess about the party's purpose and who else was invited and what were people going to be doing at this party and is that Johnny guy still staying at your house? None of the answers were satisfactory to Winslow. "Clean your glasses, boy," he said.

Jess smeared the dirty lenses on his sweaty shirt and then walked-waddled away.

"Clumsy damn kid."

Now it was dark. Jess and Beehart could've gone the long way home, but the street running between Beaker Mansion and the cemetery was the most direct route. They talked it over trying to decide which of them was scared and which wasn't. Beehart said let's go the long way around, and Jess called him a sissy.

So many houses in Beaker's Bride were abandoned that the emptiness of the stone mansion didn't frighten Jess, but he had heard stories of how that place was infested with snakes and of some bride haunting the house, waiting for her lover to return—but what truly horrified the boy was this: that someday he might have to live there. Please, anything but that. What was wrong with *their* house? Jess hoped against hope that Bonner would never finish Beaker Mansion so that they would never have to move into that awful place.

How could anyone even *think* of living in a house that overlooked a cemetery? In his peripheral vision, Jess could see figures moving among those odd stones and monuments; he could see them as clearly as he could see Beehart, who remained close to his side—on the side opposite the cemetery, of course.

Perhaps it was because of what he could see peripherally that teachers had told Alva Jess might be retarded or suffering some brand of autism. Bonner suspected something was wrong with the boy each time he found him riding the big marble bird that Bonner kept in the shed behind their house, Jess in some sort of trance on that statue so that his grandfather had to pry him loose saying, "Child, child, child."

But Jess simply occupied a world that did not coincide at all points with the world we know.

"What you got to do," Jess instructed Beehart as they approached that terrible corridor between haunted mansion and populated cemetery, "is walk real slow no matter what we hear or see. Grampa says nothing can chase you if you don't run from it."

But as soon as they were within striking distance of their own brightly lighted home, like always Beehart ran on ahead and Jess had to race for his life.

6

AS ALAN WINSLOW got ready for tonight's party, he thought about the hailstorm of a week ago. A crazy September hailstorm, and he had taken his wife's dog into that hail, a hail bad enough to put marble bruises on the backs of Winslow's small hands, but he didn't mind, not when he had as compensation the suffering of Alphonse.

His wife's dog. A cowardly and sneaky poodle dog. What satisfaction it was to watch Alphonse hit by ice bullets from which there was no escape, the poodle jerking at his leash and trying to hide next to Winslow's legs but unable to avoid that heavy bombardment, being stung as if ten thousand bad boys tormented him with no recourse finally except to hump up his skinny cyst-infected back and whine and then howl—howling long and low in the hail.

Ho! What dee-light. Until, *until* the French poodle suddenly squatted to lick maniacally at his genitals. Winslow was incredulous that the creature would perform this hated act in the middle of ice popping and clicking all around them, ice bad enough to kill chickens.

"Even in the hail!" Winslow shouted. "Even in the hail, you little Froggy bastard, you!" He jerked hard on the leash, causing the dog to roll off his haunches and fall on his side in the manner of a small and very stupid panda bear.

Alphonse was as relentless as the hail. He dropped his rear end to the ground and began scratching it along the grass, propelling himself with front legs only—a sight so offensive to Winslow that he picked up the dog and headed home. It had been on the way to his house that he had seen Johnny standing out in the middle of the road in front of Beaker Mansion.

. . . . .

NOW IN HIS upstairs bedroom getting ready for tonight's party, Winslow could hear the poodle licking at itself somewhere in the house. "Stop it," Winslow muttered wearily, knowing the dog would never stop it. He stepped out into the hallway to see Alphonse balanced on haunches with back legs in the air to lick like a cat at stomach skin that was permanently hairless and a bad purple from so many cycles of being licked raw, crusting over, licked raw once more. Its tail was exceedingly ugly: a hairless and angry-purple wet stub. "Stop it!"

The dog looked up from his licking but did not change positions.

Winslow retreated into the bedroom, shutting the door but knowing exactly what was going on out in the hallway: that incessant licking of stomach, genitals, anus, tail.

Alan Winslow treasured an image of himself. That he favored Fred Astaire not only in debonair manner of dress but also in body build and elegance of carriage and a certain brand of haughty class. That he was a man offended by crudity. The presence in his life of that eleven-year-old, foul-smelling, gas-passing, bladder-weakened poodle wounded him more deeply than anyone could have guessed. His wife's dog.

Winslow tried to recapture the mood that Jess's invitation had summoned—a mood of hope that maybe his wife wouldn't return from shopping in time and he could get out of the house alone for once and maybe a woman from the city would be at the party and . . .

But how can you dream about dancing with a beautiful stranger when that goddamn dog is slurping at his ass out in the hallway? "Stop it!" Winslow screamed, rushing to open the bedroom door but not finding Alphonse there. He locked the door.

Now I have to take another shower, he thought. The dog had made him all nervous-sweaty, and Winslow couldn't tolerate the thought of not being absolutely clean and sweet-smelling, especially when he and some sophisticated lady might dance in front of everyone tonight.

People would have to cajole Winslow and the lady into dancing, saying about him that he's Fred Astaire and to her insisting this was an opportunity not to be missed. Winslow and the lady would shrug, lift eyebrows, nod—and dance.

When the waltz is over, Winslow bows to *her* and then to the audience. *There is applause.*

To a full-length mirror, Winslow bowed.

"Al! Are you using the toilet?"

Once again his wife had not been killed in a car accident. Winslow kept his eyes tightly closed. The sophisticated lady from out of town would be demure, soft-spoken, and she would weigh no more than one hundred and five pounds. One-ten tops.

"Al, did you fall in or what? I been waiting to use the toilet. Come on, unlock this door, I need it bad!"

When she started rattling the bedroom door, Winslow unlocked it. With his velour robe wrapped tightly around him, the little man sat glumly on the bed refusing to talk to his wife as she patted his shoulder and asked what he was doing, trying for a kiss before she went into *his* bathroom, the hated Alphonse trotting snottily behind her. *Why does she take that dog into the bathroom with her?* Winslow listened, disheartened, to sounds that no sophisticated lady from out of town weighing one-ten tops would be capable of making.

"We're going downstairs to watch television," his wife

announced when she and Alphonse reemerged. "You come join us and I'll make a nice snack for you to eat while I show you what I bought. Okay?"

Winslow said nothing.

"He *wants* to be alone," she said good-naturedly to the dog.

When he finally was ready, Winslow danced down the steps. He wore a muted yellow jacket, brown slacks, white linen shirt, brown-and-yellow wool tie in a perfect Windsor knot, and two-toned shoes. Tiny little shoes, brown and yellow.

"I'm off," he said quickly. "Might be late, so don't wait up." Winslow opened the front door but didn't make his escape.

"Off where?" She was alarmed, and the poodle shook nervously.

"Oh, didn't I tell you? Bonner asked me to drop by this evening. Probably wants to talk business—go over his policies, I guess."

"Why are you all dressed up?" She was suspicious.

"I'm not all dressed up."

"*Al.*" She was relentless.

He hated to be called Al. "I guess some other people are coming by, too," he said softly. "Maybe they all want me to explain some of their policy provisions."

"They're having a party, aren't they?" She was sure.

"I don't know if you'd call it a party, exactly. A little get-together maybe. The kid came over to invite me and you can't ever get a straight answer out of him."

She screeched. What about me she wanted to know. You were going to leave me here alone weren't you? I didn't think you'd be interested he replied. I'm going she said. You're not ready he pointed out. She insisted she could be ready in ten minutes and he knew it was true and that truth broke his heart.

"It won't be much fun for you!" Winslow shouted as she went up the steps. "I thought you said your legs were bothering you."

But she was already upstairs in his bathroom. Winslow waited standing so he wouldn't wrinkle anything. He was a retired insurance salesman.

Alan Winslow's first wife had been a dowdy little woman who adored him and seldom spoke out of turn, and for twenty-two years they were comfortable with each other, childless. He became the world's most complacent man: never worried about not being loved, never suffered a business reverse, always in good health, no complaints, never had occasion to examine any of the premises of his life. Then his wife died and Winslow retired early, having socked away big money in annuities. He bought up Beaker's Bride property as it became available, people out of work and forced to move—forced to sell to Winslow at heartbreaking prices. He came to own most of Beaker's Bride, and as a widower in a town of widows, he grew in complacency.

Until life took a turn for Alan Winslow.

He was convinced that eventually the railroad would reopen the depot and yards, that the town would become repopulated, or at least that city folks would buy summer houses here—and then Winslow could cash in, doubling or tripling his investment. But none of what he waited for so desperately had come about and, over the years, he was being drained by mortgage payments on a devaluing portfolio. This wasn't the worst turn in Winslow's life, however. The worst turn came when he took a bus to St. Louis to see a show and *she* was along for the ride—someone's friend's sister spending the summer visiting up in Jacksonville.

That was nine years ago, and nine years ago she was a firecracker: voluptuously big-hipped and cushion-breasted, made up like someone in the theater, cackling laughter, sitting next to Winslow on the bus and slathering him with compliments about how he was a man who could wear clothes, and she liked that in a man.

"Can we bring Al, Al?" she hollered from upstairs. It was a joke of hers, calling both her dog and her husband by the same name.

He married her nine years ago because when he brought her to town for a visit, the other men poked ribs and cracked jokes—causing Winslow to grin and grin. He was invigorated by what he assumed people said about him and her, that Winslow must still be pretty hot stuff to marry a gal like that, by which they meant someone younger (though not so much younger as Winslow had been led to believe). Someone with a spectacular figure and so sassy. The woman had a mouth on her you wouldn't believe, and before they were married she did things to him that his dowdy first wife didn't know were possibilities. Those were heady days, dating this new woman and then receiving her open gratitude when he proposed marriage.

But except for her talents, she brought nothing to the marriage—certainly nothing that added to Winslow's holdings, no savings or stocks or bonds or real estate. All she owned were her clothes and poodle.

Look at him. The dog actually had balanced itself half propped against an ottoman in the living room, the better to reach way down and lick languorously at an inflamed scrotum. Ugly tongue rolling doggy testicles. That hideous dry slurping sound that Winslow awoke in the middle of the night hearing. Vet bills, pills—nothing could keep the dog's tongue away from its privates twenty-four hours a day.

"Stop!" Winslow demanded, straining to whisper as he waited at the door for his wife. But Alan Winslow knew how it would finally stop. He'd already purchased the pistol. Meanwhile, there were scores to settle—by taking Alphonse for walks in a bad hail, for example. Winslow grinned.

7

THE ONLY RESIDENTS of Beaker's Bride not in the Relee house for the party that night were Agnes, too old to move, and the occupants of those three acres beginning across the street from Beaker Mansion and running all the way down to the winding road, river road, that followed as best it could the Illinois shoreline.

Those who resided in the cemetery had once lived in Beaker's Bride or in one of the small towns from the surrounding area. There was an attraction to being buried here. Certain people had given death years of thought, were serious about it, and they appreciated the propriety of being planted in a proper location overlooking a river and facing sunsets, your grave dug with a shovel by a man who resembled Abraham Lincoln, a man who—if you made the arrangements ahead of time and if your kin didn't let the funeral director talk them out of it—would shave and peg soft pine for a dignified coffin. Certain people made these arrangements even if they had to forsake their family plots, because graveyards in other towns were weedy, rocky sites stuck out someplace on a piece of property unsuitable for farming or housing or any other secular enterprise, and in those other towns your grave was dug by a loud backhoe and they buried you in a casket made of some space-age material.

Besides, if you came to Beaker's Bride for your grave, you could buy from Bonner Relee some wonderful stone artifact to mark your spot. Ed Beaker had brought the stones and statues down from Chicago on his train, and now the Beaker's Bride cemetery was full of flamboyant and eccentric markers: white angels in reposes of great drama, stubby gray obelisks, concrete tree trunks with concrete squirrels attached scampering up, big round stone balls, massive marble boxes on which marble figures had thrown themselves in grief, crosses wreathed and rising fifteen feet, rounded headstones topped with stone hands showing one finger pointing skyward. On pedestals over the graves of infants stood wistful Madonnas, each of them holding an unclothed baby to her stone breast. During summer, you might be able to pass these mother monuments with little more than curiosity, but in winter, no one unstonehearted could look at them and remain untouched—not in winter, when stone is very cold and snow clings to those bare marble babies.

What was destined to be the cemetery's biggest monument wasn't yet in place, however, because for now it resided in the shed behind Bonner's house: a half-ton colossus that Bonner kept for himself. He already knew, *exactly*, how that giant marble bird would look when positioned correctly over his grave.

It was upon this stone bird that Jess flew: a big white marble dove that waited out in the shed, waited with one of its wings straight out and the other swept back—waited in midbeat while the party in the Relee house progressed.

8

HEAD LIKE A bowling ball, chicken wings in his shirt pocket, fingertips stained from illicit chocolate chips, and a drumstick in each fat hand—Jess sat halfway up the steps eating as he watched people arrive for tonight's party. For him, life in Beaker's Bride was the equivalent of being half asleep while someone read to him from a book of stories, and he never was sure what the next page might bring, never sure how much was recitation and how much his own dreams—always waiting for a new character to be introduced.

The chicken tasted good and he loved sucking the bones, licking his formerly chocolate fingers, pulling another piece from his greasy pocket as he sat there listening half asleep to the arriving stories.

"Where's your mother, boy?" Bonner asked from the bottom step.

Jess didn't reply to this part of the story; it exasperated Bonner the way that child could refuse a direct question. When his grandfather left the hallway, Jess arranged the clean bones in a neat pile on one of the steps and then crept down to fill his pockets once more.

Alva came in the back door and rushed through the kitchen, entering the living room in time to be struck by one of Bonner's cold stares. To avoid him, she headed directly for the big couch where Johnny sat talking with two old women.

"Where are your people from, Mr. Reace?" one of them was asking him.

"Call me Johnny, please. From Virginia, ma'am, on my father's side. On my mother's side, Irish."

"We had an uncle once married an Irish girl. My mother's brother. His name was John, too. A sweet girl. We loved her like she was one of our own. Annie, you remember Uncle John's little Irish wife, don't you?"

"Of course. She had that funny eye. Seems the Irish people always got at least one thing wrong with them." She'd been staring at the stub of Johnny's ring finger.

"This?" he asked, holding up his left hand.

"Oh, I hadn't noticed. How in the world did that happen?"

"Firecracker. We were playing with them on the Fourth of July, a bunch of us kids. My mother told me not to, but you know kids, I didn't listen to her, and one of those big firecrackers that you used to be able to buy years ago, it went off right in my hand."

The two old women clucked and nodded. "I knew it!" one of them said with gleeful satisfaction. "Kids and firecrackers come to no good, I've said that all along."

"Kids won't listen," the other agreed. "Then it's too late. Firecrackers!"

They continued clucking.

"What is it you do, *Johnny?*" one old lady asked.

Alva rolled her eyes.

"Little of this, little of that. Thought one time of taking up the ministry, but I got caught in the ways of the world—you know how that is."

"You better put your legs down, honey," one of the women told Alva.

With her knees up to her chin, Alva's skirt had dropped away under her so that those on the couch could see her white underpants. She wondered if Johnny bothered to look. Although Alva didn't really care what the women of Beaker's Bride thought of her, she lowered her legs and smoothed her skirt.

"We had a second cousin, didn't we, Evelyn, who was in the ministry. Bernie?"

"Bernie?"

"You remember Bernie. Elizabeth's boy."

"He was in the ministry?"

"You know very well he was. One of them offshoot Methodists. Lived someplace back East."

"His wife was from Ohio, wasn't she?"

"Was she? Now what was her name again?"

"Betsy, wasn't it?"

"You're thinking of Nathan's boy, killed by that city bus in Cincinnati. *His* wife was Betsy, remember? She had that speech problem."

"Nathan's boy was killed by a city bus in Cincinnati? You sure?"

"Of course I'm sure. His wife got that settlement from the city, remember? Bought herself a convertible car, don't you remember ever'body talking about her? After getting that settlement money in her pocket, she became eccentric as a lapdog."

Johnny laughed, delighting the two old women and forcing them to join him in that laughter, though neither of them was exactly sure what had elicited it.

Alva stood. "I need your help in the kitchen," she announced.

Johnny nodded but did not stand up.

"Whenever you're ready," Alva said, her voice openly sarcastic. When Johnny still made no effort to move, she stalked away.

"That little girl can be so hateful," said one old woman.

"Now, now," cautioned the other.

In the hallway, Bonner laid a giant's hand on her thin shoulder. "Better get all this food organized."

She looked at the covered dishes and plastic bowls on the table and was made sick by the sight of so much food, German potato salad and stuffed cabbages and pies—and half of the chickens killed in last week's hailstorm had been pulled out of freezers for tonight's party, except this isn't a party at all, Alva decided: it's a feed. Hadn't Jess told these people not to bring anything? That's all they do here in Beaker's Bride. Eat. When someone got sick or died, the first thing Alva was expected to do was fix food and bring it over. Looking at all the food, Alva decided she had to leave this town. But it was an old resolution.

Bonner greeted two women fussing with their dishes. "Sally, how are you? And Jenny? What's that you got there?"

"You don't think Sally'd show up without one of your mince pies, do you, Bonner?"

"I certainly hope not. Makes the best mince pie in the state of Illinois."

The two women smiled broadly.

"We sure could use some more food," Alva said.

"I know Agnes isn't able to make it to no party," one of the women said, "but I sure hope she was invited." Both women looked at Alva; they knew she never bathed or cleaned up after Agnes and they were hoping the mention of the ancient one's name would shame Alva. Agnes was the civic project of the women of Beaker's Bride, and Alva's refusal to help marked her as irresponsible, an outsider. The kind of woman who apparently saw no disgrace in being a mother without being a wife first.

When the Winslows entered the hallway, Alan immediately cornered Bonner and started talking about his latest correspondence with the railroad. According to Winslow, there was a possibility of the yards reopening sometime next year, maybe—did Bonner have any idea what Winslow's property holdings would be worth if the railroad returned to Beaker's Bride or even if they reopened just the depot? His wife, meanwhile, waddled along the food table.

"You met Alan before," Bonner said to Johnny. "This here's his wife. *Wayne.*"

"Wayne?"

The woman grinned at Johnny.

"Come on, now, that's not really your name, is it?"

"Now don't make me go back to the house and get my driver's license," she replied, with a plate already in her hand.

"I'll be. I've met a lot of women with strange and wonderful names in my life, knew a Silence in Virginia and a little deaf gal in Massachusetts by the name of Winsome, but you're the first female Wayne I've ever met."

"Actually," she said, filling her plate, "the name on my birth certificate is Elaine-Wayne 'cause I was named out of honor to a brother of mine who died in childhood that year I was born, but I've gone by Wayne since childhood and it's my official name now. You should hear the grief I get when I have to fill out some application."

"I bet they don't believe you."

"They don't!" Her plate was full.

"Brother," Alva muttered, loud enough for all to hear.

Alan Winslow also was disheartened by the conversation, by the awful truth that he was married to a woman named Wayne—a woman who outweighed him by a good forty pounds.

"Just look at this spread," Wayne said. "I didn't know we were supposed to bring something. Al gave me hardly any time at all to get ready. I just threw on this old pantsuit. He hates it, don't you, Al? Told me one time that it made me look like a big old fat cherry."

"Like a *ripe* cherry, Wayne," Johnny told her. "Ready for the plucking."

She whooped as if someone had stomped on her swollen feet. "You better watch this one, Al, he's got a mouth on him. Ain't he, Alva?"

Alva didn't reply. From a middle step, Jess watched with dreamy interest. He desired more chicken.

Later, in the kitchen, Johnny helped Alva make drinks.

"Myself, I'll have a gin gimlet," she told him. "You know how to make one of those?"

"Sure. I'll do a whole tray of different drinks and we'll see if we can't loosen up this crowd."

"The women in this town don't like me," Alva said after she got her gimlet and had sipped from it. "I think it's because I'm the only female in town still menstruating." And when that didn't impress him, she added, "The only woman in town still screwing."

He laughed as he left, carrying a tray of drinks to the living room, handing this glass to that old lady and that one to this one, teasing them into accepting what they at first refused. But Johnny always asked the men what they preferred, because he knew that while women can be talked into trying a new drink, men have liquor codes they seldom break.

In his wake:

"Helen, do you have the same kind I do? No, yours is green ain't it? Taste mine. Isn't that good? Oh yours is good too. What *did* he put in these? I never had this kind of fancy drink before, hope it ain't addicting. I wonder what that kind is. See Jane's, she's got a slice of orange in hers. Jane. Jane! Deaf as a rock. I think I'll ask him if I can't try one with a slice of orange in it."

By the time Johnny returned to the kitchen, Alva had finished her gimlet and was working on a glass of straight gin. She waited until he departed with another tray of colored drinks before taking off her underpants and putting them in the wastebasket—right there on top.

Out in the hallway, still halfway up the steps, Jess chewed on a chicken wing. He listened to Mr. Gibsner talk of flying saucers.

Johnny was fascinated, too, hearing the old ex-farmer talk about a UFO that landed in his wheat field thirty-some years ago. Although Mr. Gibsner never saw the craft itself, he had as evidence a hundred-foot square of wheat that had been burned off and if, by God, they tried that again, he claimed he was prepared to give them a short course in the sanctity of private property as guaranteed in the U.S. Constitution and enforced by one of Mr. Winchester's products.

" 'Course I know them UFO people probably got strange customs," Mr. Gibsner said. "I saw a movie once when this guy got killed for not sleeping with a Eskimo's wife."

Charlie Warden laughed. "He wants that UFO, which never landed in the first place, he wants it to come back and take him home with them so he can sleep with some green Martian gal."

"You really frost my balls, Charlie Warden! Never took a thing serious in your life. I bet you never even read the U.S. Constitution or anything at all about space travel."

"I know one thing. I don't spend my time waiting out in the middle of the night for some UFO to come back and get me, 'specially when it never came here in the first place."

The people of Beaker's Bride had heard them argue for two decades, and while the audience was comfortable with this old performance, the two veterans—troupers—played it like opening night.

When she couldn't tolerate another minute of it, Alva left the living room and went upstairs, stopping on the steps to tell Jess he had to go down and say hello to people. "Go on, dreamboat. I'll be right back."

He didn't want to.

"Go on, go on. Now you've been real good about this shyness ever since Johnny came, and I want you to keep on being brave for me. Okay?"

"*Mom.*"

"Go on! I'll come down in a second."

Jess trudged reluctantly to the edge of the large living room. He dreaded the moment when someone saw him and started a fuss—the old women flapping to offer their laps and the old men commenting "boy" this and "boy" that.

Handed from one perfumed hug to the next, patted on the shoulder, smiled upon, Jess was maneuvered to the center of the room, his eyes anchored to the floor and his belly knotted. As bad as this was, worse came in the doorway: Alva carrying the clarinet. Jess tried to signal her but she refused the message, so he squeezed shut his eyes and tried to fly.

Alva, more than a little drunk, asked loudly, "Who wants to hear Jess play the clarinet? Johnny found this old thing in the closet and for a whole week now he's been teaching Jess to play taps. Wouldn't you all like to hear Jess play?"

She offered the clarinet to Jess but he didn't take it, didn't even open his eyes. "Come on, dreamboat. It's the one you call the soldier's song. I heard you play it perfectly the other day."

Nada.

"Come on. Make Johnny proud of you."

From within Jess came a moan so low only Alva heard it.

Why would your own mother choose to torture you? Jess swayed his weight from foot to foot like a chained baby elephant, and the people in that room tried their best to look elsewhere.

Alva was sorry, but she didn't know any way out of it now.

Then Johnny intervened, making his way to the center of the room and quickly lifting the heavy child high in his arms, carrying Jess toward the hallway but stopping to turn around and tell everyone, "Foot in the stirrup, hand on the horn—best damn cowboy ever born!" He and Jess looked at each other, both of them grinning.

Johnny put him to bed and then came down to find Alva in the kitchen pouring herself another drink. "I'm the world's least judgmental person," he told her, "but that wasn't right."

"Did you happen to notice my panties there in the trash?"

Johnny looked. "You're a spooky little broad."

"I may be the only woman you ever meet in your life who's willing to do *anything*. Oh, I know you've probably known some wild women—willing to do almost anything—but I don't qualify it, Johnny. I'd do *anything* for you."

He put back his head and closed his eyes and sang as he had off-key in the hallway that day they first met: "*She's short of height and shy on weight, but Alva's the girl makes my coffee percolate. Yeahhh.* " Then he opened his eyes. "I bet no man's ever sung that for you, huh?"

"No. But once a man called me his sweet sticky thing."

Johnny laughed.

"Do you want to kiss me?"

"Let's talk about it when you're sober."

"Ah, an honorable man."

Johnny considered Alva and her offer, but he had too often complicated his life with women. "I guess I'll see if I can hustle another tray of drinks. For old geezers, they're—"

She stepped close enough for them to smell each other, whiskey breath breathing down on gin breath rising. But this was all Alva could do: stand there and offer it, because her experience came from defensive positions, yielding territory that an opposing force is then faced with holding.

"We could go out to the shed," she offered. "I got the key." Would he be aroused or offended if she lifted her skirt and let him have a look?

"What's Bonner keep in that shed?"

Alva's big eyes popped. "Oh, you know, don't you? I thought he'd showed you that white bird the first day you were here."

"White bird?"

"Oh, come on, Johnny. Bonner's showed it to you, hasn't he?"

"No."

"I swear that man keeps secrets better than anyone I've ever known. Almost as well as I do—and I *never* tell."

"Well, tell me about this white bird of Bonner's."

"Let's go see it."

But just then Helen Datterly came into the kitchen. "Oh, hi, you two. I hope I'm not interrupting anything."

"No," Alva said icily, stepping back from Johnny.

Helen Datterly asked him if he could fix her another one of those red drinks. "It comes with the toothpick, you know that one with pieces of pineapple and a cherry on the toothpick. Alva, honey, where'd you get these fancy makings?"

"You go on back to the party," Alva told her. "I'll bring it out to you."

"Thank you, dear."

As soon as the woman was gone, Alva took Johnny's hand. "Let's go."

"What about Helen?"

"Hurry up and fix her drink, then we'll sneak away—okay?"

"Yeah. I better see if anyone else needs a fresh one."

"You're not going out to the shed with me, are you? I'll be damned. Tell you what, Mr. Johnny Reace. If you suddenly get in the mood later on, get in the mood to see what's out there in that shed, then you just let me know. Give me a signal, okay?"

"A signal."

"Yeah. What was it those old hens were telling you about earlier—where Nathan's boy or whoever it was got killed by a city bus?"

"Cincinnati?"

"Right. You just say 'Cincinnati'—work it into the conversation or something—and that'll be our signal. I'll leave right away and we'll meet by the shed. Okay?"

"Sure."

.   .   .   .   .

HE FIXED Helen Datterly's red and fruited drink. Taking it to the living room, he was just in time to be pulled into a disagreement among several men about how Beaker's Bride *really* got its name.

Johnny paused until he had their attention, not only the men who'd been arguing but everyone in the room. "It so happens, I know the *true* story."

"How's that?" Winslow asked. "You ain't even from here."

"But I came down from Chicago, and up in Chicago, it's common knowledge. The truth is, your town came this far," Johnny said, holding his thumb and forefinger barely an inch apart, "from not being called Beaker's Pride or Beaker's Bride or any version of that. Big Ed Beaker wanted to call this place Florence." He nodded to himself. "Yessir, Florence."

Winslow snorted.

"Florence, Illinois." Johnny smiled. "Old Big Ed met her at an outdoor party the railroad threw at a little park on the shore of Lake Michigan. She was shivering. Middle of the summer and the whole crowd thankful for that breeze coming in off the lake, but little Florence, a wisp of a girl, she was shivering. Big Ed gave her his suit jacket. It fit Florence like an overcoat. She couldn't have been more than nineteen, the tiniest little thing. Big Ed Beaker could've tucked her away in one of his pockets."

Johnny sipped from his brown drink, looked at the ceiling, then spoke in the softest voice. He talked of a tough-hearted businessman arranging for flowers, big big bouquets of them, to be delivered every morning of the week, and how it is that innocence begets innocence—Florence so innocent it didn't occur to her that Big Ed's intentions could be anything but honorable and Big Ed so smitten that he was unable to take advantage of her nature. He wrote for Florence. This man of rails and rolling stock wrote poetry that made Florence weep and shiver. Big Ed, who'd known every indulgence a rich man can buy, was thrilled to hold that small white hand. Neither of them cared about or even noticed the snickering when they announced their betrothal. Giving Big Ed a son was what she wanted out of life, but a wisp of a girl was too frail to bear a big man's child, and the doctors pleaded with Florence, who would not be dissuaded.

Look at that fraud, Bonner thought, he's actually put tears in his eyes.

Johnny told of the pain and of the suffering suffered in silence, the secrets kept from Big Ed, who thought of the coming event as a profoundly happy one—not knowing what the doctors had said. So he built a mansion on the sweetest single spot along all those miles of right-of-way he owned, and he told Florence that's where he and she and the boy would spend their summers.

Whispering now, Johnny talked of a small woman's pain and how doctors cursed their limits—how midwives had to leave the room, it was that bad. With Big Ed downstairs boasting to his cronies: a son, a son. Tears were on Johnny's cheeks and the men of Beaker's Bride shifted uncomfortably in their chairs while women took out tissues and dabbed their noses, their eyes. But Johnny spoke on relentlessly of deathbed promises and deathbed pledges, frail bodies going limp in strong arms, an infant boy who never cried, and how god-awful black a big man's mood can become.

Upstairs Jess was inconsolable as Beehart, blond and angelic, patted the child's shoulder telling him it was only a story.

But the story became a wake in that living room, women recalling babies of their own who had died at birth and children who had died in terrible fevers. It was the way Johnny told the story, that's what made it too much, how he could say things that would embarrass the rest of us— too flowery, too emotional. Bonner wanted to tell him, have some decency, man—but Johnny talked on in that hesitant whisper of his about the infant son held around by a mother's thin arms, the two of them at repose in a rich casket overburdened with flowers, big big bouquets of them, and how it took three strong railroad men to pull Ed back from the grave. And when Bonner thought it couldn't get any worse, that's when, from upstairs, there came a sweetly punishing sound that made even the men touch their eyes. It was Jess playing his clarinet.

. . . . .

JOHNNY NEVER DID MAKE a connection between Florence and the name, Beaker's Bride, but facts no longer mattered to those who had been seduced by some truth larger than facts: they simply granted Johnny the benediction of believing him.

Except for Alan Winslow. "Where did this Florence come from, anyway?" he demanded.

Johnny looked at him. "Her hometown? Florence's hometown was in Ohio. Let's see . . . yeah. Her hometown was . . ."

And then Alva knew. No one else in that room knew what Johnny was going to say, but Alva knew. She pressed her legs together and put a hand down there like a little girl. Alva knew. Say it, she thought. Say *Cincinnati!* Say it!

"Columbus. Columbus, Ohio."

Alva yelped as if touching something electrical while wet. She stared right back at the people who stared at her. "Couldn't you just eat him up!" she said. "I know *I* could! Just eat him up!"

This party had turned out to be so crazy that the people were confused about what to do or say next.

Then Bonner stood as if it were his turn to speak. "Yes. He's something, ain't he?"

For the first time in years, Johnny Reace was unsure.

9

THAT NIGHT after the party, I couldn't sleep, plotting and knowing that one day Mr. Johnny Reace would want what I could grant him, would want it real bad, and then I'd say "Columbus" instead of "Cincinnati" and let him feel how it feels to get shocked like that. Like the shock of a ball peen hammer to the temple. He was the kind of man who'd been hit before.

I don't know how Johnny got it broken, but you could tell by the way his nose wandered a bit to the west of his face that he'd never had it properly reset, and although his eyes were heartbreak blue, they were small and closely set, and Johnny was short. He was handsome only in the way men speak of a good saddle horse or field dog being handsome—displaying a dignity and durability that overrode any shortcomings in conformation.

For me, however, Mr. Johnny Reace had a dangerous appeal, that square face and strong jaw, thick brown hair, eyes like sky, and especially his laughter. If not laughing, then he seemed always about to laugh. After my years of isolation in Beaker's Bride, I would've been put off balance by the arrival of any stranger—but for him to be Johnny Reace, laughing, who came to live in our house, well, that just lay me down.

· · · · ·

WHEN I WAS a little girl, I wanted nothing more than to have a scorpion on my belly. I announced this to my father one July day when I was eight years old. Daddy had his shirt off and I was sitting on his lap listening to his tattoo stories: how hot it was in Manila the day he got the snake put on his shoulder, what SEMPER FI on his arm meant, and the way a Mexican lady he met in Guadalajara laughed using just her eyes. "She didn't talk much," daddy said, "but she had plenty to say." MARIA was in flowery script above his left nipple, and these tattoo stories were better told when mother was out of the house.

Daddy said that instead of a scorpion on the belly, I should have my motto tattooed over my heart. Although I knew what a motto was, "Semper Fidelis" being the Marines' motto, I didn't know *I* had one. Daddy said it was what I told mother every time I got into a fistfight with some boy and she asked if I wasn't afraid of getting hurt. The same thing I told daddy the *second* time he pulled me out of the river. He said it was also what I told the boys when I got bitten by old man Crat's cocker spaniel because I was the only one who'd go over the fence to get the football.

When I still couldn't remember, daddy stood up and imitated me. "You button up your lower lip like this. Put on one of your fierce frowns. Then you say, pouting and too stubborn to cry, you say, ' 'Fraid of nothin'.' *That's* your motto, Alva."

. . . . .

I GREW UP in a town so small it isn't even there anymore. Just nine kids lived in Millerway, and I was the only girl among eight boys: six older than I was, one younger, and one my age. After I got my first period and when my breasts came, I no longer went skinny-dipping in the river with the boys, but I still played and fought with them— always fought like a boy, using my fists—and I was as tough as they were. 'Fraid of nothin'.

Then daddy died and I took up with Donny B., who lived next door and was the only boy in town exactly my age. I had just turned thirteen when Donny B. stopped throwing rocks every time he saw me. Then one summer Saturday afternoon, something happened that made me think he and I would eventually marry.

The rest of the boys were off fishing in the Illinois while Donny B. and I were out behind my house eating mulberries, staining our hands and mouths purple. He asked me to pull up my dress and show him my "panties"—which at the time I thought was the oddest request, but you do strange things for a future husband, so I lifted my hem. That was it for the moment; we returned to our mulberries without further revelation.

But as Donny B. was gripped more tightly by puberty, his requests intensified: Let me touch you down there. Okay. Take off your panties and let me see. All right. You wanna look at my weenie? If you want me to, sure. Touch it. Like this? Yeah—oh baby, *yeah.*

When we turned fifteen, he finally asked me if I would "make love" with him (I'd been waiting and waiting for him to stop fooling around and get on with it), and I said I was willing to do *anything* for him. After the first time, we were at it all the time. That little creep was a rabbit: buck, buck, buck, and then done—but an hour later, it was pebbles on my window and "Alvie, can you come out and play?"

By sixteen, Donny B. had become like a husband, expecting it regularly and not particularly concerned about my moods or schedule. Although he was low on the pecking order among the eight boys of Millerway, sex with me had given Donny B. a cocky-tough attitude. He'd meet me out back and say, "Put a lip lock on my love muscle, baby, and be quick about it because the angle of the dangle is inversely proportional to the heat of the meat." Laughing and grunting, ever the wit, Donny B.

What can I say? I was in love with him, with his blond hair and weak little angel-face—and I still believed with all my heart that we'd get married right after high school.

Then came another summer Saturday, when Donny B. called me out to the garage, asked me to take off all my clothes and lie on a packing box he'd flattened on the concrete floor. Nothing out of the ordinary so far. But when he took out his weenie, I noticed it was neither angry nor purple, and Donny B. was nervous, and something was wrong. "Can I . . ." He couldn't bring himself to ask it, whatever it was.

Then I heard them at the windows, crowded by each of the garage's two side windows: the other seven river rats, some of them laughing and some fixed with expressions of demented anticipation. I jumped up and held my clothes to the front of me, staring not at them but at Donny B.

He looked awful, and for the first time in my life I felt that superiority that comes from indignation, from being the one who's been wronged. Donny B., weeping now and trembling, reached into his pocket and pulled out seven dimes that he displayed to me like an apology, offering in the smallest of voices: "I'll split them with you."

I grabbed what was closest at hand (one of daddy's ball peen hammers lying there on a workbench) and hit that degenerate upside the head, scattering dimes and scaring away the peeping toms, who ran off convinced I'd murdered the little pervert.

Blood seeped into his left eye and the best the doctors could do was save his right.

No one ever told on me. Donny B. said he slipped and hit his temple against the workbench; the other witnesses clammed up, not wanting to be accessories before or after the fact.

· · · · ·

I REMEMBER this one time, just a month or so before daddy died, when he and I were in the kitchen and I was sitting on his lap eating mulberry jelly. When mother walked in, she said, "Jess, she's getting that jelly all over your shirt." Daddy didn't care. He said I was his sweet sticky thing.

I think he was the best man who ever lived. I remember daddy always talking about fighting the good fight. He said, "Those who got, get; those who don't, don't." Daddy had traveled all over the world and he was a union man and he told me there is no natural justice in the world—you have to beat on the scales to make them right.

I tried to make my cousin understand that. She came from Springfield, where mother's people lived, to stay with me one summer years after daddy died and just a few months after I half blinded Donny B. I was happy for the company even if my cousin did act as if spending time in Millerway was some terrible punishment.

Deep into the last night before she was to leave, I woke up hearing her weep. I asked what was wrong; she wouldn't say. But as night reached toward that dead hour when someone in bed with you will talk about anything, she finally told me. Her father was doing it with her—with his own daughter! And in spite of that, she kept referring to him as "daddy."

I couldn't believe it. This news made Donny B. seem the all-American boy.

My cousin cried that night because tomorrow she'd be going home and it would start all over again: hating her mother for refusing to take hints or do anything about it, fearing daddy, disgusted with herself for the way she used it on occasion to control him. But especially the shame of doing it with your own daddy, a shame never forgotten.

So I got out of bed, walked over to my dresser, took the ball peen hammer out of the bottom drawer where I kept it, and brought it over to my cousin.

"What's that?" she asked.

"Take it home with you." Quite a sacrifice for me, giving away that weapon of mine.

"What for?"

"Keep it under your pillow, and next time daddy comes in your room at night, cross his head with it."

"What!"

"Put his ass to sleep." I'd picked up tough talk from Donny B.

"Alva! I could never do that. You're crazy!"

I'm crazy? Go figure.

．　．　．　．　．

THE NIGHT OF my high school graduation, mother surprised me by tuning in long enough to tell me she'd saved up some money and I could go to college in Springfield—and live there with some of her people while I went to school.

I wonder now how differently matters would have turned out had I been able to complete college and stay in Springfield. I would not have grown so hungry in Beaker's Bride, and the incident with Donny B. and daddy's ball peen hammer would have been an isolated one, long forgotten as I got older and moved out of old apartments into new ones, worked in offices, had affairs, lived what might have passed for a regular life.

But mother became sick and I wasn't able to complete my first semester. Money went to doctors, and with everyone else having moved away from Millerway, I was left to care for her. Only on Saturday nights did I escape to feed at riverside taverns miles and miles from where I lived.

On those Saturday nights, I learned how it is with men—with the men who asked me to accompany them after last call for alcohol so that we could go to the trailers where they lived in postdivorce poverty or park on some lonely country road or once in a great while check into a motel. I was game for *anything* and 'fraid of nothin'.

A few times it went bad and I came home with a blackened eye or finger bruises on my upper arms, but mostly these older men were gentle with me and grateful for what I gave freely.

After mother died, I swore to myself I'd never again take care of someone who was old and sick to death—never again bathe a body as ruined as hers was. But the prospect of keeping house for two vigorous men appealed to me, so when I was offered the job of housekeeper for Bonner Relee and his twenty-year-old son, Matthew, I immediately moved to Beaker's Bride and slept down in the basement room where Johnny eventually would sleep, down there with a box turtle who ate the bugs. I was eighteen.

Matthew was a big man, almost as tall as his father but outweighing Bonner by forty pounds—and all of it upper-body weight. The thing about a big man like Matthew, when he's on top of you all you can think about is breath.

What I'd been waiting for during the first six months I lived in that house finally happened when Matthew came home late from a date, a little drunk and disappointed that one of his bimbos had said no to him. I've never said no to a man in my life.

So down to my basement room he came, smelling of beer and bimbo, into bed with me, neither of us speaking, and then Matthew hot and hard and fast between my legs while I tried my best to keep up with the race, hot and hard and fast.

These late-night visits occurred sporadically (Matthew more afraid of Bonner finding out than I ever was) until I got pregnant. I was twenty. Matthew turned cold the way a person who was spoiled as a child turns cold—cold and mean and sealed up so tight you can't talk to him. "If you have it," he told me, "I'll drown it."

But it was Matthew who drowned in the Illinois, his body never found.

Jess was my ticket out of the basement and into one of the upstairs bedrooms down the hall from where Bonner slept, and when nights are long—winter nights—and there's a woman sleeping just down the hall, a man gets to thinking, and that's all I've ever needed—for a man to start thinking.

But when Jess was four, I went crazy in Beaker's Bride. It was an unrelieved life, watching the river flow where I wanted to go, and I was only twenty-four. So I took off, leaving Jess with Bonner as I traveled around the country working as a waitress or a secretary or whatever I could get, having adventures with men but still 'fraid of nothin' involving men because I learned about landing men the way a marlin fisherman in Key West taught me how you boat half-ton predators on an eighty-pound test line: by denying them nothing they truly insist upon and then just working the slack.

I never promised anyone anything, never complained, never explained. It was a life.

．　．　．　．　．

BEING AFRAID of nothing isn't enough, however, and two years of banging around got old and I was broke and I missed Jess, so I came home to Beaker's Bride and slipped back into the sameness of that dream for two more years before the arrival of Johnny Reace and that bad winter.

Johnny Reace. If I had met him when I was a teenager, he would've been leaning against a Chevy with an unfiltered cigarette in his mouth and James Dean in his eyes— the kind of boy who looks like he can't be touched, so, of course, you want to touch him.

And if you can imagine that kind of boy all grown up and

coming to Beaker's Bride as a stranger to live in our house, then you know why he lay me down.

He was the kind of man who just had to be named Johnny, and maybe what I should have had tattooed over my heart was not my motto but his name, because I fell in love with him three or four different ways.

10

THE MORNING after the party, Jess came downstairs to find Johnny alone at the dining room table.

"Hey, bosco. How was your dewy-feathered sleep?"

The boy walked over to stand close by Johnny's chair.

"You look rough around the edges, commander."

Like some short, eccentric English lord with thick, dirty glasses magnifying his eyes, Jess stood there frumpy in his ratty old robe.

"You know what they say, don't you?"

He smiled as if Johnny were entertainment commissioned solely for his delight.

"When you sleep, you dream life is beauty, but when you awake, you find that life is duty, so the secret is never dream, or, dreaming, never awaken. Do you have any idea what I'm talking about?" Johnny asked, laughing.

Jess didn't bother to answer; he just stood there wishing for unwise power because here was a morning laugher.

"Hey, kid, you know what—you were born to that licorice stick. Natural born to it, and you played taps right on cue for my story last night. What a team we make."

Jess didn't know or particularly care to know the meaning of what Johnny said; the fun was in listening to him talk.

"I'd give anything to have your talent. The only thing I can play is the radio." Johnny laughed; Jess smiled more widely. "I wanted to be a jazz musician and play the blues. I can close my eyes and hear it the way you play it, so sweet it's punishing, but that's the only place *my* music sounds right—in my head. But you! Something about the way you play taps on that clarinet, child. Low and moaning. Like some old Canada goose, stayed too long north and he knows that the cold end has arrived. Never again to fly. Not like you and me, huh, boy? Both of us natural born to flying, right?"

Jess nodded.

"You want eggs for breakfast?"

"Just cereal."

"Well, that's already on the table, help yourself."

Jess wanted him to say it again. "What you said last night," he whispered.

"What? I didn't hear you."

"You know, about a cowboy."

"Oh." Then in a big voice: "Foot in the stirrup, hand on the horn . . ." He pointed his finger like a gun at the boy. "Best damn cowboy ever born."

Jess pushed up his glasses. He figured the horn meant the clarinet.

"You see how that milk's in a glass pitcher instead of a plastic jug? Well, I bought it fresh from a maid this morning, some maid who named all her cows individually and promised me the one who gave this milk did so gratefully— was fed on timothy hay, sweet clover, blackstrap molasses, and was sung Irish ditties to put her in the giving mood. That's why it tastes so sweet and unagitated—not like store-bought milk. Can't you tell the difference?"

Jess said he could, though in fact the milk tasted unremarkably like milk. Bonner had entered the kitchen from the hallway a few moments before; he quietly checked the trash until he found a crumpled carton and a pair of Alva's underpants.

"You want me to teach you some rules of life?" Johnny asked Jess, who nodded.

"First off, you got to learn how to hold your mud. You know what that means?"

Jess nodded. Then he shook his head.

"Like last night when you were in the middle of that room and didn't want to play your horn. At such times, you must learn to hold your mud. Okay?"

"Yes."

"Good. What else do you want to know about life?"

He wanted to know how he could grow up to be just like Johnny.

"Here's something to know. When a man says it's not the money, it's the principle—he means it's the money. You understand *that?*"

"Yes." In a tiny voice.

"Never bet against a man playing his own game, right?"

"Yes." Almost inaudible.

"You sure you understand me?"

A nod.

"Okay, let's say you and I are having a drink at a bar, but we don't know each other. Come on, put your elbows on the table and loosen up a little. What are you, a Scotsman? Lounge a bit." Jess tried to lounge, making Johnny laugh and drawing Bonner to the doorway so he could watch.

"All right, so you and I are at this bar having a few rounds and I buy you a drink. 'Here, have one on me, partner.'" Johnny poured him another glass of milk. "Then you buy me one and soon enough we're old buddies. So I hit you with it. 'Tell you what, pal. I'll bet you ten dollars I can whistle "Dixie" through my ears.' Now. What do *you* say?"

A spoonful of wet cornflakes waited in his mouth, Jess unable to chew or swallow. Johnny was going to whistle through his ears? This man who made quarters appear and perfectly real eggs disappear, who said he could fly. *Now* he was going to whistle through his ears!

Beehart stood outside at a window, watching and nodding his head. He wanted to hear it, too. Take the bet, Jess, take the bet.

"So what do you say, bosco? Ten dollars."

"I don't have any money!" Jess shouted in distress, losing cornflakes and milk from the corners of his mouth.

"What are you, a comedian?"

But the child was desperate. "*I don't have ten dollars!*" Jess looked out at Beehart, but *he* never had any money. Ten dollars was a fortune. Jess began swaying on his chair in the manner of a blind person moving to music.

"Okay, pal-o'-mine, okay. Calm down. I was just—"

Bonner stepped out from the kitchen doorway and tossed a ten-dollar bill in front of Jess. "Bet him, son."

The boy immediately brightened, as if he could see again. Eager now, he offered the bill to Johnny. "Here."

"Wrong answer, fart blossom! Wrong answer. Remember what I told you. *Never bet against a man playing his own game.* A man won't offer a bet he can't win, so no matter how outrageous the wager seems—what an easy deal for you to win—never take that kind of bet. Understand? It's one of life's rules."

But Jess continued urging the money on Johnny. "Go ahead—do it."

"Do what?"

"Whistle through your ears like you said."

"Don't you get it, kid? I'm trying to teach you a lesson."

Jess looked at Bonner and then out the window at Beehart. Didn't they agree with him that it would be worth ten dollars to see someone whistle through his ears—wasn't that a good deal? "Here," he said, placing the bill directly in front of Johnny.

"I think the lesson the boy's trying to teach you," Bonner said, "is that sometimes it ain't a bet at all. Sometimes it's just the price of admission."

After Johnny reached into his pocket and gave a ten-dollar bill to Jess, Bonner retrieved his own money and said to the boy: "Coming down from Chicago don't necessarily make the man brilliant, does it, son?"

Just then Beehart took off running.

"Soon as you men stop burning my daylight," Bonner said, "we can go over to the mansion and get started."

But Jess jumped up and headed for the door.

"Where you going?"

Going down to the river.

. . . . . .

"BEEHAAAART! *Beehart!* Damn your eyes, Beehart."

Jess had heard Mr. Gibsner say that, and it was a wonderfully shocking thing to say. Damning someone's eyes. Where was he? Playing some kind of hiding game, the dumb little brat. Damn his eyes, Jess thought, shivering with the power of words as he trudged riverside. So much he didn't understand. What is your mud, how do you hold it, and why would you want to hold it?

It was Sunday, the last of September and a day overcast with mustard clouds, a day that was damp cold, unseasonably so, Jess rich only because the Illinois shoreline offered a treasure in stone: of precisely the right shape and weight to fit naturally comfortable in that crook along thumb and forefinger, flat on the bottom so they'd skip six, seven times easy. Too bad stone skipping wasn't a sport they played at school, because Jess would've been the school's stone-skipping star. Here, he *was* a stone-skipping star, river rich and Jess at wrong only with a world that valued what he was not.

"Beehart!"

What did it mean to be lonely, Jess didn't know—something close he supposed to the way people acted at those graveside services. He wished he'd brought the clarinet with him to the river today.

Six, seven, but seldom eight. Jess kept trying for eight. And when he finally made eight, he looked around for Beehart, who would have been impressed. Then Jess went for nine. It was a tournament, and crowds cheered him on. Trying for nine.

Touring for hours along the shoreline of that river that ran straight past the lower end of Beaker's Bride, Jess examined the driftwood and flotsam and upstream curios that washed ashore here. How could you be lonely with a river like this at hand? There goes a long and serious barge. It was a route that, if you chose, could take you where Matthew went—and Jess had seen it from the air. He never made nine.

"Beeehaaaaart!" He searched silently, looking among the whitened trunks of large dead but still-standing trees the Illinois had cut in on, soon to uproot and carry off as hazards to navigation. The boy glanced downriver after the barge.

When Jess returned to the house for lunch, Alva told him the two men were out in the shed but that he shouldn't bother them because they were in a mood. She was in a mood. After he ate, Jess took the clarinet back to the river and stayed there all afternoon, watching the current play games with debris. When it got dark he played taps, confident the tune would draw Beehart from wherever it was he hid.

Jess never saw himself growing up to be like Bonner, who was too tall and as remote as history, and Matthew wasn't real to Jess, was only some golden godlike story people told and retold. But Johnny. Jess thought maybe he could grow up to be like Johnny, and what a trick that would be—to know all those strange things to say, how to make people laugh, the secret of holding your mud.

Then it was dark enough that he should've been home instead of staying riverside pissing away treasures in stone until night trapped him there. Jess was too scared to walk home alone past the dead but still-standing trees. Desperate in that way an eight-year-old can become, Jess played taps frantically in hopes of summoning Beehart. *Damn his eyes.*

Then he heard something come crashing hard through the brush up the hill from where he stood.

All your life you conjure these fears until you've granted them enough power that they actually can come crashing hard through the brush toward you. Maybe it was whatever had bitten off Johnny's finger, this thing making its way through the night toward Jess, who mourned now whatever it was he was about to lose.

It came out of the brush and he saw it walking along the mudbank, calling in a voice that spoke not English exactly but some terrifying amalgamation of English and chant, real and magic, what can be understood and what can't. Speaking exactly like a night monster of the kind Jess had always hoped didn't really exist outside of his mind, not outside of his mind where they were free to roam about, so that if you tarried too long by the river, you could meet them—not in your mind but for real—as he was about to meet this one.

"*Beehart!*" Not wanting to see what he saw, Jess wished his own eyes had been damned.

11

THE TWO MEN had worked all morning putting up drywall, reconstructing a walk-in closet off the mansion's master bedroom. Johnny didn't talk while he worked, which impressed Bonner.

" 'Bout time for lunch," the older man said.

Johnny went into the closet to measure a length he was unsure of.

"Jess is something else, ain't he?" Bonner asked, awkward about being the one trying to make conversation.

Johnny, still in the closet, grunted.

"So different from Matthew, though. My boy was strong and good-looking and he played ball in high school and everybody thought the world of him. Jess takes some getting used to. Nobody outside me and Alva ever put the kind of attention on him the way you do."

"Ready anytime you are, chief."

"Yeah, Alva should have dinner on. I need to check something on the roof—you want to come?"

"Sure." Johnny followed him outside and up the ladder and across the slate, moving carefully because of the roof's steep pitch and because the land below the house fell away toward the river. Bonner, however, walked like a man who was still on the ground.

At the peak, Johnny straddling it as if mounted on a horse while Bonner stood there holding on to nothing, they watched the Illinois, which was flanked by full green trees that made the river appear deceptively gentle.

The two men held their thoughts close, let them out slowly.

"Jess needs attention," Bonner said.

"Yeah."

"He sure has put his heart out to you."

"I know."

The day offered a sense of something coming. Winter. Something.

They both began thinking about Alva.

Bonner wondered about the underpants he'd found in the kitchen trash. Johnny had been living with them such a short time. Was there cause for offense?

And Johnny thought about asking if Alva had any boyfriends, but what he really wanted to know was if Bonner and Alva were lovers. How do you ask that of Lincoln?

"Alva and the boy sure are enjoying your company."

Johnny nodded. "It's been good—this week here has been good for me."

Bonner walked along the peak until he reached a tall chimney and then stood next to it storklike on one leg.

No way Johnny could match that; he scooted along still straddling the peak until he reached the chimney, which he used as a handhold to stand. If there was a fight here, Johnny thought, I'd lose.

Bonner watched a train slow for the bridge and then race through Beaker's Bride as if dreading the idea of stopping. "Both of us working together," he said, "and we could finish off this place before summer."

Johnny said nothing.

A big coal barge pushed downriver.

They waited.

Then Bonner said, "If you could see your way clear to stay with us through winter, you and me could have this place ready to move in come spring. Always promised Alva and the boy I'd put them in the mansion someday. I'd pay you, of course—whatever I can afford. Plus room and board. Teach you roofing. A good roofer can always make a living. That's something you could do traveling around the country. Earn your way."

Johnny rearranged his standing position on the peak. "I need to be in Florida before winter."

Not replying to that, Bonner stared downriver, toward the brambly forest where in the distance Charlie Warden and Mr. Gibsner were stacking wood.

"I'll be leaving soon," Johnny added, to end the silence.

"You told Alva yet?"

"No."

"The boy?"

Johnny shook his head.

"Well, it's a wonder you stayed at all."

But truth be told, Johnny was in no particular hurry to leave. From here he'd go to St. Louis, where he had some names, and then from there to Florida. These, however, were destinations: St. Louis, Florida. What Johnny liked best was the in-between, traveling and stopping temporarily at some unscheduled place, as he had here, although never in four years on the road had he found a place quite like Beaker's Bride. After this, it would be the complications of St. Louis and of Florida, finding respite only during the in-between.

Eating up the in-between. The road simplified life. See how Bonner has started to complicate matters, asking Johnny to stay the winter, and Alva wants to bed him and Jess is becoming dependent—you never had to worry about any of that on the road. What am I going to do today? Going to St. Louis. The road gave purpose, direction, destination. Going to St. Louis today. On the road, people didn't ask you what you did for a living or were you married or did you have money in the bank or how long would you stay with them. On the road, only one question was asked: Where you headed? Headed for St. Louis. And you never thought to ask yourself what you were doing with your life, because you knew the answer implicitly: going to St. Louis.

But then you got there.

"You ever do any slate roofing?" Johnny asked.

"Some. Mostly people can't afford it, so the slate work I've done is mainly replacement work. When someone cracks slate by walking on it or a tree falls on it. Otherwise, there's nothing you have to do to slate. Makes the best roof there is if you can afford it and if you've put up a reinforced frame to hold the weight.

"This here is ribbon stock. See the bands of color in it? They'll change with time and exposure—been changing all along. What you call a weathering slate.

"There's a natural cleavage to slate and that's why you can work it so easy, split it and all that. Gets tougher and harder the more it's out in the weather. Slate's perfect.

"Won't absorb water and isn't bothered by smoke or chemicals in the air. Slow rains, hard rains—nothing bothers slate. Hard freezes and quick thaws will eventually tear up most roofs, but not slate. Fire. Nothing. What a roofer says about slate is that it'll outlast him what put it on.

"All you have to do is be careful not to crack it. That's why when you're nailing it you want to drive the nailhead so that it's just barely touching and let the slate *hang* on it. You start nailing flush and you'll get some little shattering around the nailhead, and that's where trouble begins.

"Put on a slate roof right and if a tree or something don't crack it, that roof will be good for a thousand years."

"A thousand years?"

"True! There's a slate roof somewhere in England that was laid on a chapel back in the seven hundreds, and now the roof is all covered with moss but that slate is good as ever. Getting better, tougher. More than a thousand years old and still not leaking, allowing no rot." Bonner knew what he was talking about.

"Didn't realize you were such a slate expert."

"Don't it appeal to you, leaving behind something that could last a thousand years?"

Johnny shrugged.

Bonner didn't like to see that. "What *does* appeal to you?"

"Lunch."

Posing there on the peak, Bonner looked at Johnny and shook his head. "No. I've worked with you, and a man as serious about work like you, he ain't driving around four years on the road just to see the sights. No. It's something else."

Johnny began making his way down, off the roof.

Bonner was sorry he'd said it; a man's business is his own. "I been laying roofs twenty years and never had one come back on me!"

"So I've heard!" Johnny shouted back. He was already on the ladder.

Bonner came after him. "I got a shingle roof to lay over at Bluffs next week. You help me and I'll show you how it's done."

Johnny didn't reply until they both were on the ground. "Don't lecture me."

Turning away to keep that famous face riverward, Bonner said, "Fair enough."

They walked home.

. . . . . .

ALL SUMMER, Charlie Warden and Mr. Gibsner had worked cutting and splitting eight cords of wood, piling it in a jumbled mountain against the forest side of the old collapsing stone fence that ran along the back boundary of their property. Now it was time to make sense of that heap: stacking the foot-long pieces (cut small to fit their kitchen and Franklin stoves) on top of the irregular stone, eventually creating a wood wall three hundred feet long, one foot wide, three feet tall—a wood wall constructed so tightly that it would come apart only through the same means by which it had been put together: piece by piece.

Looking at the finished wall, perfectly plumb and perfectly flush, granted you a profound sense of satisfaction because here was a thing right with the world: orderly and good.

The two old men invested themselves in that wall of wood. Mr. Gibsner, having sold his farm decades before and losing with it his definition, he directed the work, cursing and damning and ever dissatisfied with Charlie's efforts. Charlie Warden, retired from the railroad, followed orders as best he could—arguing back and laughing and asking if it wasn't time to take a break. They'd lived together for a long time, two old men retreating into a single household for one last defensive economical stand against the years.

The hard work was done: summer months out in that timber beyond the stone fence, applying ax and saw to fallen trees and downed limbs, getting bee-stung and ivy-poisoned, laboring on hardwood trunks that had to be crosscut and sectioned and split with wedge and sledge, working slowly in tune with their age, arguing about how much wood was needed to complete a wall that would outlast winter.

Now came the satisfying part. Like having cut and assembled a cabinet, now to shave and polish and sand it smooth. Now was the time to stack. Because the stone fence ran so unevenly, they had to fill holes and gaps with kindling and pie wedges of wood and pieces specially cut to fill some empty spot, chinking and propping and arranging until each irregularity was accommodated and a flat base was laid on top of the stone, a flat base of wood from which a wall could rise rightly with sides and top so true you no longer noticed the stone fence's out-of-kilter nature, which had been made good with wood.

They stacked with obsessive precision, two pieces running this way and the next two running the opposite way and every available space filled with stove wood until there were no holes left unfilled, and come winter Mr. Gibsner would fetch from the west end while Charlie started on the east end: consuming the wall a foot or two each day of winter.

The wall didn't need to be loose for air, because the wood they stacked was summer cut and dry and, being up on the stone fence away from the ground, it stayed dry; the wall's complete impenetrability made a tarp unnecessary.

When they finished the wall, Beaker's Bride could begin marking winter's progress. At the beginning, that wall appeared good enough and strong enough and long enough to hold out against any winter, no matter how cold. Sometimes you'd walk over there just to look at the wall, it was that handsome on the field before the war.

Because the two old men used thin-bladed and well-oiled saws that did not rip through wood with the thick brute force of a chainsaw, the ends of the wood pieces that formed the perfectly flush side facing Beaker's Bride shined with flat-sliced polished grain. And that made you confident, too—as if winter were an enemy impressed with bearing. As if winter were an enemy against which you could build a wall.

Come January, buttons missing and salutes sloppy, Beaker's Bride still rallied behind that wall because it still stretched forever and people thought for sure Charlie and Mr. Gibsner couldn't possibly use up all that wood before a spring victory—that there couldn't possibly be that much winter left to fight.

But deep into January and then February, too, you came to appreciate how wearily determined winter promised to be. Burning that wall of wood and, yet, still cold. Bitter cold. You wondered how much more you could take.

That much and more.

Waiting it out, waiting and building hope day by day as the wall diminished foot by foot—nibbled at from the ends and working toward the middle, victory's anticipation increasing as the wall's length decreased. Until one day you walked down that way and saw only a small section remaining: still waxed flat and plumb but only ten feet long now straddling the middle line, and you thought: My God, we won.

And then like always you put it out of your mind, all that wood burned and gone, what does it matter now that it's spring again? But those two old white men never forgot about fighting winter, and even in summer's heat they were out in the timber cutting wood for the next war, working in a triumph of experience over hope.

. . . . .

"HOW'S THE WORK GOING?" asked Alva, small-boned and dark-haired and playing eager to please this noon, preparing great quantities of food for the men and serving them. "You think we'll be living there by next summer?"

"Could be." Bonner's voice was empty.

"He promised me I'd live in a mansion someday," Alva told Johnny.

"Money in the bank." But his voice was no more hopeful than Lincoln's.

She asked where Jess was, getting shrugs in response, and Alva wondered if they'd been arguing about her.

"Didn't the Winslows look stupid last night?" she said. "That little guy pushing the hog around the floor. I don't know why she even made him dance. He certainly didn't want to and it made them both look so stupid."

"If it wasn't for Alan Winslow buying up property when folks were leaving town," Bonner said, "a lot of families wouldn't have got a dime for their houses."

"Bought them for next to nothing because he thought he'd make a killing if the yards ever opened up again. Trying to cheat honest working folks, making a profit off their misfortune."

"Alva, you don't know what goes on in another man's mind, what makes him do as he does—leave it be."

"Don't *you* talk to me like that!" She said it hissingly, like some venomous animal that's confident it can hurt you bad if the warning's ignored.

Johnny wondered what had transpired between the two of them that they could bargain with each other in such a deadly manner. After Alva left the dining room, he asked Bonner, "What're you keeping out in that shed behind the house?"

It seemed he had no intention of answering.

"Bonner?"

"You ever been struck by white lightning?"

"Once."

"I got a jar."

"Never turned down a drink in my life."

"It's out in the shed."

"I'm right behind you."

They walked without talking to the two-story tin-roofed building; Bonner unlocked the large sliding door. What Johnny first saw when the light hit inside caused him to pull up like a startled horse.

Oh, there were other items in that shed: cracked tombstones, tools, one section given over to a woodworking shop, an old panel truck with ROOFER in large white letters on its flank and four tires flat. But you noticed all of that later, after you saw what you saw first: a giant white marble bird roped tightly to a low steel trailer of the type used to transport race cars.

Bonner immediately headed for a far shelf from which he brought down a jar of gin-clear liquid, but he watched Johnny, too, and appreciated the way the man took his time and did not immediately exclaim, the way most people did upon seeing the roped bird.

Bonner offered the jar, Johnny took a drink, winced, then walked around the trailer examining the sculpture with his eyes: running them over the surfaces, feeling the bright whiteness. He walked around the bird once more, and when Bonner opened the far door, this additional light on the marble led Johnny to put his eyes *and* his hands on the creature. So grand to the mind and spirit was this sculpture that, upon touching it, Johnny half expected the marbled flesh to quiver.

The bird looked as if it were taking off: seven feet long from marble head to marble tail, six feet high from beak to base, caught in marble in mid-wingbeat—wheeling with the right wing out from the body at a swept-back right angle while the left wing dipped low, its tip lower than the marble base and extending below the edge of the steel trailer. Because of that low left wing, the sculpture could not be placed directly on the ground; it had to be *up* on something.

The immediate image was one of quick ascent: the dove perhaps startled into flight racing so fast for air that wing-beats hadn't yet coordinated, the right pushing straight back while the left spread out widely and dipped down. The heavy ropes around the bird and around its boulder-like base reinforced this image of ascent, ropes tying to earth what was trying for sky.

Johnny stroked it. The tight-grained marble was hard, smooth, glassy. Another hit of gin-clear liquid.

The sculpture was not well detailed with feathers or feet or face; its eyes were simply deeply drilled holes, giving the dove a hard and frightened expression—in a hurry to get up get away get out of this damn white stone it had been caught in. But the overall impact was explosive: to fly.

They continued drinking the gin-clear liquid that put

nasty expressions on their faces even as they told each other how good it was. The men seemed as contented as sweet-milk producers, but how many more gin-clear drinks would you have to swallow before you could squint just right, right enough to see the big bird complete that un-completed wingbeat and part those ropes like so many threads and arise, one thousand pounds of white marble dove gaining power and height until it crashed heavily through a tin roof to gain the open sky?

They finished the first gin-clear jar and began a second. When Johnny coveted a cap that hung on a nail, a cap that said RELIABLE CASKET COMPANY on the crown, Bonner gave it to him with a flourish and Johnny wore it grinning. Bonner tripped stepping up onto the trailer, grabbed a wing to steady himself, and started dusting the dove with his flannel shirt, which he had at some point in the proceed-ings removed. Johnny wished to say something important, but his message dissolved in shine.

"This is my gravestone," Bonner told him while dusting. "It was one of them Big Ed Beaker brought down from Chicago. Got it from Italy, I heard. Bought it off a city rebuilding from the war."

"He was going to put it on Florence and the boy's grave."

Bonner didn't miss a beat: "But her people took her back to Ohio to be buried. Columbus."

"Cincinnati."

"Whatever. It's my marker now. I have it all planned out. Johnny? You listening to me, old son? Do you get what I'm trying to tell you?"

"A wonder to behold." His ears buzzed with the effects of shine.

Bonner explained: The base of the sculpture would be set into the ground over his grave, sod laid all around like a thick green blanket tucked in close to the marble. Posi-tioned this way, the dove's right wing would sweep back a foot or so above the ground, the tail would touch sod, but an angled eighteen inches of that low left wing tip would have to be buried.

"Like it's coming up out of the ground," Bonner said in one of his rare unnecessary statements.

"Need another drink."

"Yessir. That can be arranged, yes it can."

Johnny toured the bird again; he'd been doing this all along—abruptly leaving Bonner to circle the dove as if his thirsty eyes and hungry hands couldn't get enough of it. "Tell me again," he said, returning to Bonner's side. "Tell it all to me again, how you're going to bury the base and stick this left wing in the ground. All of it, tell me all of it again."

Bonner did, painting from a different angle this time how that dove would look coming up out of his grave.

Their voices were low, their emotions gin-clear: these men and their love of monuments.

"Jess comes in here," Bonner said. "Gets up on the bird's back and stays there the longest time. Holding tight around the neck like he's afraid of falling off."

To fly, Johnny thought, to fly.

Then they couldn't say enough about the boy, how it's always the ones with edges who grow up to greatness, and they decided Jess was an eccentric genius.

"Don't worry about him, Bonner. He plays that stick like you lay roofs. I've never seen anyone learn to play so quickly. He'll grow up to play the blues and always have work. *A natural.*"

Bonner came suddenly to the edge; he wished he didn't have to die, but that black blood had been coming out since last Thanksgiving, and right now Bonner felt soaked all the way through by the kind of melancholy that held him close on nights when it rained—one of those slow, soaking night *female* rains that don't roll quickly enough off a roof but, instead, the water sits and it soaks down through shingle cracks and shingle splits to reach wood underneath and rot that good wood in ways that aren't obvious until the damage has been done.

"And *you*," Johnny told him. "You got magic in you, too."

Bonner shook his head.

"I know you do. I'm not sure what kind of magic it is, but you have some kind of magic in you, Bonner—and you know you do. Some kind of Lincoln magic."

"No."

"This isn't just some line of bull. You know the truth yourself. About you and your magic."

"No magic to me."

"Bonner, I didn't think you were the kind of man to deny the truth just because it hits so close to home."

He shook his head, but he believed Johnny. Bonner had to lean against the side of the panel truck to brace himself for the roll of the ground. "You tell me the truth, Johnny. Tell me how you lost that finger."

"Can't. The facts embarrass me."

"Tell! Goddamn you, Johnny—the truth!"

"Four years ago. Drunker than this. Going to shoot myself. Fumbling with the pistol, trying to load it. Shot off my finger trying to load the damn thing. Failed at suicide, hit the road. Four years traveling. Truth."

Bonner put his arm around the younger, shorter man's shoulder and Johnny jammed the Reliable Casket Company cap low on his head so it wouldn't be blown off and, like that, the two of them rode out this storm.

Bonner didn't remember how he and Johnny became separated or how he found his way back to the house, to his chair by the window. Alva knew something was wrong because, for once, Bonner was reclined in the recliner and she had the devil's own time bringing him around. "Where's Jess?" she demanded, flapping and fluttering against Bonner to get an answer. It was late, it was dark, it was night. "Where is he! Where's Johnny! Bonner, damn it, where are they!"

.   .   .   .   .   .

JOHNNY HAD LEFT the scattered lighted houses and had entered this darker section of Beaker's Bride. He walked through the long-abandoned neighborhoods to cross the tracks and reach this place he had never been before. He stopped and looked around. Here's where he'd been heading, even though he didn't remember having in mind a destination.

A freight signaled far away, leading Johnny back toward the wooden platform of the boarded-up depot. He tripped, falling facedown to collect splinters in his knees and palms, then staying there, prone, as the train shook past the platform and loosened in Johnny a memory of how as a boy he could fly. Suddenly he remembered how.

The train had to slow for the bridge and then it was gone, leaving behind a silence so total you could hear the Illinois slipping by: that rushed hush of flowing water. Johnny heard something down there crying.

.   .   .   .   .   .

STUMBLING MUMBLING falling and sobering up, he made his way to the river, paused, heard the wail again, walked toward it.

To Jess, it was something unnameable coming for him— something he dreaded naming. Worse than a bear, some creature able to chant.

" ' 'Twas brillig, and the slithy toves did gyre and gimble in the wabe; all mimsy were the borogoves, and the mome raths outgrabe.' "

Jess shook, wetting his pants a little. "Beehart!"

"What're you doing out here, Benny?" Johnny asked.

"Playing that licorice stick in the middle of the night—you *are* too much. Who's this Beehart you're hollering for?"

Johnny stood so close now that Jess could smell on him some kind of fuel.

"I've heard about him, you know. Beehart. Why don't you introduce me?"

The eight-year-old still shook, trembled, and wept.

"Hey. Come on now. You got to hold your mud, kid."

But what is it and how do you hold it!

"I came down here to get you."

Jess dropped the clarinet and threw himself to Johnny, nearly knocking the both of them to the ground. He held on as tightly as he could. Saved!

"Yeah," Johnny said, comforting the child. "I came down here to show you how I can fly. But it won't work unless both of us can hold our mud." Keep your eyes open, Johnny told himself as he weaved and caught his balance and used Jess to keep himself upright. Hold my mud, hold my mud. "Can you hold your mud?"

"Yes!" Screaming it.

"Then pick up that stick and let's go."

Leaving the river, walking away from jaws that bite and claws that catch, Johnny said to the boy, "I'll bet you ten dollars I can fly."

Jess remembered the money. He didn't hesitate, finding the ten in his pocket and thrusting it at Johnny.

"Chief, one of us ain't learning a damn thing," Johnny said, pushing the bill back toward Jess, who let it drop to the ground because he didn't care, didn't understand, wanted nothing except to keep this magic man close to him like a vorpal sword as they moved away from the scary toward the sublime, whistling Dixie.

· · · · ·

JESS HAD NEVER been out this late in his life. They'd been waiting there on the splintered platform next to the boarded-up depot for nearly an hour, Johnny pacing off a distance back from the edge of the platform and then repacing it and looking to where the train would appear, jogging to the end of the platform, counting as he ran and finally pacing off one last distance that seemed to satisfy him. That's when they heard the train whistle coming from way down the line.

"Watch this, kid. Unbelievable, you just stand there and watch. This'll set you free." Until the whistle blew, Johnny had sounded tired and drunk, but now he was sharp and very agitated.

Making Jess nervous, too. One of the rules was don't play by the tracks, and Jess could only hope that Johnny's presence sanctioned this particular adventure.

When they saw the train's light, Johnny's voice became excited. "All of us kids knew exactly where to stand, exactly where the train had to be before we started running, how fast to run—everything all planned out. I'm estimating this one. Hope I'm right. If not, you tell them old Johnny Reace went out in glory, flying."

Flying? Jess didn't know what Johnny intended to do, except that it must be something important because he'd never seen the man so aroused.

"I saw the big white bird this afternoon," Johnny said, keeping his attention on the tracks, toward the approaching train.

"Sometimes I climb on it," Jess replied quietly, his voice calmer than the man's. "Grampa told me it was okay."

"When we did this as kids we pushed an old mail wagon on the other side of the tracks so we could jump level, but here I'll have to hit the ground rolling. Already checked it out. Should be okay over there if you hit rolling."

You? Was he giving Jess instructions? Did Johnny expect

him to follow along and do whatever Johnny was about to do? Now Jess was nervous all over again.

When they heard not just the whistle but the train it-self—those locomoting tons rumbling hard on steel rails spiked tightly to wooden ties—Jess realized what Johnny had in mind: *He's going to jump on the train!*

Was Jess supposed to jump with him?

The night was dark, the train was fast, and now the rumbling reached the platform, causing it to rattle and rock. You can't jump on a train. Not even Johnny Reace can do that. He'd be killed, and if Jess tried it, he'd be killed, too. Jess didn't want to jump and he didn't want to watch Johnny jump. How could he stop him? *"Johnny!"*

"Not now, kid. I need all my concentration. One miscal-culation . . . Here we go. Quiet, *shhh.* "

He poised like a runner at the beginning. Tensed up, coiled tight. Jess, too. The train close enough now to take on a personality: bull dragon at full charge, terribly steamed and clattering the very earth—as if that dragon knew Johnny Reace lay in ambush and couldn't wait for him to make the attempt. Just try to mount me, just try.

The train slowed for the bridge (maybe Johnny *could* do it) and sounded one last sharp and surly whistle.

What happened spanned only seconds but Jess remem-bered, dreamed, precise details because his mind slowed time, as a mind is capable of doing in an accident, for example, when you're calmly aware of and can later recall instant by instant everything that occurred.

Johnny dipping his head and then taking off, arms pump-ing, racing for the platform's edge as the big bull train roared, maddened, *no!,* he's not going to make it, he started running too soon, he's going to smack right into the side of the engine!

Jess put both hands to his face the way he did when certain music announced the scary part of some program on television.

Then—and here was the part so incredible that Jess could've been dreaming—the boy's right leg twitched in anticipation of running. It twitched as it did when Jess tried to talk himself into joining the other kids at recess, except on the platform his leg twitched a thousand times more intensely than it ever had before and his belly buzzed like when grampa drove the car fast over what Bonner called tickle-belly hills, but on the platform Jess's belly was a thousand times buzzier than on tickle-belly hills. The boy couldn't believe it, but it was true, Jesus, Jesus, Jesus, Johnny: I'm going to jump on that train with you!

Mouth open and mouth dry, Jess watched Johnny running nearly at the edge now and the train almost there, too. GO! *Jess?* GO!

At that instant, however, here came Beehart flying around the corner of the depot, his funny short legs carrying him crazily faster than what seemed possible, whizzing past Jess.

"Wait!"

But like always Beehart ran on ahead, speeding and almost catching Johnny—right behind Johnny as Johnny leapt.

An instant photographed in Jess's mind: Johnny high in the air, sprung from the platform, directly in front of the engine, blazing with the locomotive's searching light.

Then the sound: Johnny's scream cut short by the bull's high-pitched bloody bellow.

Then the action resuming: Johnny across the light beam, Beehart flying close behind, the earthshaking train speeding past like a heavily traveling wall.

Jess didn't know what to do. He was all pumped up and unrelieved and he didn't know what to do. Wait for the train to pass or run get help right now? Thirty-seven cars, forty-eight. Never ending, he counted. Until the caboose rushed by as if moving faster than everything that had preceded it.

Jess had been told stories galore about legs cut off, stories used as warnings to keep him away from the tracks, so he worried what he'd see on the grassy slope just to the other side of those still-vibrating rails. Bloody bodies and separated limbs.

But it was what he *heard* first: Johnny singing.

No, laughing. Johnny lying on his back, head on the downhill, feet facing the platform, arms spread wide, legs attached—Johnny laughing. Then telling the boy, "Come on. Jump!"

Jess could do that. Sure. Without the train in the way, Jess could jump down there by Johnny, and on his way— during that short flight down—Jess understood the truth of how rapid motion through space elates.

He landed awkwardly on the spongy sod, his glasses thrown off with the impact, but he managed to roll close to the man.

Still laughing, Johnny asked if he'd seen anything like it in his life. Jess responded by starting a scuffle because he needed to burn up the juice still in his blood and because he needed to touch this flying hero, confirming his existence, rejoicing in his magic and hoping some might rub off onto him. Jess hit Johnny with all his might, repeatedly pounding the man's thick arms and chest. When you're eight years old, you're allowed to hit a man just as hard as you can, and this grant releases something within you.

Johnny finally imprisoned Jess's flailing arms, squeezing the child tightly but not as tightly as the child needed to be squeezed. Harder, Jess thought. "Harder."

Both of them panting, they remained locked in that embrace like wrestlers who've fought each other to a draw.

"Did I hold my mud, Johnny?"

Came the warm, whispering gin-clear reply: "Yes."

12

ONE MORNING in October, Johnny got into his little blue car, which since his arrival had been left parked and unused by the side of the house, and drove off. Because that's exactly the way Johnny had arrived, without warning, Alva and Jess and Bonner believed he was entirely capable of departing in the same manner. But late that afternoon, Johnny came riding back to Beaker's Bride in triumph on the delivery truck that carried four dark oak forty-eight-inch vanities, Sears Best. One for each of the bathrooms in Beaker Mansion. More than a thousand dollars they cost.

Watching the unloading and uncrating (Johnny insisted the vanities be unboxed on the lawn in front of the mansion so that most of the town would gather to witness the event), Bonner stood there as if listening to news of war's end, he was that impressed. Alva held to Johnny's arm, Jess played in the empty boxes—space capsules from which he was repeatedly launched—and people came to find out what Johnny had done and then to touch him, pat his back, or squeeze his hand.

Alva, watching Johnny beam, understood for the first time how thin a man he was—not totally durable and self-contained as she had earlier assumed. Johnny Reace showed himself to be a mirror of a man on that lawn, reflecting what was shined on him, and that's why he needed, required, this adoration: to have something to shine back into those waiting faces all around him. Bonner absorbed light; Johnny reflected it.

That evening, Bonner asked him why he did it and where did he get the money. Sold my car, Johnny said, making the gesture all the grander. But *why?* Because vanities were the last expensive items needed to complete Beaker Mansion; the rest of the remodeling could be done with hard work and materials salvaged from abandoned houses around town. Did this mean Johnny was staying until the mansion was ready?

"I have to go to St. Louis over Christmas," he said. "I made some calls while I was waiting for the vanities. But I'll be back after that and we'll keep working on it."

And work and work—not only on Beaker Mansion but also digging graves and roofing houses in the surrounding towns. Bonner continued to admire Johnny's labor, steady and marked by close consideration to detail—similar to Bonner's own style. And Johnny was mesmerized by the older man's calm, relentless pace, by the sureness of his step on the steepest of roofs, and how he orchestrated work—snapping chalk lines like bowstrings and using tools with precise correctness—in a naturally offhand manner even though his dark eyes missed nothing.

The two men were happy with each other, but they needed Alva and Jess to listen to their stories and be impressed by what they had done or seen or said to each other during the day. Alva and the boy were producing the light that Bonner absorbed, Johnny reflected.

．　．　．　．　．

OCTOBER'S DAYS arrived one after the other like mailed gifts, and on one of those days Alva was assigned to go bathe Agnes because the woman who normally would do it that day was feeling poorly.

As soon as Alva walked into Agnes's room, smelling of ointments and dust, the old woman exclaimed directly at her, "You stick me with that sewing needle again, girl, and I'll snatch you bald!"

Alva was astonished.

"You think I don't know what you been doing when you come here, waking me up with that needle and then acting foolish all the time you're in my house? Oh, it wasn't so bad when you just danced around like a damn fool, but that needle business, when you started that—no, ma'am."

"I'm sorry. I didn't think you could feel it."

The woman's voice came out gravelly, strong. "Oh, I could *feel* it all right. I was just too far away to come traveling all the way back here to tell you to stop. But enough's enough. You're the silliest young thing I've ever seen in my long life."

For Alva, this was like finding out her mirror could talk, had opinions about her behavior in front of it, and was able to voice those opinions.

"I know *everything,* child. The other ladies who come over here, the ones who really do help out and not just dance around, they treat me like a real live living person and not a pin cushion the way you do. They *talk* to me even when I've gone traveling and can't talk back to them. Tell me what's going on around town. That's why I know everything, missy. *Everything.* "

"You want your bath now?"

"Not from you, thank you very much. I know you got a man in your house—oh, I know *that* much. They told me about him. Where's he from, from Chicago or some damn where? Cock of the walk, they tell me. Cock of the walk, this one is. Well, I don't see what he sees in you. Nothing but a piece of gristle. Lord, girl, when I was your age I had more beaux than you've had hot meals, and I wasn't skinny like you 'cause I knew even back when I was that young—I knew men don't like to feel bones when they're waltzing. You don't think I was a dancer, too? I could move lighter than you.

"It was in nineteen fifty-six, I remember it well, when I first discovered I could no longer hop. That's right, hop. I may be the only woman you'll ever meet in your life who recalls the exact day when she discovered she'd lost the ability to hop. I'd seen some little girls playing hopscotch and when I got back here, back home here in the privacy of my own living room, I tried to jump up and get both feet off the floor. *Hop.* I couldn't. Nineteen fifty-six. What a discovery that is to make—that you can't hop anymore. 'Course I was already an old, old woman even in nineteen fifty-six—already becoming like a toddler again. You ever see the way they try to hop, their bodies pushing up but their feet staying put on the ground? That was me down in my living room in nineteen fifty-six, trying to hop. And I don't even know when *exactly* I lost the ability to hop, nineteen fifty-six was just the year I *discovered* I couldn't hop. After seeing those little girls playing hopscotch.

"Oh, we had all kinds of kids in this town, years gone by. I even remember when the grocery store there down by river road stopped giving away a box of groceries to the first baby of the new year. People used to wonder and bet on who might get it, women concentrating hard if they were due around the first few days of the new year. But the last time that box of groceries was given away to the first baby of the new year, it was almost the Fourth of July. Got to be embarrassing, declaring a new year's baby on the Fourth of July—so they stopped that particular practice.

"Nineteen fifty-six was the same year I took up serious spitting. Never did spit before that because I was raised to believe it unladylike, but in nineteen fifty-six I took to spitting off my back porch and got right good at it, too. Could spit an arc. Now I don't spit *or* hop. Just travel."

She stopped talking abruptly, changing without notice from that river of words to a long silence. Alva began to creep from the room.

"The other ladies were chintzy enough with the details,

didn't want to be indelicate with a old woman, I suppose, but I gathered enough to know that man of yours from Chicago is one of them trifling men and you better learn, girl, how it is with a trifling man before he leaves you soiled. Heartbroken and soiled."

Agnes closed her eyes.

Alva waited and then said the woman's name softly.

"A man's coat has many pockets," Agnes muttered, as if already half asleep. Then another long silence.

"Agnes?"

"That's the quick of it, child." She kept her eyes closed. "That man of mine . . . called me a fine figure of a woman. . . . Look at me now, all humped over like a turtle. Uglier . . . uglier than a bar of homemade soap. But no man ever left *me* except for death 'cause I always knew . . . Knew the truth and worked within it. Yes . . . You . . . A man's coat has many pockets and he keeps you in only one of them."

. . . . .

INTO NOVEMBER THEN and into winter, the wood wall being nibbled at the ends by Charlie Warden and Mr. Gibsner, while Alva waited for Johnny to make his move and use her and use her and use her until he owed her and owed her and owed her. Then she'd see just who'd say Cincinnati.

But Johnny didn't come sneaking up to her room of a night, and when Bonner went to bed early, leaving Johnny and Alva alone in the living room, the two of them made random comments separated by awkward silences as if they were a couple who shouldn't have been left alone—two former lovers, perhaps, who have married different people after their own affair ended disastrously and they shouldn't be left alone because they have nothing good to talk about. Johnny's conversation with Alva no longer showed any of the snap and eagerness he had for Jess and Bonner; he didn't tease Alva anymore and never slapped her on the butt.

She continued suffering a bad case of Johnny Reace—so bad that one afternoon Alva opened her closet and flipped through her clothes, pulling dresses from hangers and tossing blouses to the floor: she hated everything she owned, the colors all wrong and the cuts stupid. Alva needed a new wardrobe and despaired of ever having the money to buy one.

She was hot in the belly for Johnny Reace and looked in the mirror with great regret, because where did this dusky skin of hers come from? Daddy was light; mother, a brunette. What Moor lurked in Alva's blood?

Miserable—wanting someone who doesn't want you. So she would lie in bed in the middle of the night suddenly aware that her entire body was tightly clenched—wanting so bad what was down in that basement room where she once slept that, *finally,* on an early November night Alva went night-creeping down there and tapped lightly on his door.

"Yeah?" He sounded unsurprised at someone tapping lightly on his door in the middle of the night, that kind of man.

She wore her long flannel thing, wishing she owned something more provocative. Under it, her skin was gooseflesh, dark nipples tightly erect. "I couldn't sleep," Alva said. "You either, huh?"

His little bedside lamp was on and Johnny, still dressed, sat on the bed without a book in his hands. "Haven't been trying to sleep."

Then she saw the bottle next to the lamp and the glass in his hand. Down here drinking alone. "You drink a lot, don't you?"

"No, I drink exactly enough."

Drinking whiskey straight and from a tumbler, he was that serious about it. She walked softly to sit next to him on the bed—waiting now for him to put his hands on her. Usually this was all that was required, to sit close to them when they'd been drinking and then wait.

Not Johnny, however. "You shouldn't be here."

"Why not?" All innocence, her eyes.

"What do you want?"

"What do *you* want?"

"I want to finish this glass and then pour another."

"Six weeks you've been living with us. Not seeing any women that I know of, because you work all day with Bonner and then you're here at the house every night. Don't you get horny?"

She'd expected him to laugh, but he didn't. "I have no intention of sleeping with you."

"Who's talking about sleeping?"

Didn't laugh at that either. "Go back to your room."

"Do you think I'm *that* ugly?"

It was an old routine but one for which Johnny had never learned a defense. "You're not ugly."

"Don't you trust me?"

What a child. Johnny decided to fool around with her, to bully her, to say something that might frighten this little one into scurrying back up the stairs to the safety of her own bed.

"You told me once that you'd do anything," Johnny said. "Well, you know what I'd like to do? I'd like to fuck you in the ass just as hard as I can. What say?"

"Oh, Johnny, you can cut a hole in my chest and fuck me in the heart if you want."

"Get out of here," he said, looking not at what was brown in her eyes but what was brown in his glass.

Because now there was this image to deal with, as if such a thing were possible: carving a hole in her sternum, mounting her chest, slipping his organ into something as hot as a heart, something that squeezed and pumped the way a heart did, something as tough and fibrous as a heart. As if such a thing were possible.

"Get out of here!" The three fingers and thumb that held the tumbler shook enough to disturb the surface tension of the whiskey.

She left, understanding then but still not knowing what to do with the power she had over him.

13

THE DOG'S WHINING awoke him. "What's wrong, old girl?" Jess asked, sounding like Bonner. Someone was up moving around in the house and although neither Jess nor the dog knew what time it was, they knew it was no time for someone to be up moving around in the house. Did Jess now have to worry about this, too—mom, grampa, or Johnny doing things while he slept? Something was going on he couldn't figure out, and it made the part-collie dog nervous, too.

Lady was supposed to stay outside at night—guarding the property, Bonner always said—but Jess had sneaked her into his room because he needed closer protection than an outside dog can provide. Jess hadn't had Beehart for protection since that night the train hit the poor dumb kid.

Jess floated back to sleep, Lady quiet on the floor, though *she* remained awake, her head occasionally raising off front paws as she attempted, through sound and scent, to trace the night movements in that house.

Jess's right leg twitched, awakening him with such a violent start that the old dog stood rickety quick and looked at the bed with great concern.

The same dream. He'd been having it every night since going with Johnny from the river to the abandoned depot, but it wasn't even a dream unless you can dream the truth—what really happened. Perhaps it should more accurately be called a recurring recollection that came while he slept, always ending with his leg jerking as if he were about to run, but before he ran, Jess awoke. He put the recollection out of his mind during the day and then remembered it again at night, dreaming the truth of what really happened. Jess dreamed it, remembered it, every night: Johnny running across the platform, Beehart pumping close behind, and a twitching leg awakening him before he can follow along.

He hadn't seen Beehart since then, Beehart who apparently didn't make it across and probably got smashed onto the front of the train to be carried off across the Illinois, across the Mississippi, to Bowling Green, Vandalia, Mexico.

"You have no idea how it feels," Johnny had said to Jess. "Flying across the front of a speeding locomotive like that. *Flying*. I told you I could fly."

Johnny was wrong, Jess thought as he lay in bed listening to someone else roaming around downstairs—I *do* know how it feels to fly. He called Lady into bed with him, and although she knew she wasn't allowed on beds, it simply wasn't in the old dog to deny this boy anything.

14

HE CONTINUED DRINKING after Alva left the basement, continued drinking and then went stumbling around the first floor knocking into furniture and making noise and deciding, finally, that he had to have another look at that big white hard bird, not even bothering to put on a coat—just lurching out into the leading edge of winter.

He was outside now, tripping and falling onto the cold, hard ground, ripping his pants, cutting knees that would wait until morning to hurt, Johnny maddened and made afraid by her desperate nature.

He fell twice more pushing open the sliding door, then collapsed from the effort and lay there on the cold, hard ground just this side of the shed's interior, Johnny turning over supine to look at the unfocused sky.

With not much of a moon left, the grazing stars seemed all the brighter. Down from town, the Illinois was fogged in and, overhead, Canada geese cried. Johnny stood to find them, his head tilted back as he took small steps with one foot to turn slowly. Never had much use for a man who didn't look up at night. Rotating like this and drunk, he tangled in his own legs and fell on his ass and sat there on the cold, hard ground, Johnny listening to geese grieve.

Late geese heading south. Even Jess's clarinet didn't tear at him the way these geese did. They stay too long north and there's an urgency to them, Johnny sitting there and saying aloud but to himself, "Stayed too long north."

A Canada goose will mate for life and can live to be fifty,

sixty years old, but most of them don't make it that long—
lost to adventures along the way. Johnny wondered if one
of them flying over him now perhaps was hatched on the
day he was born, thirty-four years of cold, hard flight, and
was that one up there as tired as this one down here? Or
maybe at thirty-four, the old gander remained behind this
winter, waited for the old strength that never returned,
stayed too long north, was too tired for flight. And if he was
standing out in some corn stubble right now, could he hear
his fellows overhead, and what did he make of their cry in
tonight's sky? Johnny was made to feel that way by desperate people. The way he felt at the end of the party. The way
Alva made him feel. The way he felt now.

Johnny stepped into the shed and fell. The big white
hard bird ruffled marbled feathers and strained against the
heavy ropes looped all around, Johnny down again and
closing the distance on hands and knees.

With the sliding door open, the bird can see to where a
second river runs one hundred feet deep and widely white
above the waters of the Illinois, this higher and larger
white river spilling banks and drifting over river road to
soak up valleys and finger gullies. Fed by tributaries of mist
you could see moving eerily through the trees and the
town, this fog river was in depth and breadth greater than
the Illinois and it made perspectives hazy, unreal, faraway.
Late geese looking down lowered their altitude and
wheeled as the drilled eyes of the marble bird saw now a
chance to launch off the steel trailer and rotate on down
toward a river too big to miss and too thick to be found in,
Johnny needing to fly away in that fog before he was half
buried and forever trapped, triple-trapped by desperation
and all that stone and all that dirt.

Wings beat and trailer rocked, but Johnny was too drunk
for knots and it was up to Bonner to untangle him, Bonner
who'd heard the commotion and who came to help Johnny

stand and who guided him out of the shed and then closed
the door on that big white hard bird, its eyes fierce and
intent upon this night scene, Johnny being taken back to
bed by Bonner more tender than a brother.

15

FARMERS years ago on Saturdays came to Beaker's Bride to ship hogs and buy feed and get broken crossbars welded; the big mill now dead and weeded off to the north of town did so much Saturday business that farmers would park their wagons in a long line a mile-long line and go to taverns to wait, leaving sons to move the tractors and teams a few feet at a time in that long line leading to the mill, leaving sons or hiring town boys to move the tractors and teams a few feet at a time in that mile-long line leading to the mill.

"Hey, boy, two bits to keep me in line. You know how to run a tractor?"

"Yessir."

"You come fetch me when it's my turn at the scales. I'll be at the Past-Time."

So the boy moved the tractor a few feet at a time, getting nervous trying to gauge exactly when he should set the brake and run fetch the farmer, because if the boy went too early and the farmer had to sit out in the sun another half hour before it was his turn at the scales, then the boy would have to listen to it: how he was as useless as tits on a boar and he wasn't worth two bits (though other farmers paid twice that, sometimes even a dollar) and how next Saturday this farmer intended to bring along his oldest girl because at least she's got sense about how slow this line is moving and wouldn't come get her old man until it really was time—I could've had two more beers in the least, in the very least two and maybe three.

But if the boy waited too long—perhaps a stopped freight would block his way into town—and when he got to the tavern if the farmer lingered to finish a beer and the last of his story about that Poland China sow he owned, the smartest and meanest creature God ever put down on all fours, then by the time boy and man returned to the line, certain impatient farmers—Dutchmen—would've moved the tractor and wagon over to the side and this newly arrived farmer, sweating and red and blinking from the sudden sun when all had been so quiet and cool in the Past-Time, he would curse first the boy he had hired and then all those goddamn Dutchmen who had moved ahead of him and on some Saturdays there had been threats of fistfights by the scales.

So the boy sat there nervous on the metal seat, using the hand clutch to move the tractor a few feet at a time as he looked forward toward the mill and back toward Beaker's Bride, this boy sitting there in that heat knowing that others his age were using this Saturday to put woolly bears in girls' hair and that no matter how *he* worked it, he wouldn't be able to work it exactly right.

. . . . .

AND ALVA had become so stupid for Johnny that one afternoon she filled an entire page with signatures—*Alva Reace, Mrs. Johnny Reace*—then burned the evidence in the fireplace and broke up the ash with a heavy poker.

She daydreamed rude little dramas in which she discovered Bonner's body on the floor of his room or was unable to rouse him from his recliner by the window overlooking the back lot full of monuments. Alva wanted what was wrong and she mouthed the guilt over and over: it'd be wrong, it'd be wrong—if you sing it right, like a little bird's song. She was hungry for Johnny Reace and imagined all the time how it would be: her and Johnny and Jess living together in Beaker Mansion or Florida—the Reaces—and being as happy as they were this Thanksgiving morning, playing Monopoly in the dining room while Bonner brooded around town in a cold rain.

Wearing his pain. The damp chilled all the way to the core of his long length as he walked Beaker's Bride, bowel-cold, he was that cold wearing his pain.

Bonner always thought he'd live to be an old man because in manner he was predisposed toward that condition of slow study—was like an old man even as a boy—but now he knew he'd die young, or at least that's what they always said when you died before you were sixty: *And such a young man, too.*

He had been passing black blood for a full year, but *this pain*—it was recent and it was bad and Bonner, like a gut-shot cavalry horse, he showed the pain in his eyes even as he kept standing.

Bonner could make no sense of it. He had worked hard all his life with no resentment toward others who had it easier, without anger at the bad that came his way, allowing himself none of the options that gnaw at you toward the end when you think, maybe I should've done *that* instead of this—Bonner simply didn't think about it. Instead, he went ahead like always.

When the yards shut down, Bonner found other work. When his wife left him, he reared Matthew alone or with the help of an elderly housekeeper. When Beaker's Bride fell on hard times and no one looked after the cemetery, Bonner assumed responsibility. He took care of the old people around town. Matthew's death stooped him, but Bonner went on and let Alva stay and then reared Jess as his own. But now! Now he had to fight what he had avoided his entire life: thinking about it.

Easier just to go ahead like always, because if you ever started thinking about it, all the bad that's come your way and a life brutal in its constant unrelieved, unrelenting hard work, never money for anything more frivolous than taking that strange boy on an annual circus visit, not enough hours to finish what you've begun—if you ever started thinking about it, *why?*, then you would suffer delivery of a desperation stored so long and built to such proportions that it would immobilize you with a bitter, mad hopelessness. Better to do your duty and not think about it; duty is better than thinking about it—he had tried often to convince Johnny of that particular truth.

. . . . .

IMMEDIATELY UPON ENTERING Agnes's house, Bonner could smell the staleness of rooms unmoved through, air too long in one place. Old ladies had dusted and swept, but you can't clean dead air, and when couches haven't been sat upon for years and heavy chairs remain unmoved for decades, there's a stagnation to a house that you can sense immediately upon entering it.

He had tried for years to get Agnes to live with someone in town, one of the widows, but Agnes would not be moved. She had lived in this house forever, since before Bonner was born, and although Agnes had retreated to two rooms upstairs, she held them resolutely and would not be moved.

"Agnes?" He knocked on the bedroom door before opening it, finding her in bed with eyes closed but not dead. "It's me. Bonner. How you feeling today?"

She was lost somewhere in the forties. Give her a minute to sort this out, because Agnes sometimes watched her life like a long movie jumbled out of sequence, and although the individual scenes were perfectly played, she sometimes forgot who was the baby she now held: little sister, one of the grandchildren, or her own child—maybe the boy. She waited at a train station, full of soldiers. Trains and soldiers—what war was this?

Bonner stood there hurting.

"What month is it?" she asked. Agnes didn't care about the years anymore, these new ones sounding so odd and foreign to her. Tell her it's 1969 or 1970 and you might as well say 2000—and what could she possibly make of that? The 1960s and 1970s: these were strange numbers for years and Agnes could never get used to them, was never comfortable with them—not the way she had been with the more familiar and more reasonable 1940s and 1930s and back toward the comforting 1920s.

And days? They were foolish, too. It would have been as meaningless to name days for Agnes as it would have been to name the hours of those days—what did they *mean*, poor pitiful and insignificant Tuesdays proceeding indistinguishable from Mondays.

But months. Months still meant something; months were good and durable; Agnes could make sense of months, the hot ones and the holiday ones—and which one was this?

"November," Bonner said. "It's Thanksgiving."

Oh, don't tell *her* about Thanksgiving, Agnes remembering sweet potatoes with marshmallows and big bowls of Waldorf salad and dressing by the gallon and . . . and a turkey so breast-heavy you had to start cooking it a day early. Why, she can remember this one Thanksgiving back before some war when they must have had fifty people over to the house. . . .

"I'll be bringing you dinner later on. I got to go to the store, too—maybe tomorrow. You need anything?"

"Pogey bait and bath salts."

This again. She had enough bath salts—and colognes and sprays and perfumes—to last out the century, closets full. "I bought you some bath salts last week," Bonner said weakly.

But she had cared for her mother during those bad two years when the old woman rotted away, and Agnes, who had all her life been something of a pill about cleanliness and smelling good, she still could recall the stench and still dreaded worse than death the idea that someday *she* might smell as bad as mother had.

You call on the old scents, and they come back so willingly: a morning in 1932 when baby brother got married—all those flowers. "Something lilac," Agnes suggested.

Bonner got out his pipe and watched Agnes, who did not watch him. Her husband had always told her she had a fine, fine nose, but over the years it had drooped, giving her a beaked appearance now—like a buzzard, perhaps, because her skin was loose and ruffled around the neck and Agnes's eyes when open were fierce small.

Bonner decided he would do what he'd done last time, take a jar of bath salts out of her closet and bring it back the next day like new. "Anything else I can get you?"

But already she had slipped the forties and had floated back beyond 1932 and stood now in a garden full of lilac bushes, the smell so strong as to be intoxicating, and who held her hand? Was it the man or some beau before him?—Agnes lay there fascinated, unhurried, waiting to see.

"Now you stay out of that tub until Sally or Jenny come over and help you—okay?" Bonner was concerned because Agnes had nearly broken her hip three winters ago taking a bubble bath alone one afternoon. The old woman placed unreasonable emphasis on being clean, sweet-smelling. "You hear me?"

"Huh?"

"Don't try to take a bath until someone comes over to help you with it."

"Keep that evil little Alva of yours away from me!"

Bonner stood there blinking. What did she mean by that? What did she mean by calling Alva *his*, that evil little Alva of *yours*, and how had Alva been evil? "Why'd you say that? Agnes? Agnes, why'd you say that?"

It's Willie Shellstrom! She remembered now. Willie Shellstrom who had led her out into this lilac garden, Willie who always got that funny haircut every summer, the sides of his head practically shaved and keeping just a short thatch on top. Hear the music? A dance. Willie Shellstrom had asked her to step outside for some air—step outside so he could have a smoke is what he meant, and Agnes watched him roll that cigarette, his hands moving like pieces of precision machinery, and now she could smell the tobacco. What God-wonderful details He grants us: that music to the ears as softly as lilacs to the nose, Willie Shellstrom's summer haircut, how his hands moved when he rolled a cigarette, the sweetness of tobacco not yet lighted and then its burning odor—and how it felt to be young, at a dance, with a beau.

Bonner left Agnes reviewing a life of such details.

· · · · · ·

JESS LOST EVERYTHING because he invested in utilities and railroads in spite of Johnny's advice, while the deals Johnny offered Alva seemed so foolhardy on his part that she couldn't pass them up and thought for sure he'd go bankrupt any turn now, but instead he skipped among her developed properties, always missing the hotels, and then he landed on Free Parking to replenish his account against the rules or went directly to jail exactly when he needed the respite, rolling doubles to get out and offering such deals that Alva couldn't resist: Johnny winning.

"I've never seen anybody with your kind of luck," Alva told him.

"Better lucky than good."

While Alva put away the pieces, Johnny took Jess into the kitchen, telling him you had to commune with a turkey as you cooked it—had to gobble in at the open oven and call this formerly noble bird, now domesticated dumb, by his right name. "Hello, Tom," Johnny said before gobbling. Jess, leaning to look into the oven and being made red and hungry by the heat and the meat, didn't understand everything Johnny said but was delighted all the same.

"Turkeys can't fly anymore," Johnny told him. "They bred flying out of them, gave them more meat instead. Now turkeys are for eating, not flying."

Jess stepped away from the oven; this constant business about flying had begun to weigh on him.

Alva came in. "What're you two doing?"

"Checking on Thomas," Johnny said.

"It'll never get finished, you keep that oven open. Bonner's not back?"

"Haven't seen him."

"Jess, honey, you put a coat on and go look for your grampa. We're about ready to eat."

But just then Bonner returned and, soon, all four of them were part of that last rush: setting the table, stirring gravy and filling bowls, making sure nothing was left in the refrigerator—then sitting down at this particularly detailed feast that Johnny made wonderful with his talk and laughter even as Bonner remained dark throughout the meal, reminding Alva again of how boring past Thanksgivings had been—of how deadly her life was before Johnny arrived.

She couldn't help being stupid for him, yesterday putting on one of Johnny's unwashed shirts as soon as the others left the house so she could walk around all day in that shirt, smelling him on her. But it wasn't only sex she hungered for anymore, because having him *there* was enough—to hear him talk and laugh, to watch him eat the way he did, as if always famished, and to wear a shirt of his around the house. Having him there was enough.

Late that afternoon, Alva walked into the kitchen as the two men were going out the door; their arms were full of covered dishes they would be delivering to old people living alone, people too sickly to make Thanksgiving dinner for themselves. Bonner usually did this by himself, and

Alva wondered when he had discussed it with Johnny—when these arrangements had been made. And how can two men so different be so much alike? She said nothing to them as they went out into the rain.

You had to stay for conversation and then coffee at each place, so night had come and the rain had stopped by the time they were finished with their deliveries. Bonner said he intended to walk on out north of town now that the weather had cleared, and Johnny could tell that he was not being invited along, wasn't supposed to come and would not be welcomed if he did.

Alva greeted him at the door. "I wondered if you two got lost or something. Where's Bonner?"

"Damn cold out there. You got a fire going?"

"Jess's bringing in some wood now. He forgot to fill the box again today. I must've told him a dozen times. Where's Bonner?"

Out walking where it is a summer Saturday, good and hot, and boys his age are putting woolly bears in girls' hair—out where the only trouble that troubled his mind was trying to gauge the pace of a long line, a mile-long line leading to the mill, out where he didn't have to think about it.

16

DECEMBER WAS WINTER, and ice came down the Illinois like someone upriver was in the business. Those big, long barges kept the channel open, but white and fast-moving ice ran the river along both banks; the nearest ferry, twelve miles upriver, was put out of commission. That left the bridge, twenty miles in the other direction, as the closest means for crossing the Illinois. Bluffs prevented you from reaching Beaker's Bride from the land side, and once you did get there, along that old river road, you were caught on a thirty-two-mile stretch of uncrossable river—longer than that when ice put the ferry out of commission. The railroad, with its bridge at Beaker's Bride, was the town's only good route in and out, but, of course, trains no longer stopped there.

Johnny made December, its ice and isolation, tolerable for Alva, so when the television went on the blink and Bonner decided not to have it fixed—cash was short with Christmas coming—Alva didn't argue the point.

Jess had always been a television addict, but he didn't care about the set being broken, either, because Jess was changing that December, becoming someone Alva didn't know. Now he got up early and eager for school, when always before Alva had to beg and threaten him out of bed. Now he talked openly and cogently at the dinner table like some kind of normal kid. Jess no longer played taps and Alva couldn't get him to admit anything about Beehart.

She couldn't get him to trade gossip about Johnny, either—though Alva still pumped the boy for information:

Did Johnny ever say anything to Jess about *her?* Did he ever talk about having girlfriends? Jess wouldn't say.

That December, Bonner kept waking up an aggravated man—coming down for breakfast one morning clearly intent upon fighting with Alva, when it had been years since they'd last argued so openly.

Why had Agnes referred to Alva as evil little Alva? he wanted to know. Alva wouldn't say.

Didn't she realize that taking her turn caring for the old woman was her duty? Bonner asked. Alva wouldn't respond.

She was selfish, Bonner said. Alva broke three eggs into a hot skillet and let her anger fry because she had learned long ago how to protect herself from Bonner's powerfully consumptive bad moods: by becoming as hot as he was cold, matching every drop in his temperature with a rise in hers.

She offered him the plate of eggs with toast on the side.

"Don't want no breakfast," Bonner said, voice as cold as that icy Illinois. "Just coffee."

Without missing a beat, she threw the plate, eggs, and toast across the kitchen into the sink, where china clattered, threatening to break but not breaking.

"Could've given it to the dog," he said, still all ice.

She knew, of course, that the man hated waste. "What's your problem this morning?"

Bonner ignored her. "Where's Lady?" He'd opened the kitchen door, but the old dog wasn't standing there waiting for her morning food. "If that boy put her in his room again last night . . ."

"That's it, Bonner. Go get mad at Jess, too—then you can start on Johnny. Make us *all* miserable!"

He went to the front hallway in time to meet a deeply chagrined Lady coming down the steps. "Boy!" Bonner hollered. "What's the dog doing inside? I told you about that before. You know the rules."

Jess sat on the top step and shielded his face against

window light. "I had bad dreams" came his bewildered reply.

Lincoln softened. "What you dreaming about that's bad, boy?"

He shrugged. "Just bad dreams." Though not as bad as they were unsettlingly true.

"Get dressed, you're coming with me today. I'll let your dog out."

"Where we going?"

"Little overnight trip to Springfield."

"But what about school?"

"You can miss it."

"Grampa, I don't *want* to miss school."

"I thought you hated school. You can miss a couple days, anyway—won't hurt you."

"What're we going to do in Springfield?"

"Just get dressed and come along, boy—don't question me."

Bonner wouldn't tell Alva his plans, either, and when Jess came down to the dining room she made over him to spite Bonner—asking Jess if he would be missing any important tests at school and did he think he'd get in trouble and grampa would have to be the one to write the excuse. "You look like the wreck of the *Hesperus*," she said to Jess, smoothing down his sleep-wild hair. "You have a bad night again last night?"

He shrugged, keeping his eyes on Bonner.

"I think he's scared," Alva said to the silent one. "You taking him off like this without warning or not telling anybody what you're up to."

"Let's go." Bonner had awakened thinking of those circus trips he and the boy made together each summer, and Bonner was eager to get on the road.

Alva followed them out to the old white Ford and stood there by the driver's door as Bonner got the car started and let the motor warm. He rolled down his window and spoke softly to her. "Taking the boy to Springfield to visit a old buddy of mine lives there. Him and me used to work on the railroad over by Roodhouse. I remembered he's never seen the boy—doesn't even know I got a grandson. We'll stay with him there in Springfield and be back tomorrow afternoon. I just need some time with him—with Jess, I mean. Me and the boy."

She started to lean in and give Bonner a kiss, but he had already started rolling up the window.

Alva returned to the kitchen and made milk gravy and biscuits for Johnny, who looked at that white and heavy and well-peppered mound on his plate and laughed. She couldn't tell if he was especially delighted or was making fun of the meal—but in either case, Johnny like always ate with abiding appreciation, and something about watching a hearty eater got to Alva.

·   ·   ·   ·   ·

BONNER DROVE CAREFULLY on the old gravel river road, but when he hit the macadam pavement he went fast over tickle-belly hills, thrilling Jess, and then out on the state highway Bonner pegged the speed limit exactly to cruise toward Springfield.

"You remember the circus, boy? How them bears was on leashes and tigers in cages? How that pretty lady came out riding on the back of an elephant, standing upright on that elephant like some kind of queen? You *remember?*"

"Is Springfield where the circus is?"

"No. It comes to St. Louis. But you remember the circus, don't you?"

"We going this year?"

"That ain't till summer."

"But we're going, aren't we—huh?"

Bonner never asked for anything that wasn't his by rights, but he wished to God he could take the boy to the circus one more time whether that was deserved him or not. "Looks like snow."

"Can we go sledding in Springfield?"

"We'll see."

Snow didn't damage roofs unless it was too heavy or until warm days and cold nights alternated to create runoff and then freeze it at night, making ice dams in the gutters—the ice eventually pushing up under shingles, and when that happened enough times over twenty years you're going to get leaks. No way around it. Bonner thought of traveling to see his old customers, to check on those roofs he'd laid; Bonner kept all their names and addresses in a green leather book. So much to do, so little done.

"We should've brought Johnny," Jess said. "Then it would've been all the men together."

Bonner nodded. Maybe if he couldn't be given one more summer and one more circus, at least he'd be granted another Easter, because that boy was a spectacle at Easter, barging around the yard looking for eggs that half the people in Beaker's Bride had come to hide, so they could watch the only kid in town—and Jess was worth watching, wearing that ratty old bathrobe of his and looking for all the world like some ancient member of gnome royalty gone goofy, oblivious to his audience and to everything else except finding those painted eggs and then delighting in their discovery more than what seemed right. Easter would be fine. Summer was better, because during summers Bonner and Jess went fishing, and in a boat the boy would tell such stories, speaking in a manner he came by honestly and haunting you with Alva's eyes. Summer was better but Easter would be fine, and the big-eared Lincoln cruised along right at the speed limit.

· · · · ·

THAT NIGHT was the first night she and Johnny had been alone in the house since he came to Beaker's Bride almost three months before, but Alva was determined not to beg for what she craved.

After finishing the dinner dishes, she went to the living room; Johnny had made a fire, but he wasn't there—he'd gone back into the dining room so he could look out a west window.

During winter's dusk and especially at the end of an overcast day, there comes a time between light and dark when the hour turns blue and makes you uneasy—moody and forlorn without specific reason.

"What're you doing?"

"Just standing here looking out at the end of day."

"Thinking about what?"

That damn white bird. Johnny could never get it completely off his mind, half in and half out—the way Bonner had described how that marble figure would be ascending, white stone pulling up from green grass, and Johnny wondered if he'd ever see it. That image, which obviously comforted Bonner, caused a certain disquiet within Johnny Reace.

"Thinking about what?" she asked again.

"Thinking about nothing. Just standing here enjoying the unimproved works of the Lord."

Alva looked past him across the river and into the trees. "Johnny, you say such things."

"Yes, I do."

"Take it off, will you? Makes you look goofy."

He rolled his eyes up toward the bill of the Reliable Casket Company cap that Bonner had given him that day in the shed. "I didn't wear it at dinner."

"Such a gentleman."

"When you bought all the liquor for that party we had, did you happen to get any brandy?"

"I bought everything on the list you gave me. I don't remember if you put down brandy or not."

"Be nice to have a brandy by the fire."

Alva forced her voice to be casual. "I'll go check."

Brandy! She took down two of her good goblets and filled each three-quarters to the lip, bringing in the glasses on a fancy wooden tray. When she offered the tray to Johnny, he laughed that peculiar music of his.

"What?" Alva asked.

He shook his head, still smiling as he took one of the goblets.

"Sometimes you have a way of laughing, and I can't figure out if you're laughing at me or not."

"I'd never laugh at you."

She sat next to him on the couch and they became quiet with the fire, all the lights off in that room so that the only illumination came from the hearth, and Alva hoped those flames improved her looks and that the shadows played good tricks with the largeness of her dark eyes and the smallness of her mouth and chin. "I wonder why Bonner took Jess and left us alone."

Johnny waited awhile to answer. "I was wondering that myself."

"Maybe he thinks we're young lovers who need the time alone together." Alva was sorry she said it. This brandy was terrible; if she'd been drinking gin, she wouldn't be sorry for saying it.

"Bonner's an amazing man. I wish I could learn to do one thing in life as well as he lays shingles."

"Daddy was like that—could fix anything and took pride in his work."

Johnny put on a fresh log from the box he'd filled earlier in the day. "I'm going to St. Louis between Christmas and New Year's."

"I know. But you'll be back for that New Year's Eve party we're having—right?"

"Sure. I told Bonner I'd help him until we finished Beaker Mansion."

"What're you going to do in St. Louis?"

"See some old friends." He had returned to the couch and sipped again from the goblet of brandy. "I've never been to St. Louis."

"Oh, *I* have. Daddy had to work over a lot and he stayed in St. Louis nearly a month. Mother and I went down to pick him up. While he was there, he wrote me a letter, and it was the very first letter I'd ever received in my whole life." She didn't tell Johnny it was the *only* letter she'd ever received, the only personal letter—not counting official notices and bills and such. Was it odd for a twenty-eight-year-old woman to have received only one personal letter in her whole life—and that one from her father when she was eight? Was it pathetic? I'm not the kind of person I appear to be, Alva thought. I'm not odd and pathetic. It's just that I grew up in a queer situation. "I must have read that letter a million times. But then I outgrew it."

"I'll write you from St. Louis."

She hated to hear him tease about something like that. "No, you won't."

"Sure I will."

"You won't!"

"We'll see."

She put a hand to the back of his head, where hair stuck out from under the cap. "You keep wearing that thing all the time and you'll go bald. Then none of the girls in Florida will pay you any attention."

He took it off and she laughed at him, but this nasty brandy wasn't any help at all, didn't aid Alva in saying what she was about to say. Not like gin would've. "You don't have to sleep in the basement tonight."

He put the cap back on, tugging down the bill until it covered his eyes.

It wasn't right to want so desperately what you simply were not going to get. Crying now? Goddamn brandy.

Johnny stood, put the cap backwards on his head, and offered her a hand. "Dance?"

She refused to look at him. "Don't do me no favors."

But Johnny moved her easily to the center of the room, where they held each other a moment and then danced around in the firelit and quiet shadows: eyes closed and eyes open, pretending and not pretending.

"There's no music," she whispered.

"Sometimes there's no music but you're faced with the situation anyway."

"What situation?"

"Actually, there are two situations in life." Then he didn't talk for the longest time and Alva didn't ask him because she wanted none of his stories or jokes now; eventually, Johnny told her anyway: "Dance situations and nondance situations."

"Mmm." Alva knew she was a good dancer.

"And *this*," he finally said, "is a dance situation."

Even without music, she had to agree.

. . . . .

"GRAMPA!"

"What?"

"I said do you like him too?"

"Who?"

"Johnny."

"Don't bother me with that now!"

Bonner was suffering from indecision and he hated it; he considered indecision a fault in others and was appalled to discover it in himself. He'd rather make the wrong decision and then stick with it than be undecided about what to do. His old friend in Springfield never came home, even though Bonner and Jess had waited out in front of the man's house there for two hours, went out to get dinner at a restaurant, returned to park in front of the dark house and wait another hour. Then Bonner began driving to Beaker's Bride in the night, but he worried about what he might find when he got home, if Alva and Johnny had gone to her room. Bonner pulled off the road, made a U-turn, drove back toward Springfield—but he could hardly show up at his friend's house this late at night, so he pulled off the road again to think. Jess, oblivious to these maneuvers, kept on talking.

"Do you think he'll stay with us forever?"

"Who?"

"Johnny!"

"Oh, for chrissakes, boy!"

"I'm sorry, grampa."

"No, no—it's me. Don't mean to snap at you." He drove back onto the highway. "We'll find us a motel and spend the night. That'll be fun, huh? You never stayed in a motel, did you?"

"No." But Jess was withdrawing.

"That Johnny, he's a good one, all right. Best worker I ever saw. Sold his car for those vanities—all the bathrooms in Beaker Mansion are finished and you should be living there come spring. Won't that be great, like you was rich or something, huh?"

"I like *our* house!" he insisted desperately.

"The mansion is our house too. We'll still own both places. Tell you what, you could live Monday, Tuesday, Wednesday, Thursday in one house and then Friday through the weekend at the other."

Jess seriously considered it. "You kidding me?"

Bonner laughed.

As the old white Ford droned on over highway miles, Jess slept and Bonner thought. Maybe he *should* go home, because even if Alva and Johnny were in bed together, where would the offense be in that? Bonner thought and drove and hit the steering wheel once, hard, then moved the car ten miles, twenty, beyond the limit, still heading away from Beaker's Bride.

．　．　．　．　．

A MAN CAN BE FOOLISH about what he thinks a woman treasures, shoulders or face or money or the other endowments men themselves prize.

His hands. Alva looked at the left one holding her right. Would he ever tell her the truth about how he lost his ring finger? Even with that flaw, Johnny had good hands: strong-fingered and big-palmed and calloused, but easy the way he held her thin, warm one.

It was strange but somehow better to be dancing in silence, in a silence complete except for the sound a fire makes and their footsteps and one question she finally had to ask him: "What's the name of this old song anyway?"

17

DECEMBER HURRIED ON ahead toward the day before Christmas, when Johnny left them, taking the old white Ford because Bonner and Alva insisted on it. They could borrow someone's car for a week and, besides, they wanted to ensure Johnny's return; they knew he was capable of betraying them, going away and never coming back in spite of promises he'd made, but he wouldn't steal their car—one of the peculiarities of honor.

Johnny wasn't gone a day before Bonner and Alva resumed their old ways, quietly pressing on each other with their waiting—except now they knew what it was they awaited.

Always before, their waiting had been generalized because they had nothing specific to wait for except something impossible—the return of Matthew, though neither of them ever spoke of their separately contrived fantasies about Matthew maybe surviving the Illinois and he's going to show up one of these days or maybe he got amnesia and doesn't know who he is or where he lives—or whatever it is you fantasize about and wait for when the body's never found. Alva waiting in dread and Bonner in hope.

During the last part of December, however, they knew what it was they waited for.

. . . . .

IN JOHNNY'S ABSENCE, Bonner spent time riverside listening to the Illinois talk the way water running under ice will do, sucking and whistling and causing the ice above to groan and grind—all the sounds Bonner felt like making, he hurt that bad. Everything was dying—or already dead. Matthew.

He hadn't notified the outside world about Matthew's death, because Bonner came from a heritage of people living in isolated places, keeping to themselves and dealing with the outside as surgically as possible—protecting what was theirs from what was foreign. Bonner paid whatever tribute the outside world demanded of him, but he owed no allegiance to any government and he had long ago called home all his loyalties.

Just let me finish Beaker Mansion. He'd given up hoping for one more Easter, one more summer—just live out this winter. Bonner held his lower belly with both hands and listened to the Illinois run under ice: just give me this one last winter.

. . . . . .

IT WAS Christmas Eve and Mr. Gibsner sat out on the wood wall thinking of forty zeros and the pull of the universe. He'd been reading creation stories and theories of origins ever since that night long ago when he saw lights in his wheat field and later discovered a patch of scorched ground there, and Mr. Gibsner had come to believe that the current form of the universe—planets and suns and life and all matter—was transitional, basically unstable, and that eventually everything would once again be dissolved in an infinite neutrino sea. The universe hungered for its old stability and, on occasion, Mr. Gibsner believed he could feel the pull.

Charlie Warden came out and put a blanket around the old man's shoulders, dreading to hear Mr. Gibsner talk of such things, especially when it was so cold and the Illinois competed for nighttime conversation.

. . . . .

BECAUSE the other women in town were occupied with Christmas preparations or were too sickly to go out in the weather, Alva was supposed to run over and bathe Agnes before going with Bonner and Jess to church. The old woman refused to talk but kept an open eye to ensure Alva didn't start that business with the sewing needle again. No bathing was done, of course—Alva just sat in a big brown chair by the window and read until enough time passed.

She's got a book in her hand, Agnes thought, but I know what she's got on her mind: that man. Oh, I've known them like that in my time, a man who thinks he's God's own cousin. Cock of the walk. Making twitchets itch. *I know.*

Agnes laughed, and Alva eyed her uneasily.

. . . . .

EARLIER THAT MONTH, Jess had made friends with the rough boys at school—first with Lamont Skinner, the roughest of them all.

The kids had been playing nation ball while Jess stood near the furnace room trying to convince himself to join in if for no other reason than to keep warm. His legs twitched in anticipation as he edged toward the game, waiting for an invitation to play. Then the ball took an odd bounce in his direction and, miracle of miracles, Jess caught it.

"I'll be on this side," he said, surprising everyone with his boldness, crossing one white line and aiming at the other side's best player. Before throwing the ball, Jess pointed up and shouted, "Helicopter!" The players looked (the oldest trick in the book, Johnny called it) and Jess threw the ball, hitting his target.

The kid refused to be out, of course, and continued protesting until Jess turned to one of his own teammates, Lamont Skinner, and said, "You're the best player in the whole school, so you decide. Fair or not? The best player in the whole school always gets to be the judge—that's the rule."

Having his supremacy announced like this invested in Lamont a somberness that led him actually to rub his chin before ruling: "Fair!" No one dared an appeal as Judge Skinner patted Jess's head. "You're something else—didn't know you had it in you, tubs."

To win over the other rough boys at school, however, required poetry.

Before kindergarten, Jess had been a wonderful writer. He would hold in his fat baby fist a soft-leaded pencil as big around as a man's thumb, making loops and lines and circles across the backs of advertising circulars—filling pages that he would take down to Bonner, who would say, "Now what do we have here?" Jess didn't know, but he couldn't wait to find out.

The big man—Jess's hero back then—would read what the boy had written, long and elaborate stories about bears in brambly forest and river trips and magic lands, histories of Beaker's Bride, and tales of the railroad. To think you could write such things! Jess would hurry to his room and write some more: and the best part of writing wonderful stories the way he did was not knowing what you'd written until someone read it.

At school, however, Jess learned that writing wasn't magic—it was only words, each a potential spelling mistake and all of them with meanings you had to know *before* you put them down. You can't get a wonderful story out of that.

Jess still brought his writing to Bonner, but these school stories simply said what the boy had laboriously scribed on ruled paper, and where is the wonder in that?

For the third-grade poetry assignment that was to win him river-rat respect, Jess sauntered into class nonchalantly bouncing a tennis ball from his forearm back to his hand, back and forth—the only coordinated trick he could perform, something he and Johnny had worked on for hours.

The rough boys felt especially stupid reciting their poetry in front of the class, talking like sissies about trees and truth and all that shit, so they got the biggest kick out of Jess's recitation. Something he'd heard Johnny say. Jess flailing his arms like a ham actor, earning laughs, intoning: "Beans, beans, the musical fruit. The more you eat, the more you toot. The more you toot, the better you feel."

To make it the more wonderful, rough boys chimed in on the last line (they knew Johnny's poem!) and said it along with Jess: "So let's have beans for every meal!"

Teacher sent home a note saying Jess had been cutting up in class, but he didn't care because for the first time in his school career Jess had a nickname that was affectionate, and for the first time he had friends among the rough boys, who passed him in the hallways smiling, poking him on the arm like pals: "Hey, beans!"

On Christmas Eve, Jess had plans for becoming even more Johnny-like.

18

ON THE DAY he left Beaker's Bride, Johnny crossed midwestern bridges that showed none of architecture's graces, bridges that gained strength not through design but by adding more steel: girders locked together with criss-crossing bands every six inches, steel and iron welded and riveted—these bridges didn't work with the laws but stood in defiance of them. Big, heavy, ugly, strong bridges. Fuck you bridges.

Having crossed his and running now toward the Mississippi, Johnny relaxed with the miles and became pacific with the knowledge of what he was doing: going to St. Louis. He no longer worried what storms brewed in Alva's dark and denied mind, no longer was uneasy under the influence of Bonner's brooding sense of duty, no longer fretted about whatever responsibility he owed Jess.

Johnny stopped for gas and talked with the attendant, who asked where he was headed. "Going to St. Louis."

Johnny knew a woman he could call and she would let him stay with her, but now he wasn't sure as he drove through Granite City, Illinois, then crossed the Mississippi into St. Louis, meandering through the old waterfront district near the Arch until he found a bar that was open, rare to find a bar that was open on Christmas Eve.

The Aloha Club was stuck in one section of a renovated warehouse, the inside of the place decorated to look like a South Seas joint—or someone's bad idea of what a South Seas joint looked like, with brown, dusty thatching covering the ceiling and smelly shells epoxied to the wall and expanded blowfish fitted with light bulbs to provide what little illumination the Aloha Club had. This being Christmas Eve, garland hung from the tropical motif.

The Aloha Club was full of the kind of people who go to a place like this on Christmas Eve; an official Christmas party was being held here, too—some real estate office.

Johnny stood a moment by the door, then went to the bar and ordered a dark rum drink. What the hell.

Two young women from the office party watched him. "Did he come in with anyone?" the dark-haired one asked.

"No," answered the redhead. "I saw him when he was crossing the street—alone. He came up from the river."

"From the river? There's no place to park down there —is there?"

"I don't know. He's kind of cute, huh?"

"Cute! You gotta be kidding me. He looks fresh off the farm."

Johnny was dressed in the kind of clothing they sell poor people, Big Ben jeans and a Taiwan flannel shirt and a worn-out old leather jacket and that Reliable Casket Company cap he prized so highly. He knew they were eyeing him; Johnny bought a couple drinks and carried them over to where the young women sat.

"Oh, shit, Linda, he's coming here with drinks. Don't ask him to sit down—okay? Promise? Remember what happened last time you started talking with some weirdo."

"Hello, ladies. Here's a little present from me to you— for Christmas." He put the drinks on their table; the dark-haired woman muttered thanks but wouldn't look at him. "Well, Merry Christmas." He turned to leave.

"Why don't you join us?" the redhead said. Her friend kicked her under the table.

"Oh, I don't know about that. When I first saw you two sitting here, I thought, Now there's a couple good-looking twenty-year-olds—I should go over and join them. But then I remembered I had no business being with two twenty-year-olds." He waited.

"Why not?" asked the redhead.

"Honey, I ain't wired for two-twenty." Johnny tossed back his head to laugh, laughing so loudly that other people stopped talking to look.

"Oh, brother," said the dark-haired one, unamused even by Johnny's laughter. "Besides, we're both twenty-three."

The redhead invited him to take a seat and he did. "I'm Linda Greenerton and this is Myra—"

"Just Myra."

"Johnny Reace, ladies."

"How you doing, Johnny." Linda Greenerton reached across the table to shake his hand.

"Been doing 'bout half, Linda, 'bout half. Doing that half to death, though."

She smiled all the way across her face—where did this guy come from?—but Myra made a half-turn in her chair to keep away.

"Is that for real?" Linda Greenerton asked, looking at his cap.

Johnny rolled blue eyes upward. "Yes, ma'am."

"There really is a Reliable Casket Company?"

"Jerseyville, Illinois."

"How'd you get it?" She wanted one for herself.

"I dig graves."

"Oh, brother," Myra muttered, trying to signal Linda. Then to Johnny: "Actually, this section here is for our private office party—the public is supposed to stay at the bar or over in that other section."

Johnny ignored her. Myra was one of his exceptions, a woman unimpressed by him, unamused at the jokes he made, and uncharmed by his cap and close blue eyes and odd manner. These unimpressed women made Johnny uncomfortable, the way a magician is made uncomfortable by someone in the crowd who keeps hollering, "It's in his other hand—look at his *other* hand!" Johnny Reace had no use for such women, the way a mirror has no use for an unlighted candle.

The redhead was a different story. When she laughed at what Johnny said, she showed teeth so large and white as to make you wonder if they were real, though they looked real enough, wet-enamel real and not that painted on or capped white—an entire mouthful of teeth completely goldless even in the back, where Johnny could see when she laughed mouth-open to showcase her asset.

"I guess we better go mix with some of our clients," Myra said pointedly.

"You go mix," Linda replied. "I'll be along shortly." After the other woman left, Linda told Johnny, "It's a real estate office, but we don't have anything to do with the clients—we're just secretaries."

"No one is 'just' anything," he said, trying for her eyes.

"Right," those eyes, big green ones, mocking him back.

"Real estate, huh?"

"Yeah. My college degree is in English so I'm working as a secretary—make sense?"

"English?"

"Yes."

"What a droll coincidence."

Linda cocked her head, trying to get a bead on him. She would use that phrase herself in the future—droll coincidence indeed—and in the future she often would talk about Johnny, what kind of man he was and the strange things he said and the adventures they had together during that week between Christmas and New Year's. That's what Johnny Reace was, a story people told.

"What do you mean, coincidence?"

He sipped and smiled. "I *speak* English."

Why did she keep laughing at the stupid things he said? "Why?"

"I don't know, but I like that in a woman."

"What do you do for a living?"

"I told you. I dig graves."

She hooked a finger onto her lower front teeth and let it hang there until she was ready to speak. "You're a cryptic man."

"Is that a pun or are you just happy to see me?"

She shook her head, genuinely confused as to why she found him so fetching—blue eyes and lights-on smile maybe, or the way that cap she coveted made him appealingly goofy among these other men she worked with, young soon-to-be-rich men who dressed so carefully.

Linda Greenerton was his height and wide-shouldered, her hair barely red and very fine, kept back from her face to show off its openness, the flawlessly white skin, green eyes—and that fleshy, large mouth she couldn't seem to keep her fingers out of. Linda's heavy breasts bulged to the sides of the green dress she wore without a bra, allowing those breasts to move with a fluid weight that made Johnny try to remember if now was the longest he'd ever gone without sex in his adult life.

One of the men from the office was becoming loud—some guy almost sixty, face flush, Johnny knew the type.

"That's Bob Alden," Linda said. "This year's the second time he's been passed over for manager and the guy who was promoted ahead of him this time is about half Bob's age."

Bob Alden trying too hard, slapping others on the back and speaking too loudly, joking with the bartender about putting some *vodka* for the love of God in his screwdrivers, avoiding the eyes of his nearby wife, who strained behind a smile much practiced over the years. Alden stood unsteadily as he looked around for some client to compliment, to agree with, to show how earnest he could be—desperate for acceptance, validation. "Let me get you another drink, Simpson. Come on, come on—it's Christmas, for chris-

sakes. Loosen up! Get this man another drink, barkeep!"
Playing a role he had honed over thirty years of desperation, this laughter at others' jokes, gofer, luggage carrier,
maker of arrangements, vodka drinker who played by the
book but never won and now it was too late and he was too
loud and too drunk—Johnny knew the type.

Worried about Linda, Myra had sent the newly promoted manager—the office boss—to check out Johnny. The
hotshot stood at their table, drink in his hand, and on his
boy-tough face was a wide smile that he considered to be
his personal secret to success in real estate. "Hi there," he
said, offering the free hand. "I don't think we've met. Bill
Jones."

Reflecting the false smile, Johnny shook the man's hand.
"Johnny Reace."

"You one of our clients, Johnny?" Still selling that smile.

"Well, I've been thinking about buying that big arch I
saw on the way in—you handle that?"

Gone the smile. "Actually, pal, we made arrangements
for this section of the place to be for our office *exclusively*.
That's why we have that little bar set up here—free drinks
for the office staff and our clients. But not for you."

"I'm buying what I'm drinking."

"Good, good." The smile returned. "Why don't you go
drink it at one of the other tables—then Linda will be able
to spend some time with her friends."

Johnny reached up and hit the bottom of the hotshot's
drink, causing the glass to flip back and spill its contents on
his shirt and jacket. Once he got over his surprise, the
unsmiling one looked at Johnny and saw in those eyes bad
lights that spoke in certain terms, leaving the hotshot with
one of two ways out: retreat or straight through Jack.

Making his action even more ominous, Johnny remained
sitting with casual posture—but from this position he
could easily hit the boss right below the heart to take away
his breath or, if it got nastier, Johnny would break the stem

off his own glass and cut him across the face because nothing was more effective in cowering a man than to be face-cut, which hurts truly and brings quick blood that makes you unable to think of anything except bleeding to death. These were among the truths Johnny had learned four years on the road.

Jones took backward steps. "You're out of here, mister, or I'm getting the owner to throw you out." Then he was gone.

Johnny didn't react.

"Tough guy, huh?" Linda asked, thrilled to be tempting him.

"Just tough enough."

"Do you really dig graves for a living—or did you mean that metaphorically?"

"Feel my hands. Those are real calluses, not metaphoric ones. I got them from digging real graves, not metaphoric ones."

Examining his hands, Linda first felt and then saw where the digit was missing. "My Lord, how'd that happen?"

"What? My finger? Well, I was working a coal barge out of New Orleans . . ."

Listen to him. I was working a coal barge out of *Naw'lins* is the way he said it, and she wondered if he would pronounce the name of the state *Loosiana*. Working a coal barge out of Naw'lins, just listen to the things this man says.

After he finished that story, she asked him for more, so Johnny told her stories of Beaker's Bride, how the town got its name, of a man who lives there with a pitiful dog and a wife named Wayne, of an old farmer who waits with the U.S. Constitution in hand for the return of flying saucers, ancient Agnes, and of the great stalking, brooding Lincoln who is responsible for the cemetery where Johnny digs graves. They were better stories than she'd ever heard before.

Johnny Reace was in bright contrast to the general policy among her friends: so what, big deal, I've heard it before, you're wrong, ho hum. Johnny opened his eyes in amazement at what you told him.

"The purpose of this party, *Bob,* is to be sociable with our colleagues and clients." The hotshot Jones was speaking loudly enough for all to hear. "It's not another excuse for you to get loaded."

Bob Alden looked around, but no one was willing to laugh with him, make a joke of it, let it pass.

Hit the asshole, Johnny urged silently—face-cut the little wunderkind.

But Willy Loman laughed alone. "You're right, boss—absolutely right. No more for me. Barkeep, cut me off for the night. Nothing but OJ for me from now on. The boss has spoken." Everything grinning except his eyes.

"Hey, what's wrong?" Linda asked Johnny.

He shook his head—*goddamn desperadoes,* you can't get away from them.

"Johnny?"

"Huh? Oh, I was just wondering what ever happened to all the Epicureans."

Linda had discovered long ago that when you laugh readily at what men say, they fall to you like things top-heavy, but it wasn't Johnny's humor that attracted her. She was interested in his hazard, that quality of danger Johnny owned, his capacity to be cruel. *To have someone like that for your own.* She negotiated with her mouth open.

Johnny appreciated now why she had painted her lips so red, and he kept his attention on that full red oval oral cavity of hers, singing to himself its praises, that commencement of the alimentary canal, suckler of milk, harborer of bacteria fleets, lung sucker, warm and wet whisperer of lovers' lies, kisser, comforter of bumped heads, breath taker and breath giver.

"See something you like?" she asked.

"I'd like to get my fingers in you."

She dropped her jaw. *"Well."*

"Well?"

"They're dancing in the back room."

"Dancing in Philadelphia, PA."

"Do you dance?"

"Do I—Is a fat baby Catholic?"

"Johnny."

They stood to go dance, but Johnny paused when he saw Bob Alden sneak around the temporary bar and upend a vodka bottle into a glass half full of orange juice, then suck at that glass greedily, holding it in both hands, a desperate man. He saw Johnny watching him. Willy paused, smiled, raised the glass, and winked: just a little joke between the two of them.

"Are we going to dance or not?"

Johnny put his arm around her waist. "There are two basic situations in life."

She rested an elbow up on his shoulder and let her hand dangle back in her almost-red hair. "Yes?"

He was a sucker for women who knew how to pose. "Dance situations and nondance situations."

"And this is a dance situation, right?" she asked, swaying a little with the other room's music, moving her breasts so they brushed his chest.

He slowly shook his head no.

"I'll get my purse, then."

· · · · · ·

ALTHOUGH he was taken to church infrequently, Christmas and Easter and funerals, Jess had been drafted into the Nativity play along with kids from towns downriver, where the church and Jess's school were located. On Christmas Eve, Jess was Joseph working a pious room. When Mary (née Felicity Louise Stone) nearly dropped

Baby Jesus and then went offstage to repeat her entrance, Jess-as-Joseph sighed and dangled his arms in exasperation like any husband kept waiting by a wife. The congregation stirred, chuckled.

In mid-Nativity, Mary stopped the action to primp, brushing back grandma's banana curls to show off makeup that Felicity-as-Mary was allowed somewhat incongruously to wear only on this special night. In reaction, Jess-Joseph vamped: rolling his eyes and turning his hand in a broad hurry-up signal. The audience tried to resist but could not, rewarding Jess with laughter.

· · · · ·

"OH, YOU GOT ME GOING NOW."

Johnny was fascinated whenever a woman said that: it sounded old-fashioned and fundamental, this declaration that something had begun and that it was largely out of her control and, now that it had begun, this phenomenon would have to be dealt with.

At some point during that first night they spent together, Linda Greenerton observed that it would've been easier on Johnny and her both if he had spread out his passion at a rate of a few times a week over the course of an entire year instead of storing it up as he presumably had for this annual Christmas Eve release. "Again? What a guy."

They went into her bathroom to shower together. "You want to do something strange?" she asked. He nodded and she flipped off the light and, the room being windowless, they were absolutely blind. "I don't know if you've ever showered in the complete dark before," she said, "but it's a weird experience." It was—without light, the water somehow felt different and all the old, familiar actions of washing your own body, the little peculiarities of what you wash first, and how you turn or lift to rinse, took on heightened significance. And, of course, when another body is

there in the stall with you—a body unfamiliar to you even
in the light—the blind showering becomes an exotic ritual,
so you do it in a silence complete except for those sounds
made by water and throats.

To towel off, they turned on the lights, and when Linda
left the bathroom ahead of him, Johnny said she had a
fetching vertical smile.

"Where do you get all that shit you say?" she asked without turning around.

She put lighted candles in strategic spots all around
the bedroom, a dozen or more candles, and Johnny lay
on the bed watching her, realizing at that moment she
was the most physically beautiful woman he'd ever
known, her large, open face slashed by that red-flesh
mouth and her heavy, white breasts marked by the biggest red nipples, and her legs were long, her belly soft
above light red hair. Eyes green enough for settings.
With all of Linda's colors muted and enriched by the yellow light from candles, Johnny found it hard to keep his
eyes open: too much, too much.

"Ready, Freddy?" she asked, getting into bed.

"Mmm."

Sweet This and Sweet That, she sang, invoking his name
frequently because Johnny Oh Johnny was a song you can
sing in bed, and now he tried his best to keep his eyes *open*
and make it easier not to believe all she said, How You Fill
Me Up and So Fine, Oh, So Fine and You're the Best I've
Ever Had and other stuff a woman who's good in bed will
say to make you feel right. Just stuff you say in bed, he told
himself—except that when Johnny closed his eyes he could
believe every word of it.

"I've never been like this for any other man," she said,
and Johnny actually had to struggle to stop himself from
believing her—was tempted to believe her even after she
brought out four lengths of black silk cord.

Later, the candles gone and the overhead light on: "This is the most deviant Christmas Eve I've ever spent in my life," Linda declared. "How about you?"

"Let me think."

She laughed, sprawling openly on the bed to let him see whatever he wished to see. Now her white-white skin was highlighted by red in places other than hair and mouth and nipples. "I didn't get you a *thing* for Christmas."

"I have a suggestion."

. . . . .

THE REST OF THE ACT was all shtick: Jess pointing with his thumb—get him, folks—when Shepherd One (a.k.a. Ronnie Flippo) couldn't find his spot at stage right, Jess hitting his forehead in mock amazement when the Three Wise Men entered stage left bearing bright foil gifts, Jess wise enough to abandon one particular bit (dragging his leg across the stage like a bad Charles Laughton playing the hunchback) when he sensed the audience found it unamusing, and then at the end Jess stood center stage with thumbs thrust in imaginary suspenders as he rocked back and forth on his heels—ain't I something! Even the director, who'd gone through various levels of mortification earlier in the play, came out and put her arm on his shoulder in an attempt to absorb some of his glory: because if this hadn't been church, the ovation Jess received would have been standing.

. . . . .

"WHAT?"

"Paint your toenails and let me watch."

"Sure," she replied without hesitation. "Kinky—I like that in a man. What color?" But then she spoke quickly, before Johnny could answer. "I know. Of course. How stupid of me."

When she returned from the bathroom carrying a tiny bottle and still naked, he threw her his T-shirt and asked that she wear it. "What you do, see, is you sit on the edge of the bed and bend up one knee by your chin and really concentrate like you're home alone and I'm not even—"

"I *do* think I know what you have in mind, dear."

Right. Tossing her head to get the hair out of her face but allowing a few strands to catch in her mouth, one hand holding the bottle while finger and thumb of the other hand squeezed that tiniest brush, concentrating so intently that a wet tongue tip parted her lips, Linda created perfectly the illusion of a woman by herself, engaged in the dreamy act of slowly brushing red onto her toenails, blowing soft breath to dry the wet red—then dramatically breaking the illusion to smile at him watching from a nearby chair. Something alluring in her eyes. "Johnny."

"Here's *your* present." He removed the only item he was wearing, that Reliable Casket Company cap, and put it on her head.

Linda stretched out one leg, inspected it at a distance, then bent the other foot close to her face. She spoke as she painted, saying she knew you weren't supposed to say it because saying it just gets in the way but she was going to say it anyway. "I love you."

．　．　．　．　．

ON THE DAY after Christmas, Johnny mailed a letter to Alva, who'd had so little confidence in his promise to write that she'd simply forgotten about it.

"Something for you," Bonner said coolly when he brought in the mail in the middle of that dead week between Christmas and the new year.

Although the hand was unfamiliar to her, his name was written right there in the upper left corner. No return address but his name in black ink: *Johnny Reace.*

Alva held the letter close to her chest until she saw Bonner's face, then she ran to her room and shut the door and waited a full five minutes with the envelope in her hands before opening it. She started reading it three different times, stopping herself because she was going too fast. She finally decided to go ahead and read it through quickly, then start over and read it again more slowly—then again, then again.

His letter sounded just like him, making jokes and saying outrageous things about what he was doing—how he wanted to see the view from the top of the Arch and it wasn't until he'd climbed all the way up and almost fell off several times that he found out you can take a train that runs on the *inside*. A three-page letter that made Alva eager-eyed, the way a person looks when he's watching something good: his children playing or the arrival gate at a train station.

Without knowing his address in St. Louis, Alva couldn't send Johnny a letter, but she wrote one anyway—working on it for two days to get the tone right, filling it with sugar kisses and BigBear hugs, multiple !!!'s and inches of underscoring, ellipses for intrigue and quote marks for wit. It was not the kind of letter that came to her naturally but the kind she thought Johnny would get a kick out of reading upon his return to Beaker's Bride. Alva sealed the letter in an envelope with his name on the outside and put it on his bed in the basement room.

Later, after rereading his letter to her, Alva went down and retrieved her reply so she could rewrite it again—and then once more after that.

·　·　·　·　·

DURING THE WEEK they were together, Johnny and
Linda asked around for anyone who might be going to
Florida come spring so that Johnny could catch a ride.
They were an item at parties. He didn't bother calling the
other woman he knew in St. Louis.

Johnny loved watching Linda get ready for a party, walking in and out of the bathroom trailing the scents of a
woman so freshly bathed he could smell her wet, clean
wake and then the rasping of her stockings as she hurried
around trying on different outfits, asking his opinion but
not following it, finally tossing through an amazing collec-
tion of shoes searching for a pair to match the dress or her
mood or whatever it is a woman tries to match her shoes
to.

In her apartment, she was always brushing against him
when they worked together in the kitchen or passed one
another in a narrow, short hallway, and she found ways to
bump against him at parties, too—leaning into Johnny
when reaching for a drink and holding his arm against her
as she introduced him to friends.

He asked her if a woman was always aware of her breasts
or could they sometimes be like packages she had in a
crowded elevator, inadvertently pressing them against you,
unaware of what she was doing.

Linda didn't even answer, mildly charmed by how like
a child, stupid and guileless, a man can sometimes be.

Then it was time for him to leave and no amount of guile
could make Johnny agree to stay for the New Year's Eve
party they'd been invited to.

"You haven't found your ride to Florida yet."

"I've got until spring," he said.

"Will you be coming back to St. Louis between now and
then?"

"Could be."

"When do you have to leave?"

"Right now. I want to get to Beaker's Bride before dark."

"Why don't you come back here and stay a week or two before you go to Florida, huh? I might be able to get some time off in the spring and we'll drive down there together."

"Sounds good to me."

But he was waiting by the door as he spoke, eager to go, and she knew the truth about that. Linda began working on his trousers—belt, button, zipper.

"Hey." He tried to haul her upright, off her knees, but she simply would not release what she had ahold of. This was one of those acts that had less to do with sex than with something else, Linda working at her need with a fierceness unmatched by anything they'd done during the previous week, careless now with her teeth and choking herself, and then she began crying, sobbing in a big, shameless way, the sobbing and sucking getting all mixed up together so that Linda sounded as if she suffered some respiratory distress, lungs heaving while she gagged and sucked and wept and would not—no matter how he pulled on her shoulders and arms—get up off her knees.

"Fine," he said sarcastically. "*Fine.*" Then he grabbed the back of her head with both hands. Johnny was that kind of man. On the outside all shiny mirrored surfaces but, underneath, he was the kind of man who could fuck you in the heart.

"What was all that about?" he asked when it was over.

But she wouldn't let him take it out of her mouth even now.

"Come on, come on," he said, losing patience, and when he finally was able to pull her away and look at Linda's face, Johnny saw that it was red and puffy—as if someone had handled her roughly.

"I just wanted the last time to be one you might remember for a while," she said.

"Not necessarily the last time. Maybe in the spring—"

She was shaking her head. "Don't bullshit me, Johnny. You leave now and I won't ever see you again."

Not having been asked a question, he said nothing.

"Here's something to consider," Linda said, lying flat on the floor. "I could take another two weeks off, tell them it was a family emergency or something, and you and I could drive down to Florida. My car."

"But I'm not going to Florida until spring."

"Change your plans. I'll give you two weeks you'll never forget. You'll be on your deathbed when you're an old man and there'll be this little smile on your face and it'll be because you're remembering the two weeks you and I spent together."

"I can't leave until I finish that job I'm working on in Beaker's Bride."

She got off the floor and went for his ear, dry-eyed and ruthless she went for his ear and whispered such things that Johnny Reace could've been listening to himself tell a story—of living in a beach house close enough to the ocean you can hear it breathe in and breathe out, hot nights, lush vegetation, lots of sweat. And when you hear a story like that in the middle of winter in Illinois, on New Year's Eve in Illinois . . .

. . . . .

ALVA HAD TOLD JESS that if he intended to stay up tonight until the new year came in, he'd better take a nap. Jess thought he was too excited to sleep—with Johnny due back any hour now and just wait until he hears about the church play—but within twenty minutes of lying on his bed, Jess slept.

And came the same old dream: standing on that splintered platform, bull dragon charging in from stage left, Jess telling himself he could do it he could do it—then being saved from doing it when like always Beehart ran on ahead taking Jess's place.

But not this time. In this afternoon's dream, Jess jumped. He ran after Johnny, Beehart never made an appearance, and Jess jumped. Leaping from night across the light, it was as Johnny had said: flying. Then hitting the ground and being chased. Exit, pursued by a bear.

19

EVEN BEFORE the old white Ford had stopped dieseling, Alva was outside—bumping against Johnny when he got out of the car to stretch, brushing back at the temples his windy brown hair, reaching for a kiss, trying to catch his eye, and generally on and about him like a momma dog gratified but suspicious at the return of a puppy who's been handled by strangers.

He pulled away from her and opened the car's back door. "Look what I got you for Christmas."

"A television! Johnny. Where'd you get the money?"

"I still have some left from selling my car. Where's Bonner?"

"You're so generous with things." All she'd bought him was a shirt.

"Generous to a fault."

"Come on in out of this cold. Bonner's over at Helen's, she took awful sick last week."

"Really?"

"Yeah. I guess I should've gone over there with him. You have a good time in St. Louis, did you?"

"It was all right."

"What'd you do there for a whole week?"

"Oh, you know—bummed around."

"Did you stay with people you knew?"

"Not really."

Not really? "I got your letter."

"Yeah?"

"You kept your promise!"

"Yeah."

What's wrong with him? "It was a wonderful letter," she said. Alva decided not to spoil the surprise by telling him she'd written a reply—let him find her letter when he went to his room. "I read it a couple different times."

"Good. I guess I'd better get this set inside."

She held the doors open for him and called upstairs to Jess. "Hey, dreamboat, come here and look what Johnny brought us for Christmas! Now we can watch New Year's Eve on television."

At dinner, eaten earlier than usual because of the party to be held that night, the talk centered on Jess. "Something's come over the boy," Bonner said. "Now he speaks right up and looks you in the eye—don't you, boy?"

Jess snapped to. "Yes, sir."

"His teacher sent home a note saying he'd been cutting up in class," Alva told Johnny, "and I hope that doesn't mean he's going to be giving her trouble but, all the same, you got to be proud of him for coming out of his shell."

Jess grinned.

Said Bonner to Alva, "Tell Johnny about Christmas Eve."

"Oh, Johnny, you should've seen it. Jess had the whole church in stitches. I never knew he could be such an actor. Where'd you pick that up from, honey?"

Jess, grinning, shrugged. "I wish you could've seen me, Johnny."

He looked across the table and pointed a finger-gun at the boy. "The heart of Beaker's Bride."

Something about the way he said it, however, caused Bonner's gaze to deepen and darken.

After dinner, Johnny went downstairs to change clothes for the party; everyone in town had been invited and those who could walk would come. Seeing the envelope on his pillow caused all the air to leave Johnny and he ripped open the letter nervously, reading rapidly down the pages. He tossed the letter on the bedside table and found his whiskey but not the glass, which meant he had to drink from the bottle.

. . . . .

"NEXT PARTY we have'll be at Beaker Mansion." Bonner stood at the door saying it to everyone who came in. "Be finished with the place come spring, then I'm throwing a party like you ain't ever seen." Saying it loudly enough for Johnny. "Yessir, next party will be in Beaker Mansion in the sweet of the year."

Johnny managed to avoid him until just before the new year swept out of the Atlantic briefly to excite New York City—that's when Bonner came over to sit next to Johnny on the couch, with Jane who couldn't hear sitting there, too. The sound on the television set had been turned down.

"When're you going to tell her?" Bonner asked Johnny.

"Tell who what?"

The big man winced.

"Is that a new TV?" Jane asked the men, who ignored her.

"When are you going to tell Alva you're leaving?"

Johnny shrugged.

"You leaving in the morning, next week—when?"

"You're just fishing, Bonner."

"I believed you, I admit that. Hook, line, and sinker. Selling your car to buy those vanities put me off, 'cause I figured without a car you wouldn't be making any fast getaways. But now this new TV—just your way of softening us up for the good-bye."

"Happy New Year!"

"Not yet, Jane!" Bonner shouted at her. "It ain't the new year yet!"

This confused her to no end because the silent television clearly was flashing the number of the new year, flashing it superimposed over people in New York who were kissing and hollering and hugging.

"When she coming to get you?"

Johnny looked at him quickly. He didn't know; how could he know? "Who?"

"Whatever woman you hooked up with in St. Louis."

Keeping his eyes on the New York new year, Johnny said, "Tomorrow. Around dinnertime tomorrow."

Bonner got up and walked over to listen to Mr. Gibsner and Charlie Warden, who were arguing whether recent winters received less snow than the winters they remembered from when they were boys or did it just seem that way?

"Can I get you another drink?" Johnny needed one bad. "Jane! Can I get you another drink?"

"Think about what?" she asked.

"Another drink!"

"Eighty-two this year. Birthday's in September."

"Okay."

She nodded, keeping a wary eye on the television, and when midnight in New York City was instantly replayed, she stood up and shouted, "Happy New Year! Happy New Year!" With her wrinkled lips puckered, Jane went around looking for someone to kiss.

"Not yet!" people shouted at her. "It ain't New Year's yet!"

So she sat back on the couch and resumed her watch.

Alva found Johnny, grabbed his arm, and pulled him over to where Bonner stood drinking. "You know what this one told me once? He said there were two situations in life. Dance situations and nondance situations." The phonograph played big band music and Alva's happiness was gin-clear.

"Don't keep the lady waiting."

Johnny found no leverage with those Lincoln eyes.

They danced around the living room, Alva smiling at the

people watching her and Johnny, while the television, its sound still kept off, was ignored by everyone except the one determined to catch this adroit new year.

"Remember the last time we danced? What *was* the name of that old song?"

Johnny stopped.

"What's wrong?"

"Need another drink."

"Oh good—fix me one too. Let's get drunk tonight."

Now here comes Jess wearing that ratty bathrobe of his, Jess allowing old women to kiss him and Jess heartily shaking the hands of men—Jess who did a few little dance steps himself before making his way to the television set. People couldn't believe it, how much the child had changed; several of them mentioned to Johnny they thought it was his influence.

Taking the boy on her lap, Jane warned him, "Now you got to keep your eye out. It comes and goes, just like that."

"Why's the sound off?"

"I think so."

Alan Winslow shouted over the music: "I don't *want* to dance with you! You're a terrible dancer!" Then he left the house, his wife Wayne remaining to blubber about a ruined New Year's Eve and how strange Al's been acting lately—she doesn't know what's gotten into that man. Charlie Warden took it upon himself to ease the awkwardness by piloting the weeping, leaking vessel about the room.

Having heard this commotion but not clearly enough to discern its cause, Jane asked Jess if it was the new year yet. "I don't think so," he replied. She nodded. See how elusive it is?

With midnight sweeping toward them across Ohio, Alva arranged to stay near Johnny so he'd kiss her first. When that time came, the phonograph was shut off and the television's sound was turned up. People counted down the last ten seconds.

"Happy New Year!"
"Happy New Year!"
"Happy New Year!"

But Jane, fooled before, remained cautious. Jess hugged her and shouted into one old hairy ear, "Happy New Year!" She still wasn't sure, her watchful eyes remaining on the television—waiting for confirmation.

Alva kept her arms around Johnny's neck so that he wasn't able to get away even after he gave her a second quick, hard kiss; she wanted more and put her small mouth up to his, but Johnny, looking down at those thin lips parted now by a tongue tip, acted as if that mouth intended to feed upon him. "Hey, no PDA—okay?"

"PDA?" she asked.

Johnny didn't answer, trying as he was to use his own blue eyes to plead across the room at Bonner's dark lights, which returned nothing that a mirror could reflect.

People began leaving immediately, everyone gone before the new year was half an hour old—Jess assigning himself to stand by the door and say the good-byes, then kissing Bonner and Alva and Johnny before going to bed. Lady stayed outside and Beehart was nowhere around.

As Alva carried dishes to the kitchen, she wished Bonner would go to bed, too, so she and Johnny could have some time to themselves by the fire in the living room—just the two of them with the new year. Maybe they would dance some more. It was good having him in the house again.

After she straightened up the living room, Alva sat there with the men, who said little, drank much. But she wasn't going to leave the two of them down here by themselves, not tonight. Whatever happened or whatever was said, she intended to be a part of it. Meanwhile, more gin.

.   .   .   .   .

AS WAYNE kept talking and kept asking Al what was wrong and why had he been acting this way lately, Winslow continued cranking himself all the tighter until not even exquisite torture could have loosened a word from him. Finally, she turned off the light and, even as worried as she was, Wayne soon snored.

He had reworked the year-end calculations four times: bankrupt. Again, right at this moment in bed with Wayne and the new year, Alan Winslow knotted up inside just as he had when first arriving at the figure, the fact, the truth, the awful news that was worse than any news he could've received: *poor!*

All his adult life an insurance man, Winslow had preached and preached about preparing for your retirement years and, practicing what he preached, he had socked away big money in annuities so he could feel superior to the other retirees in Beaker's Bride, trying to live on Social Security while *he* bought nice clothes and a new car every third year. But Winslow couldn't leave well enough alone. Couldn't pass up buying Beaker's Bride real estate at heartbreakingly low prices, using everything he'd saved and then borrowing against future income and, by God, if the yards ever *did* start working again or even if the depot reopened and trains once again stopped in Beaker's Bride, then he would be rich and could once again rise above all the dumb, careful hicks in this town who now probably laughed at him because he was bankrupt, these fools who kept their paltry dollars in savings accounts that lost money to inflation each year while Alan Winslow had a vision: a man of property!

He couldn't leave well enough alone: marrying Wayne when his life as a widower was perfectly fine.

He had added and subtracted four separate times, taking all he owed from all he owned and arriving each time at that horrifying negative, the very sight of it on paper chilling him more than a death warrant would have. Winslow was a man of property in a place where property was worthless—so worthless that the bank might not even try to foreclose on the worthless houses he owned all around Beaker's Bride, but, still, he was ruined.

He felt clumsy, stupid, cheated.

Out in the hallway, Alphonse was licking, licking.

"Stop it," Winslow demanded under his breath—not that the dog could hear or, hearing, would obey, but Winslow used it as a curse anyway: *"Stop it."*

He considered the many ways that cur had offended him; even watching it eat in the morning was an outrage.

Once, long ago, the dog's collar chain had caught on the edge of his metal feeding bowl, flipping it over with a clatter that elicited from Alphonse his usual response to calamity: squat and piss. After that, the dog approached his morning feeding as if the bowl were an enemy and he didn't know when the next attack was coming—a pitiful thing to watch, that humpbacked poodle trying to sneak up on his food, carefully placing one trembling leg in front of the other, taking one gingerly bite and then retreating, gripped equally by hunger and fear, requiring nearly half an hour to eat each morning, eating timidly and hopelessly like some creature so thoroughly whipped that it no longer believed it deserved to eat—a Jew in Winslow's SS eyes, and when Wayne wasn't looking, he sometimes kicked the bowl to terrorize further the mongrel, though terror wasn't enough, he wanted the dog dead, dead, dead.

In the otherwise quiet house (now that Wayne had rolled over and no longer snored), Alphonse's groin-and-ass snuffling was loud but, worse than hearing it, Winslow could smell the dog's foulness. Seeing and hearing Alphonse were aesthetic offenses, but when you smelled the dog it meant that actual molecules of the beast entered your nose, your blood, your brain—and for years now Winslow had been inhaling dog shit molecules and dog hair molecules and licked-raw dog skin molecules. This crap was *inside* him, no wonder he was going crazy with a brain full of dog shit, dog piss, dog stink molecules.

Wayne stirred and, with the terrible new year barely four hours old, Winslow funneled the soured disappointments of his life onto the despicable animal out there in the hallway, a canine without one redeeming trait: no personality, lacking in loyalty, rug-pissing, no man's best friend, nervous, ugly, poorly postured, smelly, frightened, dumb, sneaky, greasy to the touch, trickless, *French*.

"I'm caught," Winslow moaned. "I'm caught."

No dream, this. It happened when he was a boy, helping his uncle on the farm; they were bringing a tractor and wagon out of the back pasture, it being Alan's job to close the gates behind them. In that stupidity of adolescence, he closed the last gate with himself on the wrong side and had to climb over, catching his pantsleg on a nail in a way that caused him to fall forward and hang there upside down from the top of the gate. He dared not call for his uncle, a man as dour as Winslow would turn out to be, but no amount of struggling or yanking on his pants could free him, so there he hung until his uncle came around to see what was wrong.

In bed remembering it, Winslow saw again the look of profound disgust on his uncle's face. "I'm caught," Alan had said, but his uncle did not reply, just stood there and watched the way a crowd might stand and watch some public drunk unable to rise from his own vomit.

Winslow held both positions now: he was a stupid boy caught upside down unable to get free, ashamed of himself, *and* he was the man standing apart witnessing it, being shamed by his own blood.

"Stop it."

Alan Winslow no longer talked to the dog. "Stop it!"

Tears running from the corners of both eyes, he cried to God, please *"Stop it."*

· · · · ·

ALVA TRIED drinking with the men and she tried listening to them, but the drunken arguments of men are like Chinese opera—you can't even make a good guess at what's going on and you suspect that the participants don't know either.

What *were* they arguing about?

As the gin carried her away, Alva thought maybe Bonner and Johnny argued about her. Bonner jealous?

For years she and he had lived together in that house, alone except for the baby, the boy—and when a man and woman sleep down the hall from one another for years, even the strongest taboos erode, seem to apply out there in the world but not here in the house where we're the only adults—so maybe when Bonner watched Alva and Johnny kiss at midnight, he remembered how it was the first time he came to her room and she feigned sleep as he got in bed and lay next to her, Alva pretending to awaken only after they were in the middle of it, with Bonner behind her and the two of them moving wordlessly against each other, the sounds they made fascinating them both with shame and secret delight, this dead-of-night act not exclusively sexual, not when you both are suffering, are desperate, hungry, and you own certain needs that you both put together tightly, squeezing to a point and then holding it, then past it, done. Waiting for words that never came.

She slept; the men argued.

Alva no longer dreamed of Bonner's night visits, hadn't dreamed of them since Johnny's arrival. Now it was all Johnny, Johnny bright and Johnny laughing, offering the risk of a man who's only visiting and might be gone on any given morning—a man you watch with such pride, the way everyone loves him.

But Johnny had never come to Alva in the night, so in

her gin dreams on that couch with the argument no longer
heard by her, Alva was mounted by Johnny *and* Bonner—
not taking turns, but both men the same man, this one man
all men, Matthew and the men from taverns, Donny B., all
men this one man Alva dreamed of in heat.

. . . . .

WHILE THE OPERA played on.

"I told you the first day you came to town I didn't want
you bringing any bad into this house. We've had more than
enough to last us."

"I know, I know."

"Now you got her crazy about you—and that boy too.
How you think they're going to feel, you leaving tomorrow
with no warning?"

"I'm an asshole."

"And promising me you'd stay until we finished Beaker
Mansion. If a man's word ain't good, what's he got left?"

"Nothing."

"I don't want to hear it! Too easy for you to say it and
then just go on your merry way like saying it makes things
right again."

"I know."

They were just drunk enough, any drunker and they
wouldn't have been able to speak in sentences.

"Why do you do it?"

"I don't know. I'm sorry."

"I told you—saying sorry don't make things right. Besides, I don't see *no* sorry in you, none at all. Just saying it."

"Bonner, I can't do what you do—I'm not tough enough.
I can work as hard as you do for a while, weeks or months,
but if I had to look at an entire life of work the way we've
worked since I got here, I wouldn't be able to get out of bed
in the morning."

"It ain't the work."

"It's everything—the work and trying to keep this town alive and living with Jess and Alva, digging graves and being isolated out here where you don't see anyone except the same people, day after day. I don't know how you do it."

Johnny waited for something from Bonner and then said, "You want to know why I hit the road? The truth?"

"You wouldn't know the truth if it came to live with you."

"It started at a birthday party for one of the secretaries. I used to work in an office. I was a hotshot.

"I knew this secretary vaguely, got talking to her at the party, just chitchat, and she said she liked French restaurants, so I told her I knew some great ones and, kidding around, she said I should take her to one for her birthday and I said, sure. We left it at that. Then I went off on a trip to the city, and when I came back, they told me she'd quit work. Off on disability. Cancer."

Johnny poured more brown stuff into their glasses and then continued quickly with a story not told like his usual stories, not artful or well crafted: his words simply spilled.

"People already knew about the cancer, that's why they'd made such a big deal out of her birthday party, but I didn't know it because I never paid much attention to what was going on with the secretaries, at least not the older ones. She came back for a visit and, Jesus, Bonner, she looked dead already—the treatments, you know—and she comes into my office and closes the door and says, 'I'm dying.' Just like that. Shit, she hadn't even worked in my department—why was she telling *me?* What do you say?

"I mumbled something dumb about there always being hope, but I was pissed at her for dumping this on me when the two of us barely knew each other well enough to say hello in the hallway.

"So she tells me she's dying and I can see that's the God's truth and I'm nodding my head and shaking my head—

sorry, so sorry. Finally she gets to the point, says it with a laugh like it's all a big joke. 'I guess if you're going to take me to that French restaurant,' she says, 'we better go now.'

"I laugh too, tell her it's great she's kept her sense of humor and that she's being such a good sport, but then I see she's dead serious.

"She wore a cheap damn wig, like something for Halloween, and I'm trying not to stare at it—trying not to see what's underneath it. I had a meeting I was supposed to be running in about ten minutes and this secretary is telling me she wants to go to some goddamn French restaurant.

"Oh, I guess I could've swung it—delayed the meeting and then made reservations for lunch. But what the hell would we talk about? Who wants to eat lunch with someone, practically a stranger, dying of cancer?

"Why me? That's what I was thinking the entire time she was in my office—didn't she have any family or friends who could take her to a French restaurant? Hell, I'd pay for it if money was the problem.

"So finally I sneak a look at my watch and, naturally, she catches me looking. I tell her, 'We'll definitely have to go to a French restaurant—absolutely. Why don't we make a date for the next time you're in the office?'

"She just sits there. She knows it and I know it—she's not coming back to the office ever again. I look at my watch again; people by that time were already in the conference room waiting for me. I start shuffling papers on my desk like some kind of asshole bureaucrat and then I say, I tell her, 'Listen, I'm real sorry but I have to scoot out now—got a meeting that I'm late for already.'

"She says *nothing*. Doesn't call me a coldhearted bastard, doesn't start crying. Nothing. Just sits there.

"Still the asshole, I bustle around the office and tell her I simply must go. I ask if she'll be around later—so we can talk some more. No response, her expression hasn't changed or anything. And she makes no signs of leaving either.

"I finally just took off and left her there. After the meeting, I came back expecting to find she'd set my office on fire or had gone around to the secretaries telling them what a bastard I am, but nothing—no notes on my desk and no messages left with the secretaries. *Nada.*

"Then a few weeks later I heard the news, she died. I decided to go to the funeral and everyone thought I was a champ for doing that, going to the funeral of someone I barely knew. On the way to the church, I'm still cruising— you understand what I'm telling you? None of this is getting to me. More than anything, I was just curious to see how I would feel—like maybe I would jump up in the middle of the services and start screaming, 'All she wanted was to go to a French restaurant but I didn't take her! She was dying but I went to a meeting!'

"I didn't do that, of course. Said nothing, felt nothing. No tears to hold back because no tears came. Nada. And after the services, people come up to *me* and thank *me* for coming."

Johnny waited for a response from Bonner, but Bonner sat there like something carved.

"I should've taken her to France, for chrissake! 'Here,' I should've told her, 'at least you get a week in Paris, all expenses paid, before you die.' But, no, I go to a meeting."

Still nothing from Bonner.

"For months after she died, I told this story—like I'm telling you right now. And you know what? People comforted *me!* Me! They would say they understood, that we all wished we'd done certain things differently, before it was too late, *and they sure can appreciate why I feel so bad about the whole thing.* I still tell the story. People are still sympathetic.

"I've told them I can't even remember the woman's

name, that I have to think about it and think about it and
even when it comes to me I'm not sure I got it right—like
maybe it's Janet but maybe it's not. Something close to
Janet—Joyce or Jane or Jannette, I don't know. This con-
fession never fazes people, never. They just tell me about
how sometimes they can't recall exactly what their own
mothers' faces looked like—and they feel bad about that
too, so they certainly can understand *my* feelings."

Johnny stopped and looked pointedly at Bonner, but the
old man wasn't giving anything.

"Say something!" Johnny demanded, squeezing his glass
and hitting it on the arm of his chair. "Goddamn you, say
something."

But Bonner was thinking: He would have been perfect.
A man like Johnny could keep Beaker's Bride alive, maybe
even convince the trains to stop here like they used to and
talk families into living here so there'd be children in
Beaker's Bride once again. Someone as hard on himself as
Johnny, he'd make sure the cemetery didn't grow up in
weeds and he wouldn't let happen to Beaker's Bride what
happened to Millerway, south of here, where salvagers
bought houses ten cents on the dollar and took all the good
stuff first, copper and marble, then scavenged everything
else, lumber and bricks, leaving the rest to rats up from the
river and to teenagers who'd come around to drink beer
and screw—the town rotting until someone with enough
meanness or pity starts the fires and what's left of the town
burns three or four different times until nothing but blackened husks stand.

Johnny had it in him to save Beaker's Bride, but he
wouldn't do it—and Bonner hated him for that.

"Ain't saying nothing to you," Bonner finally conceded.
"You're too scared to listen."

"Scared?"

"You heard me. Scared like you were that time you tried
to load a gun to kill yourself but then accidentally shot off

your finger—remember telling me that when we were out in the shed with my white bird?"

Johnny had stopped hitting his glass on the chair arm. "I gave you too much credit, Bonner." He held up his left hand. "When I was a kid I had a friend whose old man brought back some souvenir machine-gun cartridges from the war, and my friend and I were trying to pry them apart for the powder when one went off and blew away this finger. That's all it was, Bonner—a childhood accident. No significance beyond that. Oh, I've told people everything, that I did it trying to kill myself or trying to save a friend from killing himself—but I never dreamed *you'd* fall for one of those old stories."

Johnny became agitated again, pounding his glass again. "Jesus Christ, I told Jess a bear bit it off but at least the kid had sense enough not to believe me—but you! You!" He hit the glass on the chair arm, hit it one time especially hard, hard enough to shatter the glass and, squeezing it the way he was, a jagged shard embedded deeply into his right palm.

The pain was immediate, but the sight of all that sudden blood, down his wrist and quickly onto his shirt, was just as bad. "Oh, God! *I cut myself!*"

Muscle deep came the second wave of pain, perhaps the worst pain he'd ever felt in his life—pain shocking enough to terrify Johnny. "Jesus Christ, Bonner, don't just sit there! I'm bleeding!" He held up that cut hand as if to prove the point.

Bonner stood slowly. He hurt, too, but Bonner was used to it. "Think of this as some new story you can tell."

Then he went off to bed, leaving Johnny in a panic intensified by alcohol and emotion and blood and hurt and the realization that he wasn't such a hard man after all, not compared to that hardened butcher Lincoln—this singular moment of desperation pressing down on Johnny with the weight of a big, heavy, ugly, strong bridge. An iron weight of desperation. He couldn't get his breath.

"Alva! *Alvie!* For chrissake, Alva, wake up, I'm bleeding to death!" His left hand holding the bleeding right, Johnny had to nudge her with his knee. "Goddamn it, honey, wake up."

"Johnny? What's—Oh, God, what happened?"

"I broke a glass and cut my hand. Alvie!"

"Okay, baby, okay." His panic scared her fully awake. "Let's get to the kitchen so I can wash it off." She led him by the arm, ruthless in forcing the injured hand under cold running water—it hurt!—so she could see the extent of damage. "Where's Bonner?"

"That asshole went to bed! He saw me bleeding but he went off to bed anyway. Can you believe that?"

Alva was more concerned now with stopping the blood. She used dish towels and direct pressure. "You need stitches. I'll get Bonner and we'll drive you to the hospital."

"No! Leave that bastard out of this!" The cold running water was anesthetizing his hand, helping Johnny to calm himself. "Just bandage it. I'll be okay."

"You have to see a doctor."

But now he'd regained his old composure. "No, it's not that bad."

"It is!"

Alva used all the gauze she had in the house making a well-padded bandage, telling Johnny he'd better go to a doctor if not tonight then first thing in the morning because it *was* that bad.

With the wound dressed, she led him back to the living room, where they sat on the floor near the fire to absorb what warmth was left in the ash-covered embers. "You want me to put on some more wood?" she asked.

But he was soaked with sweat, stained by blood—pretending he was trying to remember: "I know it's not Sandusky."

"What's that, honey?"

He grinned the old Johnny smile. "Cincinnati."

She didn't get it, then she got it. As he reached for her, Alva asked, "But what about your hand?"

"Got cut fending off a saber, protecting your honor." Then he moved to lay her down.

"Johnny?"

He had her dress up and, when he ran into difficulties working at her underwear with three fingers and a thumb, Alva helped. "You're crazy," she said, scooting to get under him.

"Crazy about you."

"Oh, Johnny." Said it scoldingly, laughing.

He was half laughing himself until he got his pants open and then tore at the top of her dress, roughly pushing up the bra without bothering to undo it, exposing her small dark-nippled breasts, which she mumbled an apology for and which he gripped hard, first the left and then the right—hurting her. Neither of them laughed after that.

Johnny bucked hard and hard against her, but he was doing no good.

She reached down and fiddled with things. *"Now."*

"Now what?"

"Anything you want, Johnny."

"Anything?"

She thought she had him now. "Put it in me."

He did. Johnny became a hilt and his mind filled with blade words: pierce, thrust, stab. Put it in her *now*. Drive it home. To the hilt. Home, hilt. Hurt, hard. Stab this dark desperate bird fluttering beneath him. Hard and then hard. Again and again, making them both bleed. Johnny's passion reopened wounds old and new, making them both bleed.

20

EVERYONE was careful at breakfast.

Johnny and Bonner kept their heads down, eating not speaking. Although Jess wanted to know what had happened to Johnny's hand, the boy was perceptive enough not to question the somber and very adult faces at that table. And Alva, when she finally spoke, spoke quietly: "Soon as you finish, Johnny, I'll drive you over to the hospital. Jess, honey, you can come with us if you want." Then smiling. "One time Jess told me he wanted to be a doctor, didn't you, dreamboat, and I was going to be the nurse working in his office."

Bonner looked up from his plate like a judge looking up from the jury's verdict, which he is about to read. "You didn't tell her?"

Johnny stared at the milk gravy congealing on his fork.

"Tell me what?" Alva still smiled. "Tell me what, Johnny?" Then to Bonner: "Something about last night?" She was full of last night. "If you two have a secret . . ." Then she got it, and the expression on her face collapsed.

"Alvie . . ."

She shook her head. "I don't want to hear it. Whenever you're ready to go, just go—don't tell me good-bye. Just go." Before Alva left the dining room, she started in on Jess: "You better cut some kindling, young man. And bring up the firewood—it's been a week you haven't kept that box full. Look at me when I'm talking to you! I got a bag of chocolate chips in there and for once in my life I'd like to start out making some Toll House cookies and find a full bag of chocolate chips, so I'm warning you—don't touch them. Don't go tearing off one little corner of the bag like I won't notice how you've squeezed out one chocolate chip at a time. I know all your tricks. You better start worrying about your chores and leave those chocolate chips alone, you hear me?" Then she went upstairs.

Johnny stood.

"Where you going?" Jess asked. Alva had figured it out, but he hadn't.

"Pack my things."

"Why?"

"I'm leaving."

"Leaving?"

"Going to Florida."

"Florida? When?"

"Leaving after dinner tonight. So, uh, you hang in there, all right, Skeezix?"

"That ain't my name!" Jess screamed.

Bonner, softly to Johnny: "Congratulations."

Johnny immediately left for the basement as Jess ran from the house while the big man remained there alone, forcing himself to continue eating.

. . . . .

ALVA WISHED she had her letter back, regretting now each sugar kiss she put in it, all those !!!'s, every BigBear hug, all the . . .'s, and every inch of underscoring. That letter's animated contents mocked her: What a *fool!!!*

After last night!!! Knowing that he was leaving, how could he have done what he did last night? If he were here in the bedroom with her right now, Alva would have used the ball peen hammer on him. But Johnny stayed wisely in the basement all day.

That afternoon, Bonner came to her room and said Johnny was leaving *today*. Did she know that? Some

woman from St. Louis was picking him up around dinnertime. Alva's anger wasn't strong enough to support what
she felt now: Johnny leaving *today*, going off with some
woman from St. Louis.

No. It was as bad as it could be finding out he's leaving
at all—surely not today and not with some other woman.
It can't be. Bonner's gone crazy and is making this up to
torment me. No, God, please—not after last night, not
today.

. . . . .

JESS STAYED at the river all morning thinking how un-
fair it was that adults know these things and don't tell you.
Johnny *leaving*.

Back at the house for lunch, no one was around so Jess
fixed a baloney sandwich but only played at eating, finally
giving it to Lady, who was grateful for everything except
the mustard. Adults were in their various rooms, refusing
to come out. He pinched open the bag and stole three
chocolate chips.

Jess walked to the shed, unlocked and slid open the door,
climbed up on the white bird's marble back. He closed his
eyes but went nowhere—not like it used to be, not anymore.

He tried to remember how it used to be, how he once
flew on that bird holding tightly to its cold neck and keeping his eyes shut as the stone lifted out of the shed and
wheeled riverward, flying south and ever higher until Jess
could see blue line boundaries the way they were shown in
his school books.

But no more. Now Jess felt no sensation of flight or
height, nothing. This, he thought, is the difference between
the way I used to fly and the way Johnny can, me just
pretending but Johnny really flying 'cause I *saw* it, I was

there and saw him go off that platform to fly right across the front of the train—precisely the way Jess did it only in his dream.

Johnny's flying was real, not just closing your eyes and pretending.

He left the shed door open.

· · · · ·

IN THE EARLY-EVENING DARK of January, Johnny stood in the middle of the road in front of Beaker Mansion, a suitcase at his feet. That hand of his, the newly hurt one, was hurting bad.

But it was that hand he waved when he saw Linda Greenerton's car. "Have any trouble with my directions?" he asked while struggling to fit his suitcase in the backseat, crowded with her stuff.

"I got lost seven different times." She grabbed him by the hair and gave Johnny a kiss, her tongue in his mouth already. "What happened to your hand?"

"Got in a fight."

"Really?"

"Some crazy hick came at me with a broken beer bottle. Had to put up my hand to save my neck—as any man would."

"How awful."

"Yeah."

She put the car in Drive.

"I'll show you where it happened—a few miles down river road there. It looks like a regular house, but it's one of the local shebeens. Let's get going, I'll show you."

"All right." She drove slowly in this town, where all the streets looked like private roads on which you shouldn't be trespassing. "Are you going to be able to share the driving—with that hand like it is?"

"Sure. You want me to drive now? Come on, I'll drive first."

"Actually, that might be a good idea. I don't do so well on these country roads." She stopped at the edge of town and they got out to switch. Meeting Johnny at the back of the car, Linda hooked onto one of his belt loops. "Everything okay?"

"Sure."

"Your friends going to be able to find someone else to help them finish remodeling their house?"

"No problem."

She looked around at the abandoned, boarded, darkened houses. "What a godforsaken place."

When they were back in the car, Johnny told her she possessed magic.

"A week in bed with you and any woman gets magical," she said.

"No, I mean it. First time I saw you, I thought, now this one's got some magic in her. I bet you *can* do something magic, can't you?"

"You had a week to find out."

"I don't mean *that*. I mean something else, something I sensed the minute I laid eyes on you."

"Yeah, yeah—let's go. This place gives me the spooks."

"Well, we'll find out. Between here and Florida we'll find out what your magic is."

"There is one thing. Oh, I know you're just feeding me a line, but there's one thing I'm capable of that's like magic."

"What?"

"I had a boyfriend once who called me a witch because of it. Sometimes . . . sometimes I can tell what's going to happen before it happens."

"Me, too, buckaroo—me too!"

He put the car in gear and eased down to river road, pausing there to glance north before heading south, but

Johnny drove only a few yards before he stopped the car abruptly enough to knock Linda against the dash. He had looked back.

"Ow! What—"

But Johnny already was out of the car, leaving the door open and running north.

"Johnny!" She started to go after him but it was too dark and this place was too frightening for traveling on foot, so Linda turned the car around, searching for Johnny in her lights.

· · · · ·

"COME HERE! Come here quick!"

Wayne ran to the front porch, where her husband stood, pointing north. "What is it, Al? What's wrong?"

"Not a thing *wrong* in the world. Look over there—at the station. See? It's a passenger train, too. I *knew* my letters were getting through, I knew it!"

"I don't—"

He kissed her unusually hard and slapped her on the butt and called to the dog. "Come on, Al, come see the train that's going to make me rich. Here, Al, here, boy, here."

But the poodle remained suspicious, approaching Alan Winslow as if he were a potentially diabolical food dish. Winslow finally went to the dog, sweeping him up in his arms and carrying him out to the porch. "Wave to the train, Al." Winslow waved Alphonse's front paw. "You'll be eating steaks from now on, pooch."

Although still not absolutely sure what this all meant, Wayne beamed: at long last her two Als were getting along famously.

· · · · ·

ALVA STOOD at the back door screaming into the dark. "Jess! *Jess!*" Where was he? When Bonner came up behind her, Alva told him, "I'm going to beat that boy black-and-blue."

Seeing that the shed door had been left open, Bonner added his complaint: "I told him and *told* him to keep that shed door closed."

"He's just getting too smart for his own good, that's all there is to it. Thinks he's a hotshot. After I warned him about those chocolate chips, he's been in the bag already. You're going to have to discipline him, Bonner—or *I* will."

At that moment, either one of them could have slapped the little bastard's fat face.

Alva began complaining how Jess never kept the box full of firewood as he was supposed to, but Bonner no longer listened to her because he had just then seen the train stopped by the station. "Jess," Bonner said, immediately long-striding away from the house, heading north without even bothering to put on a coat.

Alva, who hadn't noticed the train, wondered if Bonner was angry enough actually to strike the child.

21

CHARLIE WARDEN reached the boy first—Charlie who'd been out walking when he saw the train stop and hurried over toward the station, climbing the embankment and coming upon the boy right there. Charlie was a railroad man.

He quickly covered Jess with his long brown coat and then bent over the child, saying Jess's name and his own name. "Jess? It's Charlie, Charlie Warden. Jess?" He ran to get his station wagon, this tall thin old man actually running so he could drive Jess to the hospital, which was thirty-two miles away. Charlie wasn't the type who could stand there doing nothing, nothing but waiting, so he ran to get his Chevy station wagon even though he'd seen what had happened to Jess and knew that thirty-two miles were too many miles. It would've been better to have found the boy dead.

Jess couldn't understand why he'd been left alone again. He'd been alone there on the cold slope, on frozen brown turf, for what seemed like hours—was it close to morning yet?—and when Charlie Warden finally showed up, Jess thought everything would be okay, that adults would be gathering around doing adult things and he'd be taken care of—but now Jess was alone again, cold in spite of Charlie's heavy coat over him, feeling no pain yet but still scared.

Actually, Beehart was the one scared of the dark, except Jess couldn't see Beehart clearly because he'd lost his glasses and that's what bothered Jess—he'd lost his glasses and couldn't see anything.

Beehart sat up on top of a passenger car, his short legs hanging over the edge and his angel's face resting in his hands—watching as if he had nothing to do with what had happened. Mr. Innocent.

Then pain. Jess opened his mouth and there came a silent scream, his eyes wide and unblinking, calling out but only in his mind. Beehart! Where *was* everyone? Mom? Why had they left him alone like this, terribly cold and now in pain? Grampa! Had Johnny already gone to Florida, where it was warm? *Where it was warm.*

Johnny and Alan Winslow arrived at the same time.

"*Jess.*"

"Charlie Warden's coat," Winslow said. "He must've gone to get help."

But where do you go to get help in Beaker's Bride?

Johnny leaned close to the boy's face. "Where are you hurt, Jess? *Jess?*"

My legs.

An awful weight pressed pinching Jess's legs, which hurt. *Now* they hurt, all the way down to his toes. The child's arterial pressure dropped in response to the blood he'd lost; his pulse became fast and thready. His legs hurt—not an unbearable pain but bad enough, something fiery and weighted as if the train itself rested on his legs.

That train seemed so out of place there, stopped just past the station. Living in Beaker's Bride, you get used to trains—trains signaling their fast approach to the bridge, then slowing for the crossing, all those train and track sounds that you've become accustomed to and no longer take note of, the way you fail to note after a while how well sunsets treat the town, painting with light. But all that changes when you see the big train *stopped* there before the bridge, making you suddenly aware and causing you to become self-conscious, especially with the passengers watching out of tinted windows.

When Johnny lifted the heavy brown coat, he and Winslow saw it at the same time and immediately looked at each other, seeing in their faces horror reflected. Winslow had to turn away, walking to the train stopped there, not so iron-hearted after all. He put his forehead to the cold steel skin.

Johnny carefully laid the coat back over the boy; he wanted to tell Jess it would be okay but he couldn't speak. Johnny put his bandaged hand gingerly to his own eyes.

People at the train windows watched with the indifference of spectators: they were inside and the drama played out there in the cold.

Then something happened.

Jess's body pulsed and arched as if a current had been sent through it, and Johnny was frightened to see that Jess's face now held an expression of profound astonishment—pupils dilating into big black circles and his breathing suddenly rapid. Jess sucked for air: something was happening to him.

Johnny looked around. "Help," he started to scream but managed only to state it because what was the purpose of screaming, who was there to help and what could anyone have done?

Bonner arrived with Mr. Gibsner close behind.

"Jess." Bonner said the name as a confirmation. He immediately lifted Charlie Warden's coat, and the sight under it caused Bonner to make a sound. Not a word but a sound, a sound worse than any word.

Mr. Gibsner hadn't seen it yet. "I ran into Charlie. He's bringing his car so we can get the boy to the hospital. Charlie should be able to back up this slope, don't you think? Otherwise we can carry—" Then he saw it. "Sweet Christ."

Before Charlie got there with the Chevy, a dozen more residents of Beaker's Bride gathered along the tracks in two groups, one group a few yards up the line where the engineer lay, also stricken. He'd come running back from the locomotive and thought the boy was under the train, so he pulled on the legs and then dropped them when pain radiated down his neck and left arm and he had to sit, couldn't get his breath, his face almost as desperate as Jess's. People were helping the engineer down off the embankment so he could be taken to the hospital; someone had thrown a piece of plywood over the severed legs.

The second group of residents gathered around where Jess lay, the men staying close to Bonner either to receive or to provide comfort—no one seemed sure which—while the women kept off a few paces whispering news they'd heard and overheard. "His legs." "It's his legs." Some prayed; passengers on the train asked each other if the kid was dead or what.

Jess had fallen to an abiding confusion, no longer knowing where he was or what had happened, and although the pressured pain on his legs lifted, his hunger for air deepened; he couldn't get enough. Breathing deeply, he still couldn't get enough. This is what put Jess in a panic, because no matter how fast and hungrily he breathed, he couldn't get enough air. No air and no spit: Jess dried out. Like being skinned and then heavily salted down, the boy had every element of moisture sucked from him—mouth dry so he couldn't talk and throat dry so he couldn't swallow. No air, no spit.

Bonner got down there on the ground and cradled the child's heavy, whitened face—skin cold and sweaty and bad to the touch. Keeping his large hands on Jess, Bonner looked up at the people standing around: "Where are they?"

People knew what he was talking about but said nothing.

"Where are they?"

Someone pointed up the line.

"Go get them."

No one did.

"Johnny. Go get them, Johnny."

Johnny didn't move.

"For the love of God, man, his mother's coming!"

Nada.

Bonner had to do it because no one else would. The big man strode on up the line, people following him and the people already there greeting him. "Bonner," they said. "Bonner."

He saw the plywood, lifted it, shook his head, and tossed the wood on down the embankment. Bonner looked at the people. "Someone take them." No one did. "Johnny. Carry them back for me. Don't make me do it. He's my own grandson, please don't make me do it. Someone carry them for me." The passengers on the train watched with these eyes you could see at the windows, terrible in their fascination.

Bonner picked up the legs, one in each giant hand, feeling the corduroy as if this were the first time in his life he'd ever touched corduroy, the corduroy still warm. He carried those surprisingly heavy legs, holding them away from his body—horrifying and compelling the spectators above in the passenger cars, where it was well lighted and warm, men and women and children *with those eyes*, men and women and children who either moved away from the windows or pressed all the closer.

When Bonner reached Jess, Johnny pulled back Charlie Warden's coat. Bonner put the legs down.

"You got them wrong," Johnny whispered as if they were onstage and Bonner had mishandled a prop. He didn't understand and then he understood, reaching down again to put his hands on those two horrors once more, switching the legs, then carefully positioning them so that the severed bone-exposed ends were close to the boy's red-wet thighs: corduroy to corduroy.

Things were better as soon as Johnny replaced the long

coat over Jess—the boy's head sticking out from the coat's collar and his feet extending beyond the bunched-up end of the coat. Almost normal, as long as you didn't know.

By the time Alva arrived, Jess was somewhere far away and although the people standing near him might wish to think he held in his mind some last good image, he did not. Jess possessed no final sensation of flight—off the edge of the platform flying from the dark into the dragon's single searching light, like flying really like flying. No. Jess held nothing in his mind except those still-firing fragments of fear, of pain, of panic, of being too dry, and of that constant awful hunger for air.

She was instantly on the ground next to him with her face and hands on Jess's face, trying to find his eyes. "Where are you hurt, baby? Jess! Where's he hurt, Bonner? You got to find his glasses, he can't see a thing without his glasses." Alva told herself that's why she couldn't recognize anything familiar in his eyes. "Don't anybody step on them!" People searched around because this was an assignment they could handle, but no one found his glasses. "Where's he hurt, Bonner?" She started to look under the coat but Lincoln knelt on it.

"His legs."

"What happened?"

"Don't know. Charlie Warden's bringing his car so we can get him to the hospital." Bonner wouldn't look at her straight on.

"Do you think they're broken?" Alva asked.

He nodded.

"Johnny? Both of his legs broken?"

He nodded, too.

Something these men weren't telling her. "What is it?" Then to Jess: "Can you hear me, dreamboat? Hey, little Junie bug." When he made sounds deep in his throat, Alva wept.

Bonner steadied her shoulders.

She tried again to look under Charlie's coat but Bonner wouldn't move off of it.

"Where are his glasses?" she asked again and, again, everyone started looking for them. "Bonner! Get off the coat so I can see."

"Nothing to see, just a lot of blood."

"Blood?"

"We'll get him to a doctor."

"You have to stop the bleeding right away!" She knew that much. "The hospital's thirty miles away—we have to stop the bleeding!"

"I already done that," Bonner lied. Thirty-*two* miles, he thought, though it didn't matter. One mile would be one mile too far.

Johnny stood there with his left hand gripping tightly to the wrist of the wounded right hand, which he held close to his chest. Next to him was a woman no one knew, dressed in bright clothes and watching all of this with a face that made people think she was a passenger who'd disembarked for a closer look. But Alva knew—some St. Louis woman.

Johnny wished Linda hadn't shown up, wished she would stop trying to talk to him, stop asking questions about who the boy was and what, exactly, had happened.

Here comes Charlie, backing the station wagon up the embankment, making tires spin wildly enough to sing and causing the car to fishtail. As soon as he stopped, people rushed over and opened doors; someone brought the sheet of plywood to be used as a litter; everyone kept slipping on the big gravel by the tracks.

In his own car and driving fast on river road, Alan Winslow asked the engineer what had happened, but the man was too stricken to speak. "You haven't heard anything about the railroad's plans for reopening the depot, have you?" As soon as Winslow asked it, he felt self-hate, glad the engineer didn't answer, and then Winslow drove the rest of the way in silence. My God, what have I become?

It began to rain on Beaker's Bride and with that January rain came a change for the worse when you thought the worst already had happened. People who were cold became cold and wet. Lights from the passenger cars fragmented. Men and women from town stood stock-still in the cold rain, hunching their shoulders and holding collars closed at their necks, keeping heads down to look at shoes and boots. Alva leaned over Jess to protect him from the rain. Linda Greenerton told Johnny she'd wait in the car because she wasn't dressed for weather like this.

They were careful—Bonner, Mr. Gibsner, Charlie, Johnny—moving Jess onto the plywood and transporting him to the station wagon, making sure everything stayed together and the coat remained over the boy covering him completely from head to feet. For Alva's sake, they told themselves.

Jess no longer made any noises.

"Brave boy," Mr. Gibsner said.

Holding his mud, Johnny thought.

But Jess was too confused to worry about dying well, about holding his mud even if he knew what it was and how exactly you hold it. His quiet owed not to composure but to shock, Jess's body so appalled by what had happened to it that systems were being shut down, preserving blood and life even as the mind recognized the utter futility of what it was doing and began therefore to sound—deeper and more deeply, refusing to accept further reports from bleeding thighs and air-hungry lungs, the mind allowing itself some final moments of peace.

Everyone outside, however, remained frantic: getting Jess into the station wagon, its backseat folded down, Charlie Warden behind the wheel ready to go, Mr. Gibsner climbing in beside him, Alva and Bonner in the back with Jess. Johnny wanted to come along, too, but Bonner said, "No. Let's go, Charlie—now."

Charlie drove fast. Alva tried to soothe her son, telling him he was her baby boy and he had to hold on until they got to the hospital because, there, the doctors would fix him right up—and she couldn't live without him, life would be too lonely without a boy in the house so you have to hold on and not give up.

Except there was nothing left for him to hold on to. And only at the final moment—Jess's mind knowing this was its final moment of existence—did he find some degree of composure, enough to hear what his mother said about being lonely and to remember how it felt to be lonely when she was gone for those two years and to wish that whatever was next, Beehart could like always run on ahead. Then there was a sense of flight and Jess was gone. Alva saw the precise point at which he went blank behind his eyes.

The major muscles of his upper thighs had been tightly contracted, like knots, acting as natural tourniquets to squeeze closed arteries, but now in the warmth of the Chevy and with unconditional mental surrender, those muscles relaxed and blood flowed from the child as if from a loosened bladder, wetting Alva and Bonner, staining plywood and Charlie's heavy brown coat.

With all that blood suddenly there, Alva screamed and threw herself on Jess.

"Careful!" Bonner hollered at Charlie when he took a turn too wide and slid on the muddy shoulder of river road. *"Slow down."*

Alva folded back the coat to see it, flesh and bone and blood and the space between legs and body. "Oh. No."

"I said, slow down. Charlie!"

But Charlie Warden continued driving as fast as he could in the rain, driving in a fever to get to the hospital because he didn't know what had happened in the back of the car and because all he had to hold on to was hope.

. . . . .

WHEN BONNER AND ALVA returned toward dawn to Beaker's Bride, mornings always late there because the sun had to get above bluffs, they went into the house and sat by the dead hearth not bothering to turn on any lights or to remove their wet, cold clothing. Thinking about a fire, Alva remembered that the woodbox was empty and she became momentarily angry with Jess, able to separate in her mind the funny kid who didn't do his chores from that bloody mess they'd delivered to the hospital, but when her mind finally could no longer hold on to that comforting contradiction, Alva wept again.

Bonner went to the basement, finding Johnny sprawled on the bed dead drunk, his hurt hand turned up showing the formerly white dressing to be stained through with blood and mud.

"I want you out of my house," Lincoln decreed.

A few minutes later, Johnny came upstairs. Alva sat alone in the dark and unfired living room.

"Johnny," she said softly. "Hold me, Johnny—*please.*"

"Where's Bonner?"

The anger. "You! You men! What is it with you two!" She wanted to say more but it got caught in her throat, making Alva choke on curses.

Johnny lurched out into the rain, seeing Bonner by the shed pulling on the steel trailer's tongue until the big white bird came into view like a magnificent float, rolling slowly across the backyard—something pulled to war—then onto a street that led between Beaker's Bride and the cemetery's wrought-iron gates: Sisyphus hauling his load to the hill.

Johnny fell in behind the trailer, pushing on it until Bonner reached the large plot he had long ago chosen as his own, high in the cemetery with a sweet river view and first dibs on the setting sun.

When Bonner came around and saw Johnny, he said, "Get out of here. Go on, before I hurt you." Then the big man loosened ropes tethering the white bird while Johnny stood there in the rain watching, waiting.

Upstairs in her bedroom, Alva retrieved the ball peen hammer from under the edge of the bed. "Bastards, bastards," she kept muttering on the way out of the house.

The men tried to get the bird off its trailer but could not, the two of them heaving against a marble heaviness that simply would not be moved.

Alva came running toward them. "I lost my baby!" she screamed over the steadiness of rain—then she hit the dove with her hammer, chipping off from the heart of it a fist-sized chunk. "I lost my baby and you bastards are out here, out here . . ." She hit the sculpture again. "Out here thinking you're, you're making some kind of goddamn gesture . . ." And hit it again, again, harder, knocking off pieces. "Some kind of goddamn gesture, some damn God gesture." Strangling on her anger, hitting at half a ton of marble with a two-pound hammer, chipping away, chipping away.

Bonner walked over and knocked her to the ground, into the cold mud. Then he pushed again against that half ton, Johnny hurrying in to help but, still, they couldn't get it off the trailer and onto Bonner's plot.

Alva was up, swinging the hammer with both hands, trying now for the bird's drilled eyes, being stung each time the tempered steel banged against that hard marble. When Bonner approached her, she hit him.

He screamed an obscenity at her, the first time Alva had ever heard him scream.

She hit him another glancing blow on his arm, but Bonner didn't even acknowledge it.

Made slick by rain and being pushed hard by men, the white bird fluttered from the trailer and halfway to the ground, remaining half up and half down like that because its low left wing tip stuck in the mud: the bird kept cockeyed trying for the torn and tearing sky.

Then it was over, the rain having slacked off and finally stopping when the temperature dropped to that bitter range where it's too cold to rain, too cold even to snow, and all three of them were exhausted, were done, and they stood there like predators giving up on some glorious quarry, the prey not elated by victory and the predators not disheartened by defeat: everyone just tired—muddy, cold, cockeyed, and tired.

Except Bonner wouldn't give it up. After Alva and Johnny left for the house, he kept trying to set the bird right by himself—pushing as hard as he could against the sculpture as if to push into reality that perfect image he still carried of the white bird positioned perfectly, coming out of the earth, left wing tip not yet free of sod, rising from a deep warm blanket of green, all pieces in the set either gleaming white or dark green. But it was over. Bonner might not give it up, but it was over.

Johnny built a fire while Alva collected what she needed to put a fresh dressing on his hand. Without speaking to her, Johnny struggled against what she was trying to do for him—struggling against this comfort of women.

It had been the same with Linda Greenerton. After the station wagon carrying Jess had departed, Johnny went with her to the car and retrieved his suitcase, telling Linda she should leave without him, and then he knocked away her hands when she tried to touch him. "Why are you taking it out on *me?*" she had wanted to know. "I didn't have anything to do with this. Johnny? We still have the next two weeks." She tried again to comfort him, put her arms around him and get Johnny to talk to her about it.

"Leave me alone," he finally said in a voice cruel enough to be clear. "Get out of here and leave me alone."

That's what he told Alva as she wrapped cloth around his hand. "Leave me alone."

"Fine. I hope it gets infected and drops off. *Bastard.*" She moved away from the fire to sit on the couch, staring at the same flames Johnny watched.

Bonner came in, collapsing heavily into the recliner by the window.

They all three sat there with their wet clothing dripping and cold, silent and watching the fire, the only illumination in that room.

Outside came the dawn, but not so as you could tell, not with the bluffs being in the way and the sky remaining low and thick this morning. But at least that bad night which promised never to end had at last ended. It was day and that night was over.

"You should've let him eat the goddamn chocolate chips," Bonner said quietly.

The pain caused Alva to hold her stomach and lean forward.

Every Bitter Thing

22

THE HEART went out of the town after that. Everything was different. It had been cold in December, but January was shattering. Forget December. *This* was winter.

Bonner worked all month on the sculpture, refusing help, using pry bars and block-and-tackle until finally the bird was moved, placed in a hole Bonner had dug and the bird anchored there in concrete, in place, the upward angles right even if the scene still didn't match what Bonner had in mind because the bird emerged from bare dirt and not a soft cushion of grass—grass thick enough to accept like willing green flesh a blade of white wing tip. Sod wouldn't be laid until spring.

Jess had been buried in front of the sculpture, his name and dates on a brass plaque bolted over the large chip in the bird's hard marble breast.

Long after the funeral, people kept bringing covered dishes, pies, meat salads, hot soups to the Relee house, returning to their own homes to talk about how strange things were: the death of a child always is bad, but the three adults in that house lived somewhere beyond sadness. They were sick, head sick and heart sick.

They went around hollow and hollow-eyed in that house, that house emptied of laughter, the hours lying on the three of them as heavily as the delivered food, which they didn't want to eat and then, eating, felt it undigested and fist-heavy, high enough in their stomachs to pressure their hearts, giving them heartburn and headaches, making it difficult for them to breathe.

Not only because a child had died but because it was Jess, fat and strange and full of wonder. Not only because it was Jess but because of their lost investments in him—because of what they'd done to one another before the boy's death bound them together in that house. They hated the sight of each other and avoided mirrors.

Bonner kept telling Johnny he wanted him to leave, but Johnny neither replied to the demand nor left. Alva said nothing to either man; at some point she stopped crying.

Alva cut her black hair even shorter—short and severe, chopping at it with scissors that weren't meant for that kind of cutting, too blunt.

The men did not comment on her new hair; they did not work on Beaker Mansion; they seldom left the house. Bonner refused three requests for burials that month, and it turned out that this January was the driest in two decades despite the rain on the night of the first, morning of the second.

No one bothered feeding Lady regularly, and for the first time in her life the dog begged table scraps.

Their three lives were threadbare, no love among them, plans wrecked, futures uncertain. The sides of their triangle were of bridge iron, sharpened to razors. They were like the bitterly divorced forcibly reunited. They were desolate, more wretched than desperadoes.

But finally there aren't words enough and the words there are come too light to convey, carry, that is, the load the three of them bore. They lived to watch one another suffer.

23

ON FEBRUARY SEVEN, Wayne heard two shots and went screaming up the stairs to find Alan on the floor at the end of the bed. Wayne couldn't bring herself to touch him, so she ran to the one person in town who'd always taken care of everything.

Bonner told her to stay at his house, he'd go take a look.

Even though Alva and Johnny still were mourning, Wayne thought they would make a fuss over her, seeing as how her husband was in all likelihood dead and she was an hours-old widow. She thought Alva would offer coffee and then fix a little bite to eat while that nice Johnny Reace might try to lift Wayne's spirits by telling her maybe Al's not dead only hurt.

Wayne was wrong. Alva just glared on her way through the living room, and Johnny stayed in the basement well away from where Wayne sobbed all by herself on the couch. People as bad as they can be.

· · · · ·

DURING THAT FIRST WEEK of February, Alan Winslow had come to believe that he stank—that the dog smell throughout the house came not only from Alphonse but from Winslow's own perspiration. He took showers, several a day, but showers don't help when the stink is inside of you. Winslow emerged from those showers to be confronted by the poodle on the bathroom floor—licking at an inflamed scrotum.

It was in that first week of February that the dog changed from a kind of natural affliction delivered upon Alan Winslow and became, instead, malevolent. Waking up in the middle of the night, Winslow would find Alphonse right there staring at him. Looking Winslow directly in the eye—following him about the house, plotting, remembering hail. The dog knew. *The dog knew.*

Wayne suffered from cabin fever and pestered Alan, who was bankrupt. She left old urine unflushed in his upstairs toilet, maddening Winslow, while the dog began snuffling at Winslow's crotch in pursuit of some familiar scent.

On February 7, fresh from a shower, Winslow sat on the edge of his bed sniffing. He didn't know where the poodle was but he could smell himself. He dressed in fresh clothes, went into the bathroom to flush the toilet again, and fetched the gun from under his side of the bed. Sat there a long time thinking about it.

Alphonse came in, trotted to a spot directly in front of Winslow, and squatted to lick its ass. Winslow patted the bed, but the dog wouldn't jump up; he had to lift him and, while being lifted, Alphonse licked the man's face. Think where that tongue has been! Winslow cocked the pistol, held the barrel right by the French poodle's mouth. "Lick this." When the dog did, Winslow pulled the trigger, nearly blowing off Alphonse's head and propelling the creature in a backward flip onto the floor between bed and wall.

The second shot followed quickly. Because Winslow still could hear the dog slurping and still could smell the filth, he tilted the barrel toward his own head and gently squeezed the trigger.

· · · · ·

BONNER carried the surprisingly light man out to the old white Ford, which Bonner had left running in front of the

Winslow house. Steering with one hand and holding a heavy towel to Winslow's head wound with the other, Bonner drove fast on that thirty-two-mile trip, speeding twenty miles over the limit until he looked at Winslow's eyes and then let the towel drop, slowing down to reach the limit.

He talked with county officials all day, first at the hospital and then in county offices. Bonner told them it was an accident. "He was alive when I got there. Told me he'd been holding the pistol close to his ear, clicking the hammer on what he thought was empty chambers. The trigger had been catching and he wanted to see if he could hear what the matter was—that's what he told me. He mentioned it a long time ago, having trouble with that pistol. So he sat there listening to the hammer strike, except one of the chambers wasn't empty." Bonner didn't mention the death of Alphonse.

County officials were disbelieving. A man with a head wound like his, he was able to tell you that whole ridiculous story about listening to the hammer hit on empty chambers?

"Yes."

Maybe you're trying to cover up so this won't be ruled a suicide—avoid the shame and make sure his widow gets the insurance.

"No."

Do you realize the trouble you could be in for falsifying an official report?

But it was like threatening the bluffs behind Beaker's Bride.

Bonner had long ago called home all his loyalties, and when he was forced to take a Beaker's Bride matter into the outside world, as in the death of Alan Winslow, Bonner did what he had to do—protecting what was his from what was foreign. He not only was willing to lie under oath to county officials, Bonner considered it his duty.

Alan Winslow's death eventually was ruled accidental because county officials couldn't prove otherwise, saw no profit in proving otherwise, and when a big solemn man sits there in your office, sits there with weathered hands on his knees and looks you in the eye like Lincoln from a Brady photograph, you realize finally that there's no point in questioning him further because only Bonner Relee knew the truth and he would not be moved.

· · · · ·

IT WAS DARK by the time Bonner returned to Beaker's Bride, stopping first at Winslow's house so he could take care of Alphonse and then going home to break the news to Wayne. He told her the same story he gave the county, adding for Wayne's benefit certain greater improbabilities—that on the way to the hospital, Alan made a dying declaration of love for his wife, that the gun had accidentally fired *twice*, with the first wild shot hitting and killing Alphonse.

Bonner walked Wayne home and helped her pack some things. He had decided—not offered but decided—she would stay at his house until she felt like living alone or with one of the other widows in town.

After that, Bonner took care of everything: Alan's burial, the filing of forms, closing off the Winslow house, leaving the thermostat just high enough to prevent pipes from freezing because it still was winter, February cold and snowy, the wood wall little more than half gone, leaving a long plumb-perfect length of war yet to fight.

24

"I TOLD YOU before, *Wayne,* I don't want you moving things around in my kitchen."

"Alva, honey, it just makes life easier on me if those skillets aren't jammed back in the cabinet like you had them. I'm the one fixing meals and—"

"Who asked you?"

Wayne had stayed with them through the end of February, but it was into March when she began weighing so heavily on Alva.

"I don't mind cooking and cleaning, I really don't. *Some-one* has to feed those men." She had begun to leak again. "Al was such a finicky eater. Oh, Alva, honey, I've lost my *two* best friends in the whole world! Both Als! They're dead!" She blubbered.

"For crying out loud, Wayne, put the damn skillets wherever you like!" Alva went to the living room and said to Bonner, loudly enough for Wayne to hear, "I don't want that woman in my house." He didn't even look at her.

You couldn't read him, what effect Wayne had on Bonner; the man had withdrawn completely within himself and spent his time sitting in silence or going down to stand in the cemetery by the white bird, running his hands over the marble's pockmarks put there by Alva's ball peen hammer.

But for Alva and Johnny, Wayne trivialized their despair—she in her seam-straining pantsuits, at meals talking with her mouth full so you could see the masticated food, breaking into crying like someone trying for the balcony, always talking and making it impossible for Alva and Johnny to bear down and grieve as they'd done before Wayne's arrival. There had been something noble about their grief, something blood deep that Wayne's presence dissipated.

. . . . .

OF AN EVENING, in March:

"I'm so glad Al lasted long enough to tell Bonner what happened—otherwise I might've got the wrong idea. I'll never have a gun in my house—didn't even know we had that one to tell you the truth. Home protection, I suppose. They say guns don't kill people, people do, but this was a case of that gun killing them both like it had a mind of its own. Going off twice like that, a freak accident—like what happened to Jess. One tragedy follows another. Trouble comes in threes—your Jess and then my two Als. Terrible, terrible accidents."

They sat around the fire she had built, sat watching flames and listening to her as if the three of them were mind-control criminals assembled there expressly to hear the punishing lecture.

"I just can't understand it, a man in the insurance business all his life like Al, why he cashed in those policies and left me with nothing. I don't have a head for figures, no idea at all what he was up to—and they say there are no secrets between man and wife.

"What in the world good does it do me, owning all that property but having no cash? Property rich, cash poor. Not even property rich, really, since there's nobody to sell it to. Cash poor *and* property poor.

"Not even my little Al to comfort me in the rough times ahead. He was getting along in years anyway, I know that, but I would never have him put to sleep. He was like a member of the family. I remember Al holding him and waving his little paw when the train stopped—oh, that was before Al knew about the tragedy, of course. Well, I prefer to remember the good times. How big Al took little Al for walks in all kinds of weather."

Johnny was without protection against the irritation of this woman because ever since her arrival he had stopped drinking. She took away his liquid appetite, though Johnny's cells still suffered a craving unfed and it was that cellular hunger making him humorless and rash.

On one of his temporary escapes to the nearest store (a twenty-mile round trip), Johnny stood by the cash register as the lady checked his items, and there on a display at eye level were packs of Camels, which Johnny had smoked as a young man. The little packages fascinated him as they'd never done ten years ago: Old Joe with his head up, smug; the running *A* in *CAMEL;* that quaint typeface under Old Joe's feet, *Turkish* fancy ampersand *Domestic Blend.* He picked up a pack and turned it around, pleased by the sand-yellow color of buildings and palms—pleased, too, by the elegantly aloof sentence:

> Don't look for premiums or
> coupons, as the cost of
> the tobaccos blended in
> CAMEL Cigarettes pro-
> hibits the use of them.

"You want them?" the lady asked.

"Hmm?"

"You want them cigarettes?"

"Yes," he replied on impulse, tossing the pack on the counter for her to tally.

He carried the Camels unopened in his shirt pocket until that March evening when Wayne went on and on. Sitting close to the fire she'd built, Johnny took out the package, opened it, got a cigarette, and retrieved a burning stick from the fire to light up. He smoked not yet for the nicotine but just to have something to do with his hands, those two hands maimed and scarred, one missing a digit and the other gouged across the palm: a Camel looking right in such hands.

Neither Alva nor Bonner commented, but Wayne said she didn't know Johnny smoked and had he always smoked or was he just now picking up the habit and, either way, it was bad for him and she didn't like to see a man smoke, though a pipe—like Bonner's—that was nice and from what she understood a pipe didn't give you cancer and she liked the smell of a pipe.

Then Wayne returned to her lecture on losses.

"Oh, I'm not saying you can feel as bad about losing a dog as you can a husband, of course, but it's a terrible package when you lose them both. I miss little Al just like I miss little Jess. Again, I'm not saying it's the same, especially with Jess being so young. Such a shame when they die young like that. At least both of my Als had long lives. What is it they say a year in a person's life is worth in dog years?"

"Put a cork in it," Johnny said.

That caused Bonner to rouse himself from some dream state. "You don't say nothing to that woman—not in my house, you don't."

"Oh, don't mind him, Bonner, that's not Johnny talking. It's his grief talking."

"No, Wayne, it's me talking. Put a cork in it."

"I want you gone from my house." But Bonner had said that many times before.

As if winter wasn't bad enough outside, March forced it in on them with a howling that put you on edge, ghost-ruffling curtains so you couldn't even sit by a window without freezing—that March wind making it so you were unable to think straight and could never get warm, not even in bed under covers in the middle of the night.

. . . . .

ON MARCH THIRTEEN, Johnny asked Charlie Warden to give him a ride to the bus station, but Johnny got only a hundred miles on a ticket that would've taken him a thousand—traveled a hundred miles and then he had to turn around and come back.

It happened to him in an EAT café, the bus's first stop; there would be a fifteen-minute delay so Johnny went into the café and saw that people there were ordering meals and eating them. Waitresses poured coffee and chatted behind counters. Truck drivers waiting to pay their tabs stood talking in ways that moved toothpicks up and down in their mouths. Two children at a table engaged in a mild quarrel that mother soon quelled. One man read a newspaper.

All wrong.

A soldier tried to strike up a conversation about how good it is to be traveling south when the weather's like this, but the PFC gave up talking when he saw Johnny's small eyes, how dark-ringed they were and how they seemed permanently astonished. The bus driver, meanwhile, watched Johnny because during the first one hundred miles the driver twice had to tell him not to smoke on the bus and the driver worried that this passenger, looking so exhausted and frightened, might cause trouble between here and Florida.

Johnny sat at a counter and ordered coffee, but these people here must be crazy—just *look* at the way they're acting.

He neither drank nor paid for the coffee; Johnny simply picked up his suitcase and walked out into March to hitch a ride back where he could keep an eye on desperation because it was too unsettling being out in this other world where people acted as if nothing had happened and he couldn't find the whereabouts of what he knew existed. Where were all the desperadoes now that he needed to see them? Beaker's Bride.

He hitched a hundred miles facing always away from the March wind even if that meant missing rides, rides back to where life was deadly serious and everyone acted appropriately stricken, appropriately desperate.

When he came in late that night, the kitchen was lighted because that's where Wayne reigned, but the rest of the house remained dark, inhaling winter's breath around windows and then exhaling a despair that chilled Illinois. Outside, wind moaned and, inside, so did some old seventy-eights that Alva had found stacked under the lamp on Agnes's bedside table—where Alva once kept the sewing needle she used to prick the old lady. Alva sat sipping gin in her room, spinning seventy-eights that spread their black hunger throughout that house, while Bonner in the dark living room remained unreclined in his recliner with a teacup in his large right hand.

When Johnny looked in on him, Bonner spat into the teacup and then said nothing, as if the man had never been gone.

In the kitchen, Wayne fixed him a sandwich. "Why'd you come back?"

Cold and wearier than he'd ever been in his entire life, Johnny offered her a face to break your heart.

"Charlie Warden told us he gave you a ride to the bus station, so we all thought you'd gone to Florida."

Nothing.

"How far did you get?"

He looked at the baloney–American cheese–white bread sandwich as if eating it would rend his guts.

"You know what's so strange?" Wayne's voice became conspiratorial, suggesting that she and Johnny were okay and it was the other two who were weird. "Nobody asked about you while you were gone. I was the only one who talked to Charlie when he came over. *They* didn't even mention your name all day long—don't you think that's strange? Is something wrong with the sandwich? You need ketchup?"

Please *stop it.*

"I think you're losing weight, Johnny, I really do, but of course you know sadness affects different people different ways—some can't eat and others can't stop—and it's just my luck, huh?, I'm one of those who eat, eat, eat when I'm feeling low, and I must've gained fifteen pounds since I been living here, while the three of you pick at your food like birds. I've thrown away more good food! Such a waste. At least Lady has a good appetite. My little Al was such a finicky eater, I must have tried fifteen dog foods getting him to eat right, and one brand, I can't remember the name now, it made him sick to his stomach. Look how bloated I am. Too much salt, maybe, I don't know. They say most of your extra weight is fluid, not fat, and I've always had problems with fluid retention. This sadness affects everything, even my bowels aren't right and I've tried everything—bran and prunes. No laxatives, though, because I had an aunt once got like addicted to them and couldn't go at all unless she had her laxatives and when they took her off them she got bound up something awful. Speak of the devil." Wayne stood. "You'll have to excuse me now—I feel a stool forming."

He could've wept.

.   .   .   .   .

THE MORNING after Johnny's return, the four of them gathered at the dining room table for breakfast while March filled the house with a chill no furnace could reach. Wayne jabbered as she served them, passing plates and asking questions about how they liked the food and anxiously filling each golden opportunity for silence.

Alva pushed away the plate of eggs she'd been playing with. "Shut up!"

"Sometimes I run off at the mouth, I know I do, honey, just can't seem to help myself. It was like I was telling Johnny yesterday, some people get affected different ways by sadness. When *you're* feeling blue, you keep to yourself and play those records over and over—and I don't even say a word about how they give me a headache—but I'm different, *honey*. When I'm low—"

"Shut up your fat mouth!"

Johnny clapped slowly, a mocking applause.

Bonner: "Enough!"

Alva left the table at a run, heading upstairs.

"Don't be too hard on her," Wayne told Bonner. "It's just her grief talking, Alva doesn't mean it—not in her heart of hearts she doesn't."

Johnny lighted a cigarette, inhaled deeply a few times, and then smashed it out in his plate of food.

"Now, Johnny, that's not right," Wayne said.

Bonner told him to leave; Johnny went to the living room and smoked more cigarettes by the cold hearth, tossing butts to the dead ashes and waiting for Wayne to build her daily fire.

Alva came running down the steps, grabbed car keys off the hook in the hallway, and opened the front door to let in even more March. "Good-bye, you fuckers!" Then she was gone.

. . . . .

OFF RIVER ROAD and finally onto a state highway, Alva was hit by a suddenly violent storm that made her pull to the side crying and then sobbing, this storm so bad she couldn't drive and had to pull to the side, sitting there with foot on brake, head on steering wheel, engine still running, her thin body being shaken by great sobs that Alva didn't realize she had left in her.

Twenty minutes later, a state cop car parked behind the old white Ford and one of the two Smokies got out, walking slowly to Alva's window and tapping on it. "You okay, miss?" His voice muffled by the wind and the closed window.

Alva couldn't stop crying.

Rapping harder, the cop said, "Open your window." She did. "Miss, it's not safe for you to be sitting on the shoulder like this. Your car okay—does it run?"

She nodded, still crying.

The cop went back and said something to his partner, then returned to the Ford. "Why don't you scoot over and I'll drive you to a truck stop, just a few miles up the road, and you can wait there in the parking lot till you're feeling better."

She moved to let him drive. On the way, Alva wanted to explain but, still sobbing, she simply could not speak. The cop said nothing more until they stopped in the parking lot. "Miss . . ."

He hesitated, measuring words before speaking them. "He ain't worth it, miss."

Alva's entire face was wet and the state cop thought about handing over his handkerchief, but duty goes only so far and he didn't want his wife-ironed and neatly folded handkerchief on Alva's face—looking like what she suffered wasn't heartache but cancer, that's how bad Alva looked with her hair chopped off and her eyes made wild and red from so much crying.

"I got four daughters, miss—believe me, I know. More than once I've seen them feeling like you do now. I told them what I'm telling you: no man who'd make you feel this bad is worth it."

Alva was keen to explain, to tell this state trooper with

daughters that it wasn't a man making her cry, but Alva's throat had closed up on her.

"Don't drive till you're feeling better. He especially ain't worth getting in an accident."

Alva stayed on the passenger side long after the cop had departed. When at last the storm seemed to be over, leaving Alva cried out and empty, she slid behind the wheel and turned it toward Beaker's Bride, where the kind of sorrow she suffered was so commonplace that no one commented on it anymore.

. . . . .

THE NEXT DAY, on the 15th, Johnny walked into the bathroom to find Alva sitting on the edge of the tub painting her toenails some bloodstone shade of red. She raised her head to meet his eyes but did not bother to cover herself, still naked from a bath.

"I didn't know you painted your toenails."

"Always have."

"But not your fingernails?"

"No."

"I guess I should've said excuse me for walking in on you."

She shrugged and resumed work on her toenails.

Johnny watched. Her body had become scrawny, arms especially thin, and her wet short hair was plastered to her head. But there was about her a small tenderness, sitting with one leg cocked up on tub's edge so she could get at her toes, Alva perched so tiny on that heavy porcelain vessel made for a man Bonner's size, Alva isolated as a small dark spot in that huge bathroom with all the white pieces—sink and toilet and tub—too large and too bright.

Johnny recalled her letter full of such cheer, sugar kisses and BigBear hugs, !!!'s, underscores, ellipses, quote mark twins. "Alva?"

"Hmm?" She didn't look up from painting.

I could fall in love with you if I weren't so scared. Something alluring about her small, dark tenderness, sitting there on the tub painting toenails red.

"What?" Still not looking up at him.

The curtains were pulled boldly wide to allow in whatever light was left to this dying winter's day; outside, March blew cold, but in here it was jungly warm and wetly humid—a good place to be and better if it weren't so bright. Johnny flicked down the switch.

"Cincinnati?" he asked in the shadows.

She finished blowing on the last drying toe, then reached to replace the tiny brush but, in the dim light, Alva knocked over the bottle. "Shit." Not bothering to clean the mess, she walked over and latched the door, flicked the lights back on, spread a large towel on the bathroom's white tile floor. Alva lay on the towel, supine and naked and waiting.

Unable to think of anything to say, Johnny undressed and knelt between her legs; she put her hands behind her knees, hauling her legs up and back to open herself for him in a manner especially obscene amid all that white and light. The obscenity didn't dissuade Johnny, however, and Alva kept her head turned anyway, so she wouldn't have to see his eyes—kept her head turned toward that red stain so stark on such white porcelain.

Johnny entered her, hurting her, once again not being careful with her. He hit against her so hard that she belly-grunted in response—hit and grunt, hit and grunt, but Alva did nothing to soften the blows and, in fact, kept her legs and pelvis lifted for him to hit all the more deeply inside of her. Faster now. Repetitive blows. Banging against her, both of them grunting, all the way in and then all the way out, constant, hard and fast, without imagination or variation, none of this having anything to do with pleasure: hit, hit, hit, hit until Johnny worried about hurting her and asked in a strained whisper if she was okay.

"Harder," Alva urged, *harder.*

In the dining room waiting for them to come downstairs before beginning dinner, Wayne and Bonner heard the banging; very quickly the sounds from the ceiling became so obvious as to embarrass Wayne into silence while Bonner's gut hurt bad enough he could've cried.

After that, Alva and Johnny were at each other every day, twice a day, three times—something to do, to drown out the madding wind, to keep warm at least awhile, seldom kissing, forgetting foreplay, just getting right to it, hitting against each other as hard as they could and sometimes not even bothering to take off all their clothes because it was too cold for that and too much bother, just his pants open and her pants down, Alva bending over holding tightly to the edge of some piece of furniture in her room—letting Johnny hit her as hard as he could.

And as soon as he climaxed, he was finished with her, never lingering inside of Alva but withdrawing quickly and reaching immediately for a cigarette. For something to do in these afterward moments, Alva began smoking, too, though for a long time the Camels hurt her lungs so bad that it was only through force of will that Alva picked up the habit.

. . . . .

WAYNE HAD BECOME fastidious in the Relee household, trying to impress Bonner. Every Monday she stripped all the beds to do the laundry, so it was on a Monday, March 30, that she walked into Alva's room and saw the blood: more blood than she'd seen when finding Al on the floor, blood everywhere on Alva's bed, blotting the sheets, up on the pillowcases—and on the headboard was a man-sized handprint in blood like evidence you'd find at the scene of a ritualized murder. Dark blood and still wet—Wayne could smell something like freshly turned soil down by the river.

She was frightened until she recognized the odor. Of course. Something rich turned inside of Wayne—something rich, recalling all that lunar stuff soaking up valleys, fingering gullies. Of course. She moved less frightened now back out into the hallway and toward the open bathroom door, moving now no longer afraid of making felonious discoveries but propelled now by curiosity.

Alva sat on the edge of the tub using a wet towel to wipe at dark blood that stained the entire center of her, from belly to thighs. When Alva's head jerked up, the first expression Wayne saw was one of shame, but it quickly turned defiant, the little one's eyes as fierce as the white bird's drilled holes. Too evilly proud to explain or to push shut the door, Alva just sat there staring at Wayne as if to say of these stains: Oh, look, Wayne, *look*.

Biting her lip, the older woman mumbled some apology and then hurried away.

.　.　.　.　.

LATER THAT MONDAY, in the evening after dinner, Johnny tormented Wayne with riddles and word tricks while outside the wind rattled trees like bundles of sticks.

"Okay, now listen *carefully* to this one."

"I'm listening, Johnny, but I just don't have the head for riddles."

Alva sat by the fire smoking Camels and Bonner watched her from his chair.

"You're on an island inhabited by two tribes. Members of one tribe speak *only* the truth while members of the other tribe speak *only* lies. Members of both tribes look the same. You come to a fork in the road. One way leads to safety; the other way leads to sure death in the jungle. A native is standing there but you don't know which tribe he's from. Okay, here it is. What one question can you ask him, the answer to which will result in the native pointing to the road that leads to safety? What one question can you ask that will get you to safety regardless of which tribe the native belongs to?"

"Oh my!" Wayne was giggling. "I'll never get that one. Why don't you two help me out?" Bonner looked at her but said nothing; Alva didn't even turn around. "You better go over that one again, Johnny. My mind's all a swirl—tribes and roads and . . . now did you say this little native boy will tell the truth or not?"

"Forget it." He walked over to Alva and bummed a cigarette. "Got another one for you, Wayne."

"Try Alva. I bet she's good at these."

"No, this one's especially for you. Imagine an evil genie has imprisoned your little doggy, Alphonse, in an enchanted lamp which is unbreakable—how do you get Alphonse out?"

"I don't want to play anymore."

"Come on. How do you free Alphonse from the unbreakable lamp?"

"Enough," Bonner said.

"Oh, that's not Johnny being cruel," Alva told him. "Just his grief talking."

"Enough—both of you!"

Alva threw her cigarette into the fire, took Johnny's hand, and led him out of the room.

"You two don't have to leave on my account!" Wayne called after them. "I'll play the game and I won't start crying, either—promise I won't."

But Johnny and Alva already were on the stairway, heading for her bedroom. "How *do* you free Alphonse from an unbreakable lamp?"

He laughed.

"Not going to tell me?" she asked when they were in her room opening and lowering their pants.

Johnny made a quick movement with his hands. "Poof! He's out."

"And that's it?" Alva asked, lying back on the bed, naked only from the waist down.

Johnny mounted her and they began their tribal rhythm, filling the otherwise silent house with all their truths and all their lies.

Downstairs, Bonner lighted a pipe and took it over by the fire to blow his smoke into the woodsmoke, everything up the flue together, while Wayne came over, stood too near him, and put a hand on his back. "They're just young," she said softly. "The things they do, it's not to be hateful—they're just young and not used to grief the way we are."

Bonner closed his eyes.

"But young or old, a person needs somebody to hold on to in times like these, when you've had a loss—the way you and I have had losses."

Like the box turtle in the basement, Bonner had no recourse to voice or flight and could only withdraw more deeply inside himself, keep his eyes closed, and stand the pain.

· · · · ·

DAYS COLD, nights long, wind hard—the four of them in that house finished out March leaving no tracks on time.

25

WAYNE WINSLOW departed their house on the first of April saying she felt better, could live on her own now, and was eager to return home. Wayne made something of a ceremony out of thanking them, wet eyes and long hugs, telling how grateful she was for their taking such good care of her in her time of need and insisting they let her know if they needed anything at all. Johnny and Alva felt guilty, but Bonner was the one who had told Wayne the time had come for her to leave.

With Wayne gone, the three of them once again reveled in their unfinished grief, becoming again captains of despair, CEOs in charge of mourning, returning to this state—beset and stricken—scarcely missing a beat, their eyes avoiding each other, meals no longer regular, and the laundry going unwashed on Mondays.

Johnny and Alva didn't touch one another after Wayne left; the only old habit they still indulged was smoking because there was nothing else to do: too cold to stay outside, this winter relentless in duration.

Whenever he couldn't stand it any longer, Johnny made that twenty-mile round trip to the store, using his own money for groceries because he wouldn't ask Bonner for cash and Bonner didn't offer. Upon returning, Johnny always left the nonperishable groceries in bags sitting around the kitchen and took the newspapers he bought into the cold living room, where he read only the comics and only those he never followed before—*Mary Worth* and *Judge Parker, Apartment 3-G* and *Rex Morgan, M.D.*—the ones that weren't funny. He left the papers on the floor where he dropped them, and if Johnny wasn't smoking, he was eating Twinkies, throwing the wrappings behind the couch. Didn't shave for several days in a row. Watched the rich and famous on television, staying up late for religion. Though his cells no longer craved a drink, Johnny wouldn't have refused one had someone offered. No one did.

Everything Bonner saw on his walks around town disappointed him: the Illinois full of dirty ice, goddamn noisy trains speeding through, and that white chipped bird stuck in frozen mud with no grass to soften or green the effect. At mealtimes, Bonner would sit alone in the dining room waiting for someone to serve him though no one did and he, like Johnny and Alva, had to rummage around in paper bags for something he and the long-suffering Lady could eat.

Alva's skin was dry, it cracked, and her hands stung when she washed them. Out of boredom, she visited Agnes but still refused to bathe the old woman, who had become abruptly talkative, Alva listening with only half an ear to stories of ancient courtships involving beaux long dead, Agnes giving disjointed accounts of sparking out in the brush and holding shivarees; she spoke explicitly, too, about tallywhackers and twitchets and how you sometimes had to treat certain men like barking dogs you weren't sure of, approaching slowly and making no quick movements but always keeping in mind he's more scared of you than you are of him.

Alva was smoking a pack a day, most of those Camels consumed after dark because she stayed up late enough to become bone-weary, tired enough to sleep like death until light and not awaken in the night to imagine Jess standing at the foot of her bed—never actually seeing him there but imagining how frightening it would be if ever she did, Jess standing there scaring the Christianity right out of her. She couldn't take the chance of seeing him or of glancing at a window just as some filmy white gauze went floating by, so Alva stayed up late, smoking, watching television with Johnny, falling asleep on the couch where he left her when he went down to his basement room—Alva awakening at first light to the television still on and her mouth tasting foully of old Camels.

This is how the three of them lived—but it was coming to an end, with only fifteen feet of wood wall remaining along an old property line.

26

WHILE STANDING behind Bonner's recliner, watching the rain with him, Alva placed a small, dry hand on his shoulder and Bonner responded by reaching up and covering that hand.

Moving through the house, Johnny caught Alva's eye and they both smiled—almost shyly. When they smoked the last of the Camels on hand, no more were purchased.

Bonner walked into the kitchen to find Johnny folding grocery bags. Said Bonner: "Johnny." Replied Johnny: "Bonner." Both of them nodding when speaking the other's name.

Alva began preparing meals again and they sat down together to eat.

Time.

. . . . .

APRIL'S ICE-WATER RAIN sentenced all three of them to the windows—but their grief had shifted weight, leaving empty spaces they continued to fill with expectations of spring and certain kindnesses toward each other.

Alva's bangs grew out, covering her forehead and softening the bulge of her large brown eyes to make them alluring again. She wore dresses, and April's higher humidity improved Alva's skin.

Being off alcohol had taken all the gray from Johnny's eyes, making the whites very white and lending to the blue an even more startling depth of color.

Only Bonner was the worse for wear, but there remained about the man a certain tragic magnificence: the very size of him, those deep lines cutting at an angle from his nose to meet furrows set back from his mouth like serious scars, that large head crowning its tower, big ears, a thick thatch of black hair you knew he couldn't get a comb through but had to brush, high forehead, and always and especially his eyes like the dark entrances to deep mines going how far down you could only guess. Even if he hadn't resembled Lincoln, you'd regard him as a figure with history, a man who'd won some overly expensive victory or who had been vanquished with dignity.

Johnny was reminded during April that more than anyone else in Beaker's Bride, it was Bonner who had kept him here past the time Johnny knew it was safe to stay—Johnny remaining because he was fascinated with Bonner's solemn air, his sense of duty, his stewardship of Beaker's Bride.

But in April Johnny began visiting the Illinois, and now he wished to go where that current headed. Johnny was done grieving, had put grief in one of his pockets, and now he wanted to flow like the Illinois through this heartland, get away, reach an ocean. Johnny was ready to do as the Illinois did, carry south what once had been north.

The river.

. . . . .

"YOU NOTICE how he makes a face whenever he stands up?" Alva asked Johnny one April evening while Bonner was upstairs in his room with the door kept closed.

"Yeah." A sudden grimace as if something inside was catching—Johnny had seen it. "Has he said anything to you about being sick?"

"Are you kidding? Bonner? He's never admitted to being sick a day in his life, not Bonner."

Lincoln worked at his desk all that evening and half the

next day, writing and organizing and then filling out tax forms to accompany the checks he would send as appeasements to the outside world. He walked to the mailbox in the rain and then returned to his room and took to bed. It was mid-month and Bonner took to bed.

Alva brought up his meals.

"I got some homemade soup for supper," she said, carrying in a tray. "You'll eat that, won't you?"

"Yes."

"Bonner? I made an appointment for you to go see a doctor. It's Charlie Warden's doctor, he's real nice, I talked with him on the telephone. Tomorrow morning at ten. Johnny'll drive you over."

He tasted the hot soup.

"Okay?" she asked.

"It's good."

"No, I mean about the doctor."

He looked at her the way you do a child who's proposing some childlike solution to an adult problem. "Doctor's not going to tell me nothing I don't already know."

"What's that supposed to mean?"

"Fetch me that green book over there on the bureau—next to the lamp, see it there?"

She brought the green leather ledger to Bonner.

"Kept a record of all my roofing jobs in here, from the very first one I ever did to the ones me and Johnny worked on together. Twenty years of roofing and I never had one come back on me."

"Bonner—"

He shook his head. "I ate all your sins, Alva."

"Huh?"

"After me comes the heavy rain."

"What are you talking about?"

"Soon. Soon."

"You *do* need a doctor—just listen to yourself. Johnny will *make* you go."

"Tell him I want that bird put right, he'll know what I mean."

"Bonner—"

"I want *everything* put right, you know what I mean."

"No, I don't."

"The word of the Lord is forever settled in heaven."

She just shook her head.

Downstairs, Johnny made a big fire and then fixed himself a strong brown drink that warmed him better than fire because it warmed him deep down where he was cold.

Like honey poured on soft bread, that first drink in months soaked him sweetly through. It pacified his nerves and firmed up a queasy lower tract, steadied the course of his blood, and regulated breathing. Cells that had at long last given up their appetite now recalled greedily and gratefully that old hunger.

He was on his second when Alva came down. "It's been a while for you, hasn't it?" she asked, indicating the drink in his hand.

"Sure has."

"Bonner's going crazy."

"No, not Bonner."

But the next day's doctor's appointment had to be canceled because Bonner refused to leave his bed and he didn't eat supper that night even though Alva brought it to him on a tray and offered to feed him.

"What's wrong?" she asked.

He told her he had counted the stars inside the ring around the moon.

"It's not like you to talk so crazy," she told him.

"No more circuses," he mumbled.

"Huh?"

"I'm fighting in the shade now."

"I can't understand you."

In the morning, Alva carried another tray to Bonner's

room, but she returned immediately to the kitchen and Johnny could tell that something was wrong.

She spoke nervously. "I think you better go up and check on him."

"Why, what's wrong?"

"*Please.* Just go up and check on him for me—okay?"

He did, coming back a minute later to put his arms around her.

. . . . .

PEOPLE WERE TIRED of being cold and April's icy rain made matters worse. As if they had no memory from one year to the next, people kept thinking April was when it became warm again and you could go outside without putting on a coat, keep your doors open, leave a window up at night. Yet even as they watched for signs of spring, their impressions of hot weather were less than recollections and more like stories they'd been told of exotica: lands where the sun blazes, where people sleep without covers, and it's hot all the time. How would life be in a place where it was warm and dry? Can you imagine?

Under a tent large enough to hold the entire population of Beaker's Bride *and* the white marble bird, graveside services were conducted with Johnny playing taps on Jess's old clarinet; even Agnes came, rolled to the cemetery in a wheelchair piloted by Charlie Warden, who kept a large black umbrella over the old woman.

Gone was the man who'd always taken care of everything—now what?

While the people waited out the rain, Alva mentioned that Bonner must have been thinking of warm weather right before he died because the last things he said to her were "No more crocuses" and then something about the shade.

Johnny said he was a man you could hold up to the world.

When the rain broke, Johnny stayed under the tent with the bird, everyone else accompanying Alva to her house while Johnny worked past dark—filling the grave, then wiping shovel and spade with an oil-soaked rag so they wouldn't rust, taking down the tent and hauling it in sections to the shed, where he spread the canvas to dry, putting away all the folding chairs that had to be returned tomorrow to the funeral home, then cleaning the white bird with a cloth and giving special attention to the pockmarks that had collected grime. Doing things right took time, and when Johnny got to the house, all the people had left.

He took a long, hot shower before going through Bonner's papers—something Alva had asked him to do several days before. She had a drink waiting for him.

"I assume you want this," she said, offering the glass.

"Never turned down a drink in my life."

"Oh yes you have."

They sat close together on the couch. "Bonner left a big envelope with my name on it," Johnny told her. "A green leather book inside."

"His old roofing book?"

"Yes. And something else, Alva—something you need to know about."

"What?"

"An insurance policy. From what I can tell, he bought it a long time ago from Alan Winslow, but Bonner kept up on the premiums so it's still in effect. The policy has been changed several times, but the last change made *you* the beneficiary."

She didn't want to ask.

"A hundred thousand dollars."

27

"WHAT DO YOU THINK we should do with it?"

"*We?* It's your money, Alva—do whatever you want. You're almost rich, doll."

What would daddy think? "Rich?"

"Sure. The insurance money will be tax-free—and you own this house, Beaker Mansion, everything. Bonner left you everything."

"What about you?"

"Me?"

"What are you going to do now?"

Get out, get away. "I'd like to buy Bonner's old panel truck from you."

"You can have a brand-new truck—now that I'm almost rich."

"I'd rather work on the old one, something to do."

"And after you get it running?"

"I don't know—we'll see."

Having one hundred thousand dollars emboldened Alva. "You're leaving me, aren't you?"

As quickly as he could. "I'm leaving Beaker's Bride eventually, sure. You can too—spend the insurance money to see the world."

But Alva had already seen the world—back when she was 'fraid of nothin'. "When?"

"When what?"

"Exactly when are you leaving? This time I want to know."

"I was thinking—after I fix up that old truck, I was thinking of driving it down to Florida."

"Can I come with you?"

He ran both hands through his hair.

"Whatever happened to that cap Bonner gave you?" Alva asked. "The one you used to wear all the time."

He shrugged. "Lost it in St. Louis." Johnny wanted to be gone right now. "One more drink, then I have to hit the sack."

"Are you sleeping with me tonight?"

He replied hopefully, "That's all over between us, isn't it?"

Almost, she thought—*almost* over.

. . . . .

APRIL EVENTUALLY rained itself out until nothing was left. Johnny stayed in the shed working on the panel truck and then, when the weather finally cleared, he labored in the cemetery laying sod and landscaping until Johnny created what Bonner once saw perfectly in his mind: that white marble bird rising from the green earth.

And of an evening, the sun setting across the Illinois, you could watch the great bird turn colors from bright white to a richer and more yellow white, marble head and breast and right wing already free while the lower left wing, caught in mid-beat, still was coming from, pulling up from, the thick green blanket of sod Johnny had laid—almost but not quite free. It was of an evening that the grand marble bird looked poignantly dramatic, flying out of the earth at an angle and almost free.

And it was on an April evening, almost May, that Johnny took Alva to the cemetery, where they could watch the sun-fed bird.

"What time are you leaving?" she asked, even though Johnny hadn't yet announced tomorrow's departure.

"Early."

"In the morning?"

"Yeah. Listen, I still want to pay you for that truck."

"Don't go yet." There was so much they hadn't done, especially with Johnny slipping down to the basement early every night leaving Alva to sleep alone—and now he was leaving? "It hasn't been two weeks since Bonner died."

"The panel truck is running fine."

But Alva had things she wanted to tell Johnny, stories as wonderful as Bonner's and stuff she hadn't had the chance to say. "Did I ever tell you about Nelson?" He was a crazy old guy who lived in Millerway when Alva was a girl growing up there and Nelson devoted his time to inventing hats—hats with little light bulbs attached and hats equipped with buzzers Nelson would activate when passing you on the street, hats he outfitted with motorized propellers on top or paddlewheels to the side, hats constructed from old army helmets and large metal bowls. *Nice hat, Nelson,* people in Millerway would say and Nelson, seldom speaking, would respond by pressing buttons hidden in his pockets, buttons that would light the bulbs or buzz the buzzers or spin propellers and side-mounted paddlewheels. He never held a regular job, but Nelson was something wonderful with hats, and Alva remembered him as a delight of her childhood, encountering Nelson with his hat alight, buzzing, spinning. If she could tell Johnny stories like that, wouldn't he stick around to hear more?

"I just think it's time I should be hitting the road."

But if he left early in the morning, there was no time to tell him about Dorothy, the imaginary friend Alva had when she was a girl, and no time to tell him about daddy.

"We both knew I was leaving. Putting it off won't make it any easier."

But if he was gone tomorrow morning, Alva would never know anything about him—what were his parents like and did he have brothers or sisters and where's his hometown and was he ever married and why does he keep traveling like he does?

"You can *have* the truck," Alva said.

With the sun gone, that cemetery became too spooky because Bonner and Jess were in there and because the marble bird used the darkness to turn into something rising ghostly white from the ground. "Let's go back to the house," Johnny said, taking a few steps and then waiting for Alva.

When Nelson's mother died, he didn't have anyone to take care of him, so distant relatives arranged for his commitment to the state asylum in Jacksonville, from which Nelson eventually was graduated, Alva knowing this to be true because she saw him once in Springfield, where the state employed him picking up trash from the capitol grounds: Nelson with a canvas bag on a strap around his shoulder, wielding a length of broom handle fitted with a point—Nelson working out in the winter weather, bareheaded.

Johnny didn't want to hear any of that. "Come on—let's go back to the house."

"I'll sign over the title. You're the one who got the truck running, you deserve it."

"I'd like to pay you *something.*"

"I don't need the money."

"Let's go. We'll talk about it at the house."

Seeing him so anxious to leave the cemetery fascinated Alva. "Tell you what. Let's have a party tonight, just the two of us. We'll get drunk and then sleep together. That's the payment I want, for the truck."

He agreed, leading her by the hand up the slope and through the wrought-iron gates and to the white frame house, where Johnny put on all the lights and made a big fire.

Alva got out her records. "This is definitely a dance situation, wouldn't you say?"

Yes. He danced with her all she wanted.

But Alva drank water that night, gin-clear water while making sure Johnny's glass never emptied of the brown stuff so dear to him. Relieved that Alva was festive and not pressing the issue of his departure, Johnny drank unwisely.

At some point in the proceedings, she brought down from her room a heavy quilt to lay before the fire and, after Johnny put Lady outside, he and Alva made love carefully, without any of that old hard-hitting business, but even though Johnny worked her expertly with what fingers he had left, she could recognize duty when confronted with it this way and Alva missed the old passion even if it had hurt. Johnny didn't grab her shoulders and pull down hard while thrusting up as he used to do; this time it was just a little cough and sputter inside of her and Alva couldn't wait for him to get out, though this time Johnny lingered within her while they both lay there hot only because of the fire, craving a Camel when no Camels were in that house.

"Let's have another drink," she said, pushing on his chest, desperate that he get off of her.

So they had that drink and then two more, Johnny saying he should get to bed but Alva insisting upon a nightcap— more gin-clear water for her while Johnny kept drinking unwisely.

To prevent suspicion, Alva stumbled when bringing in another round. "You're getting drunk, Alvie," he said, having already taken it as a matter of honor to outdrink her.

She laughed. "I guess so." Was she that good an actor or did he know?

Usually, Johnny held his liquor like a decanter, becoming only more golden with volume, but this night he was drunker than he'd ever been in his life and he spoke to Alva of the things he feared.

"I worked in an office once," he said, slurring his words so that Alva had to listen closely and still she didn't understand large parts of what he told her, Johnny rambling on now about secretaries. "I didn't pay much attention to them unless they were pretty, but I got to know this one and that was my mistake, getting to know this one. Secretaries who were expected to dress nice on what they had left at the end of the month just so their bosses could have something pretty to look at in the morning, while what the secretaries had left at the end of the month was less than what their bosses spent on a tax-deductible lunch. I was one of the hotshots, me and the other hotshots plotting and planning through a tax-deductible lunch while she was in the ladies' room checking for blood, willing blood where there was no blood."

"Stay with me until summer," she asked. "I'll be okay once the weather turns and it's summer again."

But Johnny called her a desperado and said he was too scared of her to stay even a day longer. He had several more drinks while Alva abandoned even the pretense of gin.

At quarter past three in the morning, she helped him outside, holding him up as best she could on their way down to the river. It was a damp night and the route Alva chose avoided the cemetery.

Johnny took a long time figuring out they were going someplace. "Where we going?" He saw the water. "I'll take you to Florida with me."

"To Florida with you?"

"Yes." He grunted the word.

"Away from here what would I be? Just some spooky woman you happened to have with you at the time and then when you left me in some motel to go off on your own, then what? The time for Florida just passed. I know you're going to leave me, so I want to be left *here*—where I own a house and a mansion and where people are used to me. And something else, Johnny—I don't want you going off to Florida telling stories about Beaker's Bride like we're just one more story for you to tell." Alva tried to help him into a rowboat tied there at the Illinois shore.

"No."

And if Johnny had resisted, it would've ended there because Alva was too small to force him; but when she urged Johnny to get in, he got in. "Tired," he said.

She pulled the outboard's rope seven times before the engine started, its noise surprising Johnny, who had fallen asleep in the bottom of the boat. "Where we going?" he asked.

"Taking a little nighttime cruise on the Illinois," she replied, heading against the current because it was important to Alva to have Johnny upriver from Beaker's Bride.

"Tired," he said.

"Go back to sleep. We don't have that far to go." When they were a good distance north, she cut the motor and let the rowboat drift with the current.

"We there?" Johnny asked, propping himself to look over the gunwales. "Are we there?" He could see nothing out on that river at night.

"Almost there, Johnny. Almost there." She sat and watched him. "I couldn't believe you actually were leaving me—only two weeks since Bonner died and you were leaving already. So soon. Too soon. And I would've done *anything* for you."

"Don't give me that shit." His head hurt bad.

They drifted in the eerie dark, eerie because it was so complete and because of the water sounds all around. From under her seat in the stern, Alva took out the ball peen hammer. Johnny saw it. "I'll stay," he said.

"I know you will," Alva replied, patting his leg. "I know you will, honey."

"You got magic in you—you know that, girl? Sure you do. I recognized it the first time I laid eyes on you. Said to myself, This one's got magic in her." But he had lost his enthusiasm for it.

"Did you ever love me?" Alva asked. "Were you ever in love with me when we were making love so hard the way

we did all those times while Wayne was living with us?"
She would have accepted anything he was willing to give
her: false promises, well-told lies, that Johnny Reace version of truth.

He shook his head, giving her nothing.

"Why'd you stay in Beaker's Bride as long as you did?"

"Bonner."

"You bastard."

"Oh, go on."

What did he mean? Go on with what? Did Johnny know?

"Desperate women," he said, still unable to focus his eyes
properly.

"I'm not a desperate woman."

Now he looked at her directly, clearly—and when he did
that the old Johnny smile returned to his face. The way he
smiled when he first came to Beaker's Bride. A light in the
otherwise dark river. "Desperate for me." He grinned
more widely.

"Don't start that old shit of yours," Alva warned.

"Yes, ma'am, winsome little Alva—*desperate* for me."

"Not anymore."

"*Hungry* for me."

"No more."

Then with all of his power he laughed, mean music rolling across the surface of the Illinois. "I fucked you in the
heart, girl!"

With the two-pound ball peen hammer gripped tightly
in her right hand, Alva pictured the sequence precisely:

Swinging the hammer as hard as she could, cracking him
just above the left temple.

You watch a movie and see someone get hit on the head,
and he goes "Ugh" before collapsing, out cold, and you
think that's the way it works when people get hit on the
head—but Alva knew that's not the way it works at all. It's
worse than that. A hammerblow to the head shocks him
with pain and it's the pain that stuns him, the pain that

would make Johnny grab his head with both hands and fetal-up, crying because of pain and trying to wrap both arms around his head *because of pain* that hurt so bad he couldn't stand it.

Then she would hit him a second time right on top of his skull, one hard overhead blast right on top of the skull that wasn't protected by his arms, and Johnny would make sounds you wouldn't think a grown man was capable of as he rubbed his head and cradled his head with arms and hands that weren't arms and hands enough to provide the comfort or the protection he needed.

Then she would hit him again in the temple and *then* Johnny would become desperate enough to cry out her name and that of Cincinnati.

Columbus, Alva would reply, *Columbus.*

Waiting Hard

28

I WANTED to close the door on Charlie Warden: no more bad news, I'd had enough.

In the two weeks it took for May to heat up, Lady died, and now Charlie was at my door with that look in his face once more, the same look he carried when he announced the news that he'd found Lady down by the river—and now he was here with more news he would've come to tell Bonner if Bonner had been alive.

"Mr. Gibsner's dead."

"Come on in and have a cup of coffee." I had nothing else left with which to comfort a man.

He told me how Mr. Gibsner always talked about feeling the pull of the universe—how the universe was hungry to have all of its wandering parts back together again and Mr. Gibsner said he sometimes could feel that hunger pulling on him and that it was a terrible thing to feel.

I had no reply. We sat there with our coffee cooling.

"I'd like to dig his grave myself—the way Johnny did for Bonner. But I can't. My back, you know. If I call the funeral home and let them handle it, they'll bring in a backhoe and you remember what Bonner always said about that."

"Yes." Said it was like folks were putting in a sewer line.

"You been through so much yourself, Alva, more than anybody else in town, and I hate to burden you with something new but I just don't know what to do. Who else I could go to."

I told Charlie we'd get the work done ourselves. "I'll hire

someone to dig the grave and you can pick out a stone from the lot and I'll hire someone to set it." I had the money.

"I appreciate it, Alva—I really do. You're going to turn out to be just like Bonner."

"Not me."

"Oh, it's been a winter, ain't it?"

. . . . .

JESS DEAD. Alan Winslow dead. Bonner dead. Johnny in the river. Lady and Mr. Gibsner dead. But still that bad winter wasn't over.

Although I had never taken my turn bathing Agnes, I was the one who found her dead. I'd been going over to visit her every day, not to clean up after her but just to sit in that foul room and listen to the odd things she had to say: "Seen too many sunrises through too many kitchen windows. . . . I'm in favor of action words—twenty-seven, seven. . . ."

On those few times when she seemed aware that I was with her, Agnes gave me advice about men. "Oh, I know that man of yours thought he was high cotton all right, but that's the kind of man I always was soft for myself—bad to the bone. The blues ain't nothing but a good woman feeling low. Precious Lord, take my hand."

Then I walked in one afternoon and there was no mistaking her condition for sleep. I wanted to get out of there and go fetch one of the old ladies who'd been caring for Agnes—let someone else handle this final mess—but I couldn't make a decision about leaving or sitting or covering her face with the blanket. So I just stood there for the longest time.

Finally I went to the bed and touched her. There was no disgust or fear. I wished then that I had taken my turn, that I had bathed Agnes at least once. She put such store in being clean.

Taking the time I needed, I removed the covers and then her gowns, unlacing what was laced and unbuttoning what was buttoned until I had her naked. Agnes's body was the second most shocking thing I've ever seen in my life—a body with which time had finally had its way. Her skin horribly bruised.

Using cloths and soap and several pans of warm water, I washed her completely and then patted her dry with a large soft and white towel. Rolling her gently to one side and then the other, I changed the bedclothing.

In a closet, I looked among dresses unworn for more years than I'd been alive, dresses covered with an early plastic that was thick and so yellowed as to be barely translucent. Under that old plastic skin, however, silks and cottons waited like new. I chose something light. In bureaus, I found undergarments and stockings never worn; I laid out everything at the foot of the bed and then dressed her.

Gently, I brushed her fine white hair and applied to that ruined face certain amounts of color. Finally, I put the fresh sheet and covers up to her neck.

Too late, maybe, but there was something about preparing Agnes's body that seemed to counterbalance my own troubles. It was among my last moments of equilibrium.

. . . . .

IN THE SURLY SPRING at the end of that bad winter fifteen years ago, I asked Charlie Warden to go through Beaker Mansion and list what still needed to be done, then I hired the work and moved in that summer. I had a large screened-in porch built to the side of the mansion, and that became my favorite spot to sit and wait.

With time and money and nothing else to do, I became the queen of Beaker's Bride—a spider queen, the center of my web at the screened-in porch with strands radiating all over town along weeded streets where old people lived and reaching into their unremodeled houses and even to the closed doors of their sickrooms: I could feel the pull when something somewhere was wrong.

Outsiders still presented themselves for burial in Beaker's Bride, so I negotiated with funeral directors and paid the wages of young men who dug graves and rode on riding mowers while Charlie Warden oversaw their work. He never let them get close to that rising white bird, however; Charlie took care of it himself, keeping the green thick and the marble polished, knicks and chips and plaques and all.

. . . . . .

YEARS PASSED like the river's flow and all the original residents of Beaker's Bride died except for me and Charlie Warden. Then Charlie died.

By the end of the first decade after that bad winter, I had bought all the property in Beaker's Bride; I bought from the relatives of those who died, from banks, and I paid Wayne enough for her holdings so she could travel to Albuquerque, where a brother of hers lived and where she died.

Then the state of Illinois decided to build a bridge across its river near my town, and that new bridge put our sweet spot within commuting reach of jobs on the other side. A real estate company out of St. Louis began bringing in clients who offered me double and triple what I'd paid for the old tumbled-down houses, which the new buyers remodeled and sometimes resold for even greater profits. I began hiring out the remodeling of the houses I still owned, and that's when I became rich in real estate. I invested money elsewhere and learned how easy it is to make money when you have money.

No wonder the wealthy are so wise.

. . . . .

BEAKER'S BRIDE repopulated itself. Stores, gas stations, churches, shops, and schools opened. One thousand people.

You should see the place now. Sidewalks newly laid are lighted at pleasing intervals by gas lamps on black poles wrapped in thick green coats of flowering clematis. The front yards of Beaker's Bride are well tended now and the houses tastefully decorated. These current residents are young and childless or one-child couples who collect at impromptu gatherings in those well-tended yards and on the newly built porches and decks of those tasteful houses. I watch them smiling as they sit on white wire chairs or stand casually elegant with hands in their linen pockets. They are pleasing to look at but they have no edges or vices or hungers; they gossip about my eccentricities and speculate about the extent of my wealth.

Even if I tried to explain everything to them, they wouldn't understand why I wait or what it is I'm waiting for so hard; they await only the new sewer system and city water and the depot's reopening—all of which has been promised us and all of which will cause property values to climb even higher. We'll make out like bandits.

But society rests on a thin shelf, that's what daddy used to say. And what's wrong in this world exerts a pull as strong as the universe's.

29

NOW I AM the only person above ground who remembers that winter fifteen years ago, a winter so bad that I carry it like something still within me, and on some mornings I awaken to find four angry marks in a line along the bottom of each palm where my fingernails have dug into my hands during the night: waiting hard even as I sleep.

Of an evening, Beehart and I sit on the large screened-in porch to the side of Beaker Mansion and watch Junie bugs. The small light I've turned on attracts them, and they crash against the screens, get knocked to the ground, and then buzz as if to talk themselves into flight—these fat blunderers buzzing like revving engines until they become improbably airborne, whirring around until hitting something that knocks them again to the ground, sobered briefly by these collisions but ready soon to fly once more. They are given to indefatigable flight.

They start life as dirt grubs born in the soil and then dig deeper to safety below the frost line, spending three years in the dirt as grubs, and then comes a May that takes two weeks to heat up until finally the newly June sun draws them from the earth hungry—hungry for foliage and hungry for flight. Hungry, whirring, flying, flying all night. Hungry, eating, flying until it's morning, when Junie bugs return to the holes where they've spent the last three years, return there to the ground to wait out the day, wait for twilight and flight. No wonder they're so undeterred: after years in the dirt, they have only this one June in which to fly.

· · · · ·

I still read his letter from St. Louis. But what I read in those newspapers and magazines I subscribe to are headlines screaming at all the wrong things. The SOS. In the capitals of the world, the rich continue laughing up their linen sleeves, but I also read about what's dangerous and I wait for it to end with desperation in the streets. I wait for the arrival here in Beaker's Bride of the small, the odd, the lonely, the bulb-headed and bulge-eyed, those who measure their steps, the quietly enraged, the foreclosed upon, the lost, the disinherited meek, those who are terrified at the prospect of mirrors, sin eaters already fat, morning drinkers and morning criers. I wait for shy men who push into the hands of pretty girls they don't know letters that are too long, and I wait for regiments of betrayed women carrying ball peen hammers, their arrival more terrible than armies with banners.

I wait by the Illinois, water different but river the same—carrying down what had been up. Always going, never gone: time and the river where I wait for various troubles in divers places.

I wait for that time when I'll no longer be able to see the precise moment that Jess went blank behind his eyes.

And I wait for Johnny Reace to come up from the river just one more time. Oh, I know. *I know.* I held him in extravagant regard, I know that now. But I was hungry—and Johnny Reace was my portion.

ABOUT THE AUTHOR

DAVID MARTIN is the author of *Tethered*,
The Crying Heart Tattoo, *Final Harbor*, and
the soon-to-be-published *Lie to Me*.
He lives on a farm in West Virginia
and writes fiction full-time.

VINTAGE
CONTEMPORARIES

V I N T A G E
CONTEMPORARIES

___ **The Stars at Noon** by Denis Johnson	$5.95	394-75427-1
___ **Asa, as I Knew Him** by Susanna Kaysen	$4.95	394-74985-5
___ **Lulu Incognito** by Raymond Kennedy	$7.95	394-75641-X
___ **Steps** by Jerzy Kosinski	$5.95	394-75716-5
___ **A Handbook for Visitors From Outer Space** by Kathryn Kramer	$5.95	394-72989-7
___ **The Garden State** by Gary Krist	$7.95	679-72515-6
___ **House of Heroes and Other Stories** by Mary LaChapelle	$7.95	679-72457-5
___ **The Chosen Place, the Timeless People** by Paule Marshall	$6.95	394-72633-2
___ **A Recent Martyr** by Valerie Martin	$7.95	679-72158-4
___ **The Consolation of Nature and Other Stories** by Valerie Martin	$6.95	679-72159-2
___ **The Beginning of Sorrows** by David Martin	$7.95	679-72459-1
___ **Suttree** by Cormac McCarthy	$6.95	394-74145-5
___ **California Bloodstock** by Terry McDonell	$8.95	679-72168-1
___ **The Bushwhacked Piano** by Thomas McGuane	$5.95	394-72642-1
___ **Nobody's Angel** by Thomas McGuane	$6.95	394-74738-0
___ **Something to Be Desired** by Thomas McGuane	$4.95	394-73156-5
___ **To Skin a Cat** by Thomas McGuane	$5.95	394-75521-9
___ **Bright Lights, Big City** by Jay McInerney	$5.95	394-72641-3
___ **Ransom** by Jay McInerney	$5.95	394-74118-8
___ **Story of My Life** by Jay McInerney	$6.95	679-72257-2
___ **Mama Day** by Gloria Naylor	$8.95	679-72181-9
___ **The All-Girl Football Team** by Lewis Nordan	$5.95	394-75701-7
___ **Welcome to the Arrow-Catcher Fair** by Lewis Nordan	$6.95	679-72164-9
___ **River Dogs** by Robert Olmstead	$6.95	394-74684-8
___ **Soft Water** by Robert Olmstead	$6.95	394-75752-1
___ **Family Resemblances** by Lowry Pei	$6.95	394-75528-6
___ **Norwood** by Charles Portis	$5.95	394-72931-5
___ **Clea & Zeus Divorce** by Emily Prager	$6.95	394-75591-X
___ **A Visit From the Footbinder** by Emily Prager	$6.95	394-75592-8
___ **Mohawk** by Richard Russo	$8.95	679-72577-6
___ **The Risk Pool** by Richard Russo	$8.95	679-72334-X
___ **Rabbit Boss** by Thomas Sanchez	$8.95	679-72621-7
___ **Anywhere But Here** by Mona Simpson	$6.95	394-75559-6
___ **Carnival for the Gods** by Gladys Swan	$6.95	394-74330-X
___ **The Player** by Michael Tolkin	$7.95	679-72254-8
___ **Myra Breckinridge and Myron** by Gore Vidal	$8.95	394-75444-1
___ **The Car Thief** by Theodore Weesner	$6.95	394-74097-1
___ **Breaking and Entering** by Joy Williams	$6.95	394-75773-4
___ **Taking Care** by Joy Williams	$5.95	394-72912-9
___ **The Easter Parade** by Richard Yates	$8.95	679-72230-0
___ **Eleven Kinds of Loneliness** by Richard Yates	$8.95	679-72221-1
___ **Revolutionary Road** by Richard Yates	$8.95	679-72191-6

Now at your bookstore or call toll-free to order: 1-800-733-3000
(credit cards only).